HOW TO GRIEVE LIKE A *Victorian*

How to Grieve Like a Victorian

AMY CAROL REEVES

CANARY STREET PRESS

CANARY STREET PRESS™

Recycling programs for this product may not exist in your area.

ISBN-13: 978-1-335-01406-1

How to Grieve Like a Victorian

Copyright © 2025 by Amy Carol Reeves

All rights reserved. No part of this book may be used or reproduced in any manner whatsoever without written permission.

Without limiting the exclusive rights of any author, contributor or the publisher of this publication, any unauthorized use of this publication to train generative artificial intelligence (AI) technologies is expressly prohibited. Harlequin also exercises their rights under Article 4(3) of the Digital Single Market Directive 2019/790 and expressly reserve this publication from the text and data mining exception.

This is a work of fiction. Names, characters, places and incidents are either the product of the author's imagination or are used fictitiously. Any resemblance to actual persons, living or dead, businesses, companies, events or locales is entirely coincidental.

For questions and comments about the quality of this book, please contact us at CustomerService@Harlequin.com.

TM is a trademark of Harlequin Enterprises ULC.

Canary Street Press
22 Adelaide St. West, 41st Floor
Toronto, Ontario M5H 4E3, Canada
CanaryStPress.com

HarperCollins Publishers
Macken House, 39/40 Mayor Street Upper,
Dublin 1, D01 C9W8, Ireland
www.HarperCollins.com

Printed in U.S.A.

For Shawn

How to Grieve Like a Victorian

Prologue

An acupuncturist once told me grief settles in the chest, pressing on the heart and lungs, squeezing around the ribs like a whalebone corset. This is why acute grief feels something like panic. But I'm also convinced now—miracle that the body is—that there's still heart-space for joy, flickering at the strangest times.

For instance, right now, in King's Cross Station, I'm excited as my train lurches forward, northbound toward Leeds and onward to Keighley, where a bus will take me to my next destination. I love this station not only because there's Platform 9¾ and my pockets are full of Bertie Bott's jelly beans, but because railways delight me. It's all a webwork of tracks and sleepers and fasteners, iron, steel, wood, the old and new—nineteenth-century engineering evolved into the sleek beast transporting me. Over the next few hours, I can settle back and take in the surrounding farmlands bordered by elms and hawthorns, the towns, the rising church spires. I can nap to the engine's rhythms.

When Philip passed away and I decided to adapt certain Victorian mourning rituals, I thought it would make me a better widow. I thought I would learn how to grieve and honor him as I walked a prescribed path to closure. I didn't know the path is ongoing, the journey never really over. I didn't know I would unravel layers of myself in this process and rekindle love and relationships in new ways.

I didn't know that I would feel this happiness and peace and yet still have the bittersweet urge to tell Philip all about it. I know now that all these feelings are perfectly fine and will coexist for the rest of my (hopefully) long life.

Because there's space for it all.

1

....

One Month Earlier

OUT OF OFFICE REPLY—

Thank you for contacting me. However, for an undetermined time period, I will only be corresponding through letters. (Yes, the kind with paper.) Thank you for understanding.

Dr. Lizzie Wells
Professor of Victorian Literature—Willoughby College
Author of *The Heathcliff Saga*
she/her

After typing the message, I drum my fingers on my desk, contemplating the elegant stack of black-and-gold-rimmed stationery pages and envelopes in front of me. They seem appropriate for a recent widow like me, and I'm grateful for the niche Etsy shop specializing in antique stationery.

No more emails.

The thought of not reading or answering campus emails from hateful asshats like Bill Rhodes, chair of philosophy, feels like a giant fucking albatross has slid from my shoulders, feathers cluttering the floor of my coffee-stained office carpet.

Since Philip's sudden death last month, I've learned I don't have much headspace other than to parent and grieve. And I've *barely* time to parent. Heathcliff ate a Pop-Tart for breakfast this morning. A *chocolate* Pop-Tart, not even a fruit one. I couldn't summon the energy to cook his regular oatmeal.

What am I going to do?

I look up at the signed *Heathcliff Saga* movie poster on the wall behind my desk and stare into the glassy blue eyes of teen heartthrob Everett Dane. He sneers rakishly, dark hair tousled over his forehead, rumpled shirtsleeves open to reveal the top of his Greek-god chest. He played the role well.

When Hollywood optioned film rights for my *Twilight*-y young adult version of *Wuthering Heights*—written during sleepless nights breastfeeding Heathcliff—Philip had been so proud. He took me out to a too-expensive restaurant, the kind where the servers wear crisp, ironed white dress shirts and say ridiculous things like the wine has "hints of leather and tobacco." We split a bottle of Cabernet over a large platter of roasted duck and asparagus. We even splurged on the overpriced cranberry tartlets; the cranberries, of course, were "raised in organic, sun-kissed hills near Asheville." After dinner, we walked through a nearby pocket park. The evening sky glowed rose-hued beyond the sprawling Carolina oaks; Philip skillfully skipped rocks across a tiny, landscaped pond as we talked about a future where we could pay off student loans and take our long-postponed trip to Paris.

My email dings, and I jump, blinking away tears.

Against my better judgment, I check the message.

Ugh.
Brad McGregor.

Hey Miss Wells,

I'm really struggling with P and P. I mean I thought this chick lit was like more straightforward. But geez . . . why do they have to write so many letters? Can I like have extra credit or something if I don't pass the Final?

Thks
B

My blood pressure rises a little bit every time I have to deal with Brad McGregor. The dean's son needs one more English credit to graduate on time, so he enrolled in my spring Jane Austen seminar because it was the only literature class over before his "epic" Cancún vacation funded by his dad's bloated administrative salary. His sense of entitlement has no end. He makes little effort to disguise his distaste for my class. He addresses me as "Miss" instead of "Dr." And last, but not least, he's Willoughby College's most notorious man-slut; last year he cheated on one of my brightest students, Kayla, with her dorm RA. (Kayla sobbed during my office hours after she found out.)

I log out of my email, close my laptop, pull out one of my new stationery pages and a black fountain pen, and begin a furious response to Brad.

A soft rap on my door, and my department chair, Patrick, enters, steam wafting from the top of his Edgar Allan Poe mug.

"Letters only?"

"This first one is going to Brad McGregor."

"He's the *worst*." Patrick groans and takes a sip of coffee as he slumps in the worn leather armchair opposite my desk. "I had him in American lit last semester. He came to class smelling like weed, called Edith Wharton a frigid old spinster, and I'm pretty sure he slept with my TA."

I see red as I stare down at my angry letter.

Patrick's quiet. Although my age, thirty-nine, he sports a graying beard. He strokes it for a few seconds as he considers me worriedly. He's trying not to look at my new black blouse with ruffled wrist sleeves and black pencil skirt. I *might* have gone on a widow shopping spree for black clothes in the days after Philip's death. Patrick doesn't need to know about the small silver bird keepsake urn containing Philip's ashes in my leather satchel. That might make me too peculiar.

He clears his throat awkwardly and gazes into his coffee.

"You doing okay, Lizzie? I mean . . . I know you're just back from leave, but you can take more time . . ."

I wave my hand dismissively. "Everything will be worse if I don't work. It will be all-day pajamas, and tears, and bingeing *Outlander* episodes."

"Well, if there's anything I can do for you—watch Heathcliff, send takeout . . . If there's anything I can do to lighten your load, just let me know. I've already taken you off the Curriculum Management Committee and the Committee Oversight Committee."

"Thanks," I mutter, bewildered, as always, at how my studies of Brontë and Dickens novels prepared me for such gripping daily tasks.

I shift the topic away from me and my ongoing sadness. "Did you have your meeting with the provost today?"

He gives me the dismal summary of this month's meeting.

Each monthly provost report becomes a little more doomsday than the one before, and the jumpy junior faculty start sending out résumés to community colleges and local high schools. In our department, we just lost a fairly new full-time hire to a neighboring new technical school. (*Teaching business writing is more lucrative* . . . she'd said. I had no counterargument.) Now the tiny English department is just me, Patrick, a small army of adjuncts, and our MAGA-supporting administrative assistant, Sandra. (Every time I pass her desk, I try not to look at the framed illustration of Jesus sitting on a bench by the White House.)

"But it looks like Willoughby will stay open for at least another year?" I ask.

He shrugs. "Let's just say I'm keeping my résumé updated." He glances up at Everett Dane's searing blue eyes. "*You*, on the other hand, will have plenty of options should the ship sink."

It's true. Although *The Heathcliff Saga* hadn't exactly made me rich, as the only faculty member to appear in *People* magazine, I'm a reluctant darling to a struggling institution. And plenty of other schools will take me if we close.

After he leaves, I finish penning my letter to Brad. I worry it's a bit too harsh, so I slip it into my bag.

I can always revise later.

I TAKE A LATE LUNCH OUTSIDE, NUMB AFTER THE LATEST Fiscal Oversight Committee meeting, where the provost announced proudly that she was siphoning off 90 percent of the humanities department budgets for an Admissions Advancement Task Force. Her lipstick-rimmed Cheshire-cat grin stretched wider, looking directly at me as she said it. Everyone waited breathlessly for me, the committee chair, to retort. Instead, in front of all thirty faculty and ten administrators, I pulled my favorite lavender-scented ChapStick from my sweater pocket next to Philip's miniature keepsake bird urn. I applied it thoroughly and carefully amid the silence, snapped the cap back on, and said nothing just to show how few fucks I give anymore.

Alone, in the campus garden, I sit on a mossy stone bench in the shade of an oak. Bees hum loudly through the blue flag irises and bulblike pink blossoms of the small magnolia near me. I open my Tupperware dish of macaroni casserole. As a Midwest transplant, I'm always amazed at Southerners' culinary zest for the grieving. I have about twelve macaroni casseroles and five lasagnas in my freezer. Heathcliff can't digest dairy, so I'll be eating these myself in the forthcoming weeks.

Even in the shade, my armpits sweat in this Carolina May heat. Still, I'd choose this over my windowless office any day. Through the garden gate, I see Bill Rhodes storming into the administration building—no doubt to unload on the president about me and Patrick. I can't care. No one will ever option film rights for his latest book—*Metaphysical Intellectualism in Neoclassical England*.

Last fall was such a bright star for me when *The Heathcliff Saga* film premiered and my book spent several weeks on the *New York Times* bestseller list. Writing that book six years ago, postpartum, kept me sane. I gave everyone A's that semester. With the hormone shifts, lack of sleep each night, and an insatiable Heathcliff hanging off my breast, I'd escape into my alternative *Wuthering Heights* world. In my book, Emily Brontë's love-triangled teenagers learn that Heathcliff inherited warlock powers from a distant Yorkshire ancestor. My Linwood is less milquetoast than the original character. He bastardizes ancient Fae supernatural powers from the moorlands and starts a spell war with Heathcliff. Cathy, caught in the middle, asks Nelly Dean to train her in the supernatural arts. She teams up with Heathcliff, helping him purge Linwood's magical darkness for good. There's lots of teen angst, desperate kissing, and disengaged parents. The adults churn butter and argue with no idea their teens could destroy Great Britain with their dark fairy-arts war.

My literary agent, Sarah, took me on and sold the book in two days. I loved my editor, my only complaint being that he wanted to change the title from *The Cathy Saga* to *The Heathcliff Saga*. I groused. After all, I wanted my heroine to be the book's star. But he said "Cathy" wasn't distinct enough—it sounded like the comic-strip character—and he wanted my Heathcliff to be the new Edward Cullen.

Then I thought about my forthcoming advance check and gave in.

The timing couldn't have been better. Over the next few years, film rights sold, then foreign rights in Spain, Germany, and Japan. By the time the movie came out last year and I had my red-carpet moment, Willoughby's president offered me immediate tenure and a promotion.

Putting the lid on my Tupperware, I scroll fondly through my Instagram page. Thanks to the movie, I have about 100,000 followers, and I pick up a few hundred more every time one of the stars tags me. My last Instagram post was a repost of Everett Dane's pic of him hugging me at the premiere after-party: "*Love this woman!* Brainiest person I've ever known."

I'm suddenly back in that moment, slight champagne buzz, surrounded by the glamorous and Botoxed. I wore a rented teal Vera Wang and teetered on strappy gold Jimmy Choos; I was in this young British heartthrob's arms, and yet I locked eyes with Philip, standing just beyond the photo's edge. With his soft, sandy blond hair and glasses, my shy lawyer husband never seemed more mine than in that moment. He wasn't a crier—ever. It's a weird Southern guy thing. But his eyes shone happy tears. There was no professional or personal jealousy there; it was pure celebration of me, of *us*—of how profoundly lucky we were to have each other and that moment.

My phone dings.

Mirabel: Hi Elizabeth, you've been on my mind so much. Lunch tomorrow? My treat☺

I groan.

My Steel Magnolia, passive-aggressive mother-in-law has been trying to get me out to lunch since the funeral. Lunch. I stare down at my Tupperware of mostly uneaten macaroni. Apparently, the grieving have to eat.

There's been a persistency in her texts.

Something's off.

And I just can't even with her because it will make me think of that night—Philip was leaving her house when his car ran off the road.

There was the call from him, just before the accident. The voicemail he left: *My god, Lizzie, we have to talk.*

The spongy casserole feels like a lump in my stomach. I'd rather face ten meetings with Bill Rhodes than think about that night and all the factors involved: rain, lightning, deer, emotional shock, the million random sparks that might have made Philip's 2017 black Camry slide off the road between Summerville and our home in Columbia, South Carolina. But painful as it might be, I need to know what happened at her home to upset Philip. Mirabel's been acting cagey, and I'll have to tread carefully.

My mother-in-law loves her azalea gardens, her large home, the Methodist Women's League. She likes lipsticks and Talbots dresses.

Unfortunately, the one thing Mirabel doesn't like (besides me) is the truth.

One Month Earlier

The Funeral

My priest, Chloe, reads the funeral liturgy about committing Philip's body to the ground.

Heathcliff farts loudly.

She pauses, suppressing a giggle.

"Usually, we do that *away* from people," I hiss at my six-year-old, before noticing that everyone except griefy-killjoy me seems to think it's cute. Even Philip would have loved the idea of our son stinking up his funeral service.

Still.

"Do you need to go to the bathroom?" I whisper.

"No." Big grin, a giant front tooth next to a baby one. "I just wanted to poot!"

I sigh and drop it.

God, the sun is hot in this old church graveyard; a strand of curling star jasmine keeps tickling my neck like an insect. Sweating profusely under my black dress, I hope I remembered to wear deodorant. Widow's brain is a thick fog. Last night I left the keys in the front door.

I can't look at Philip's urn in the open two-by-three-foot niche. We made quiche together last Saturday morning. Quiche with roasted red peppers and capers. My chest tightens.

I distract myself by thinking of all the people here who loved Philip.

My family would do anything for me. I glance at my brother, Ian. In spite of his high-pressure bank job, he flew in from Indiana last night. Mom would have driven down in a heartbeat. Even while I'm grieving for Philip, my heart still *aches* from losing her last year. My quiet professor-father sent white roses this morning. He threw out his back yesterday and was unable to fly. I want him with me now like I did as a child during thunderstorms. But he doesn't need to sit through Philip's funeral. Dad's still swallowing losing Mom, and Ian and I are worried for him.

Mirabel dabs her eyes with a silk handkerchief. She's a Southern Martha Stewart, classic whiskey in a teacup. At sixty-years-old, she still sports thick blond coiffed hair and fits perfectly into a size six black tailored Talbots dress. I used to tell Philip that I really want to know the witch her great-great-great-grandmother sold her soul to for Mirabel to inherit that fabulous skin and hair.

My father-in-law, Ted, puts his arm around her. He's dry, mild, but nice enough. Mirabel runs the show. Ted doesn't get excited about much. He likes his low-fat grits and chilled berries by six thirty every morning and lukewarm tea with lemon sliced thin and circular.

Philip helped so many, often pro bono, through the law firm. At home, sympathy cards clutter my desk from clients describing how he compassionately guided them through a divorce or out of a bad contract. Many more people would have turned up, but I tried to keep the funeral attendance small. Besides family, I allowed Philip's closest friends from law school. Through a tangle of jasmine, I spot his best friend and law school roommate, Henry Lawton. He's staring stonily into the niche, jaw set tightly under his trim beard.

I've only seen Henry a handful of times in the past several years. But Philip and Henry met often—for lunch, an after-work beer, a Saturday fishing excursion upstate. And although he's in the middle of his own divorce, Henry has offered to help me close the estate. He glances up, meets my gaze, and I look quickly away. I can't face his pain.

Philip's parents, his friends. Too many grieving hearts here for me to handle.

I can only tend to my own and Heathcliff's.

I glance down at him making silly faces back and forth with Ian. His six-year-old brain can't wrap his mind around the finality of it all. His world is Batman, LEGO, and dairy-free ice cream bars. There's no room for a world where his dad doesn't come home at the end of every workday or make the world's best quiches on weekend mornings.

After the funeral, I put Heathcliff to bed and sit alone in my backyard staring at fireflies lighting up amid my overgrown grass, and I realize I don't know what to do. I have no idea how to grieve, how to mourn, and mostly—how to live without Philip.

Desperate for some widow guidance, I pull up my phone's Google Images. I stare at an elderly Queen Victoria, cheeks saggy and pale as bread pudding. When Albert died, she made widowhood fucking performance art. She set the bar high for all widows to come.

If I were a Victorian widow, I'd wear black crinoline petticoats, dresses, and gloves. I'd look like a gothic wedding cake topper. I'd tie crepe sashes around vases and doorknobs, signifying that my house would be in mourning with me. Although ghoulish, I'd wear remnants of Philip around my neck—hair in a brooch or locket. At the funeral home, I'd clipped a lock of Philip's sandy blond hair and put it in a plastic Ziploc baggy. Now I'll place the lock lovingly in a piece of jewelry. If I were a Victorian, I'd not "move on" quickly. I'd respectably wear my black. I'd never attend wild parties or show too much cleavage, and I'd most certainly keep men at arm's length.

Hopefully, I can pull it off properly. I won't be wearing crinoline or petticoats, tying sashes around every doorknob in the house. But I'll be gesturing to it all—proper grief stationery, black clothes, keepsake jewelry.

IN THE WAKE OF MIRABEL'S TEXT, I PACK UP MY LACKluster lunch and realize I don't have the energy to keep office hours or attend another meeting. I pull out my stationery and pen a note.

> Dear Patrick, please give my regards to Admin as I will be absent from the Strategic Growth Committee meeting this afternoon.
>
> Sincerely, Lizzie

I leave the letter with Sandra. "Thank you, Dr. Wells." But she barely looks up from the Fox News segment where a blowhard yells about feminists. Patrick and I tolerate it all because she makes to-die-for Christmas shortbread cookies and organizes semester schedules like nobody's business.

As I drive back home from campus, I try to think through the widow brain fog. I'll need to figure out how best to talk to Mirabel about that night. Henry sent me a kind text reminder earlier today about helping me with my legal paperwork. Important, as now I know anything can happen at any time, so I need to tie up loose ends. Oh, and the jet-black locket necklace I ordered from the antique jewelry store in Charleston should have been delivered and left on my porch. I hope I can figure out how to fit Philip's lock of hair in it.

I approach my front door (Philip painted it red five years ago because I thought storybook houses always had red front doors). I see the small jewelry package. There's also a lavender orchid, stem straight, blooms budding out like little hearts, a note attached: *Thinking of you—Dad.*

Fifteen Years Earlier

"Sorry, we don't take credit card, only cash."

I stare longingly at the overpriced cinnamon powder iced latte, my reward for turning in my monster-length research paper for the Brontë seminar.

And *drat*. The barista is Garrett. I failed him for copying shit from Wikipedia in my class last semester. He smiles smugly while I rifle through my worn faux-leather satchel for loose change.

"I'll get it."

Just behind me a guy about my age—good-looking, tanned, with blue eyes and thick sandy hair—pulls six bills from his wallet. Wikipedia Garrett reluctantly hands over the iced latte.

"Thanks," I mutter, cheeks burning. "Really."

I walk away with the cold drink, not wanting to look at the other ten people in line behind me. I pause and take a long sip through the straw.

"Hey . . ."

I jump, turn around, and it's the cute guy who paid for my coffee. He smiles warmly. He has nice teeth and a small dimple on his lower chin.

"Aren't you going to get a coffee?" I ask.

"Well, I sort of used my last change to buy yours."

"Oh . . ."

"Philip," he says, putting out his hand.

"Lizzie," I reply, shaking his hand like we're colleagues.

I'm not sure where this is going. He's cute and I'm flattered. But I don't date much. It's not that I'm *unattractive*. But my idea of a fun Friday night is sipping Malbec and reading *Middlemarch*. Guys like this guy don't usually flirt/buy coffees for book nerds like me. I've only had one boyfriend in grad school: Wes Harker. We dated last semester as he finished up his PhD thesis on Lord Byron. Unfortunately, he was a Byron wannabe. While seeing me, he slept with my thesis advisor and three fellow students in our Romantic Poets class—Jenna, Dana, and Scott. (Who knew academia was so scandalous?) I'm ashamed that I still dated him until we went with friends on a quick trip to Haworth, England, and I walked in on him having sex on a nineteenth-century icebox with Samantha. Who does that to an antique? He had to go. Seeing him in the act was the last straw. He broke my heart, and I spent Christmas vacation crying in my childhood bedroom in Indiana. I'd bawled my eyes out in my frilly canopy bed just under the shelf displaying my large show-choir trophy and rows of spelling bee ribbons.

"Ummm . . . I have class soon," I say stupidly.

I glance down and notice his worn loafers and similarly worn bag. Definitely a student. But he's wearing a semiprofessional button-down shirt, so likely a law student. Word on the street is that they're just as poor as we humanities grad students, but they pretentiously try to dress like lawyers.

"But you do owe me a coffee, so would you like to go out?"

"Yes?" Condensation from my coffee drips onto my fingers as I grip the cup.

"Is that confirmation?" He smiles.

"Yes. Sorry . . . Yes, it is."

He pulls out his phone to get my number. There has to be a catch. This kind of meet-cute doesn't happen to me. Obviously, he's a charming serial killer who lives with his mom and her thirteen cats.

I chuckle awkwardly. "You're not a psycho, right?"

He laughs. God. That dimply smile again. I need to pinch myself.

"Nah."

3

As I walk into my too-quiet house with the orchid and package, I avoid looking at Philip's dress loafers, still by the door where he left them. Dust settles around the soles, but I can't touch them—that would mean he really isn't coming home to wear them again. I place the orchid on the fireplace mantel and press an ice cube into the soil. I remember how Dad listened so well that wintry Christmas when rat-bastard Wes broke my heart, and I suddenly ache to talk to him.

But just as I reach for my phone, Sarah calls.

"Hi, Lizzie," she says gently. I never tire of her charming, crisp British accent. She updates me on Japanese sales of *The Heathcliff Saga*. She tells me we have a nibble from a Brazilian editor interested in buying rights. Then, after a pause, she asks me how I'm doing.

"Crappy. But I'm drowning myself in cheesy funeral-food leftovers and campus politics."

After a moment's pause, she clears her throat. "You don't

have to be a big girl for me, Lizzie. I can't even imagine how bloody awful things are for you now."

A lump swells big in my throat.

"Listen, well—our family row house is empty for the summer. I want to offer it to you and Heathcliff, rent-free, if you just want to get away. London is so lovely this time of year, and it is such a cute place. The beds are cozy, there's a garden bathtub in the guest room upstairs, and our housekeeper, Ms. Fernsby, is marvelous. She lives there full-time, and she's really, *really* lovely."

Sarah's late father was a lord in Parliament, and after he passed, she and her brother inherited the row house. I always picture her childhood home life like something out of *Peter Pan* or *Mary Poppins*—ruffled nightgowns and nannies. Clotted cream and scones for breakfast.

I think about Heathcliff and me flying to London on a whim. It's appealing. But I'm teaching this summer and I can't wrap my mind around the logistics at this point. There's my summer class, and legal paperwork that has to be finished. And Mirabel. And Brad McGregor and Bill Rhodes. But to fly away from it all does sound . . . wonderful.

"I'll think about it."

"Promise?"

"I do."

"Well, then . . . take care of yourself, Lizzie."

I hear the loud engine of the school bus, and the front door bangs open. Heathcliff. As soon as he gets home, he always strips off his clothes and gets into his Batman costume. It's from last year, so it's already a little too short, the fabric pilled.

"So Chloe told me at recess that I *totally* had to eat the earthworm and I was like 'No—you eat it,' and she was like 'I'll give you all my Twizzlers at lunch if you eat it.'" He pulls his shirt off. "And I was like *ewww* . . . but I really wanted the Twizzlers because you can bite the ends off and drink from them like a *straw*. Did you know that, Mama? *Did you?*"

"Yes. When I was your age . . ."

"So I *ate* the earthworm and it wriggled as it went down my throat and Ms. Hoffman—" he pulls off his pants and steps into the worn Batman costume "—Ms. Hoffman said she couldn't believe I did that, but Chloe gave me the Twizzlers and they were good and cherry and—" he puts on the mask "—and I drank *all* my apple juice with my Twizzlers *straw!*"

"That sounds great," I say, hugging him. I should be mad about the worm, but his cheek is sticky and sweaty, and he smells like little boy. He squirms away from me, one blond eyebrow raised as he looks up and down my black skirt and blouse. "Why are you dressed like the Dark Knight?"

"Well, I . . ."

But he's already tearing through the house toward the backyard. It's his last week of school, and learning is about over for him. If we don't make it to London, we should get away somewhere this summer. Perhaps to the Outer Banks. Disney World?

Painfully, I make myself look at Philip's dusty loafers. I also can't get rid of his toothbrush, or his razor, or his glasses—folded neatly on my dresser. I worry if I keep touching them, they'll lose his fingerprints and skin oil. I wonder if our son sees all these daily reminders that Philip is gone.

THE NEXT EVENING, I RIDE MY BIKE TO HENRY'S HOUSE to get my paperwork in order. After teaching my Jane Austen seminar, I fell asleep in my office, silky black sleep mask over my eyes. I dreamed that I died, and Mirabel and Ted got Heathcliff. She raised him in seersucker suits and bow ties, and he took tea every afternoon with her and Ted on the front porch. Batman costumes weren't allowed in Mirabel's home. It was horrifying.

I left a letter with Sandra to give to Dean McGregor excusing myself from an afternoon college admissions fair due to "bereavement issues." My fusty neighbor, Edith, agreed to babysit Heathcliff for the evening, and I know I'll hear from him about her "old lady" smell and how she knits in front of her "boring" murder mystery shows. I feel a little guilty. But he'll survive.

Although Henry only lives a few miles from me, I've never been to his house. Warm air whips at my cheeks as I pedal. It's that late-afternoon hour when neighbors start walking their dogs and twilight glows from above the treetops. I swapped my pencil skirt for black yoga pants and a loose black T-shirt. The jet necklace holds Philip's lock of hair at my throat, and his bird urn rests safely in my mini-backpack. My helmet is bright lime green, but, well—I have to be practical. I still text, take antibiotics, sing Spice Girls songs in the shower, and watch Netflix.

As I ride, easing away from my street of 1930s-era bungalows to Henry's "newer" neighborhood of sprawling mid-centuries with large picture windows, I remember my few interactions with Henry. He joined us once or twice for a holiday dinner. I saw him coming and going throughout the years with Philip. I definitely *remember* the first time I met Henry back in grad school, and I blush.

My coffee date with Philip had gone well. Then there was a second date. Then he called back to see if I wanted to spend an afternoon at the zoo. He just seemed too good to be true. Even after we kissed for the first time, in front of the monkey habitat, howler monkeys and toddlers screaming around us, I knew there had to be a catch. This great, laid-back guy couldn't like me and only me.

When I called the next day to see if he wanted to catch a matinee, he said he'd love to but had a dentist appointment. Likely excuse. So around the time of said appointment, I camped out in my little green Corolla, half a block from his brick duplex. Sure enough, he was talking to a cute blonde woman about our age. She wore Daisy Dukes and held a Pekingese. My jealousy flared. All I could see in my head was this blonde and Philip getting busy on an antique ice box. At least I'm ahead of it this time.

I slammed my car door and marched down the street.

"Oh, hey, Lizzie," Philip had said cheerily.

"Hey, I'm Ginger," the woman said, showing big white teeth.

"*Ginger?*" I glared at Philip. Of course her name was *Ginger*.

He seemed confused. "It was a good dentist appointment, Lizzie. I'm still a member of the no-cavities club."

Suddenly, a large dented red truck pulled loudly up to the curb, and a nice-looking guy with a beard and worn flannel shirt got out. He hauled a cooler from the truck bed.

"Good catch today," he'd said, pulling the top off to reveal about fifteen bass on ice. Then he kissed Ginger's cheek as she grimaced—"Eewwww. Please *shower*. You reek of fish and muck." Her Pekingese snarled at him.

Philip properly introduced me then to Henry, Ginger's boyfriend.

I'd been beyond thrilled.

Now I step off the bike and walk it up the driveway around the same dented truck from fifteen years ago. I'm embarrassed I ever imagined Philip to be a cheater. As I take off the helmet and smooth my hair, Henry opens the door. A large yellow Lab bursts out, big paws on my chest, tail wagging wildly.

"Whoa, Bonnie!" Henry gently pulls her back by the collar. And then he greets me, welcoming me in as he restrains the friendly Bonnie. I feel a strange wash of shyness. I've never actually visited with Henry without Philip, and yet, my husband meant the world to both of us.

Inside, I look around the neatly furnished home. It's been a few months since Ginger moved everything out, and I don't see any photographs of her. According to Philip, they were a bad match from the start but kept trying to make it work until she ran off last year with her yoga instructor.

Henry leads me to the den, his cozy at-home office for when he's not at the firm. Manila folders are stacked neatly on his desk and coffee table in front of a small gray couch. Bonnie's bed lies near a small, white-painted brick fireplace. I'm mildly disturbed by the taxidermized buck head and largemouth bass mounted above the mantel, but, well—I eat meat and fish. I'd just rather not think about how it all gets to my plate.

Henry sits beside me on the couch and opens his laptop. He wears middle age well and looks essentially the same as he did fifteen years ago. If anything, the few grays in his wavy dark hair and short beard make him look even better.

We talk about Philip as we sit together. He points to the mounted bass, telling me about the upstate lake where he and Philip caught it.

But our mutual loss hangs between us like an anvil. Weighty and unpleasant.

"I can't even imagine, Lizzie . . ." he says, voice gravelly with emotion. "I think about him every day. I cried big tears when I heard about the accident. He was *crazy* about you. Every fishing trip, every lunch—he'd talk so much about you and that poor little hurricane of yours. You two were his world."

I stare at Bonnie, gnawing on a chew toy from her bed, and then I'm blinking away tears.

We both have to move away from this.

Henry clears his throat and opens the folder in front of him. "So, I looked at the will, and everything's pretty straightforward. My only worry is Mirabel. Maybe a week before the accident, Philip called me up about a strange trust he by chance found out about. He said it was something Mirabel set up for Heathcliff, but she was acting weird—didn't want Ted or anyone else to know about it. I'll need to chase that down, make sure everything's airtight for Heathcliff as we close up the estate. Would you care if I call up Miss Mirabel?"

"Good luck with that." I tell him about how she's been trying to get in touch with me. Then I'm about to tell him about that night, the message I got from Philip. But I'd missed it because I'd been out on the doorstep with Heathcliff looking at a blood moon. I'd missed my husband's last fucking call. But the words won't come.

"What else happened, Lizzie?"

I swallow and tell him.

He nods slowly.

We're quiet for a minute, staring at the hapless buck and fish.

"Listen, I'll deal with Mirabel. I'll talk to her lawyer and figure this out. It's likely nothing, but these things—trusts, inheritances—can have a way of staying goddamn frozen for decades if they're not handled right. I only met her a handful of times, but from the stories Philip's told me and from you, Miss Mirabel Wells sounds like a piece of work. You've got enough on your plate."

He plops the folder onto the coffee table in front of us and relaxes.

We're sitting rather close.

"Are you taking care of yourself?" I notice sunspots on his upper cheeks, his warm brown eye color.

"I guess so. It's just—there's this absence. It's always there." The lump in my throat swells and I play with the jet necklace. "His fucking loafers are still by the front door."

Because I can't think of Philip's loafers, I lean into Henry. I flashback to Ginger wriggling away from him. But I like this smell. It's vaguely earthy, like he's been outdoors working in a garden. He kind of stiffens, but I feel him breathing hard. We sit like that, frozen in a strange spell where thoughts and words won't work.

Gingerly, he puts his hand, warm, calloused, on my cheek.

I lean closer, inhaling his scent, feeling his warmth.

"Lizzie . . ." he mutters as my mouth brushes his beard.

Bonnie stands up loudly, and we both jump away from each other.

"God, what am I doing?" I clap my hand over my mouth, horrified at myself.

He's blushing deeply, as shocked as I am.

"I have to go," I say, hurrying from the den, snapping on my helmet and grabbing my mini-backpack.

"Lizzie . . ." He's following me. Bonnie runs after us to the front door, sensing the tension.

But I'm out the door and on my bike.

"Lizzie! Come back!"

But I pedal away fast.

I'm shaking. My heart pounds; tears roll down my cheeks. I hear him call after me again, but don't look back.

The evening has cooled off and night settles in, stars glittering above.

I need to talk to my priest.

I've sinned.

Philip has only been gone for one month, and I almost *kissed* his best friend.

"LIZZIE? OH GOSH, WHAT'S WRONG? IS IT HEATH-cliff?" Chloe asks, alarmed as she opens the front door. She's wearing yoga pants and a coffee-stained T-shirt. She's always been remarkably cool for a priest, but it's strange to see her without her collar.

"No . . ." I mumble breathlessly, unsnapping my helmet. "I need Confession."

"We're Episcopalian, not Catholic. We're not as into that."

Her wife, Abby, walks heavily down the stairs, red-eyed, patting their newborn son's back gently. She's not wearing a shirt, and one side of her nursing bra is open, an enlarged, irritated areola on display. Abby nods wearily to me as she walks into the den, as if it's perfectly normal for a neurotic parishioner to show up on their doorstep at this time of night.

"I just really need Confession now. I sinned *big-time*. I almost kissed Philip's best friend."

Chloe's mouth twitches.

"Did you *hear* what I said?"

"I heard you. Just come in."

"You're going to let me confess, right?"

"We're going to talk."

"But shouldn't we pray or something? I mean I *need* Confession!"

She smiles gently as she ushers me along. "We're going to go on the back porch and have a glass of wine."

"Glass of wine?"

"Let's appeal to all the spirits."

Soon I'm sitting on the cushioned wicker couch in the screened back porch surrounded by potted plants. Abby's beautiful, brightly colored handcrafted pots glow in the citronella candlelight. Chloe appears with two small glasses of chilled Pinot Noir and a plate of cheese, crackers, and grapes. She sets them on the coffee table and sits beside me. She brushes the pink-dyed streak of her thick, curly dark hair from her face.

"What happened, Lizzie?"

Through tears I tell her everything, blow by blow. I feel a little guilty—I mean, she has a squalling newborn. She doesn't need a middle-aged woman weeping on her back porch. But Chloe doesn't seem to mind. She listens carefully, hands me a Kleenex box, and I wipe my nose and wail: "There was no excuse—we hadn't even been *drin . . . king*. I'm a wid-*hoe*!"

Chloe smiles kindly. "Lizzie . . ."

"Victoria would *never* have done this!"

"Victoria? I'm a little lost."

"Never mind. I just did a very bad thing, and I'll never forgive myself. What would Philip think?"

"He'd be laughing his ass off."

"What?"

"Oh, I knew the man—he had the best sense of humor, and he'd think it's hilarious that you almost kissed his best friend. Henry Lawton, you said? You know what—he did some work for a friend of mine. Nice guy. And he's *cute*. Philip wouldn't be mad."

"But we just put him to rest . . ."

"Breathe, my friend. Do you remember that meditation sabbatical I took in Tibet last year?"

"Yes."

She leads me through a few breathing techniques she learned.

In.

Out.

In.

Out.

Remarkably, it works. I cool down by the second. Even though I'm still convinced I did a bad thing, I'm feeling less panicky about it. Breaths are miracles.

Soon I'm calm enough to take a sip of the wine.

Chloe clasps my hands in hers. "Oh, Lizzie. This is a time to be kind to yourself."

"But . . ."

"This is a time where you don't feel guilty about almost kissing Philip's friend. You do the easy yoga workout. Splurge on a pedicure. Take Heathcliff to a movie, or, better yet, on a trip!"

"I thought you were going to talk to me about Jesus and absolve me of the near-kiss."

"Everyone has such high expectations of me."

She sighs and takes a long sip of wine. "Gosh, this tastes good. You know, I gave up wine to show solidarity with Abby during the pregnancy. Now, as we take shifts with Asher, it's mostly coffee for me . . . and trashy detective novels. Speaking of . . ."

She starts skimming through her Audible app on her phone. "Have you read A.D. Hemmings? Because I can't put his *Blood Oath* down."

"Ummm . . . I think I've seen the paperbacks in airports."

"*Total* airport reads. Misogynistic, Hemingway-like style where women only exist for his macho Welsh detective, Chadwick Hall. But you need to read him. Here, I have a free Audible book to gift, and I'll send it to you."

"So we're not talking about Jesus."

"No, Lizzie . . . in fact . . . " She finishes off her wine, and I can tell she's not used to it. I remember that week after birthing Heathcliff when I hadn't had a drink in nine months, and I'd felt a little tipsy after one glass.

"*Listen to this*: 'He slowly undressed her, marveling at her wonderfully sculpted legs.'"

"That's so James Bond-ish."

"I *know*! So bad it's good. I mean, I know I bat for the other team, but part of me wants to throw tomatoes at this guy Hemmings and the other part of me wants to have wild, objectifying sex with him. I can't get enough. Wait . . . listen here . . . 'Her lacy black bra cupped her size-double-D firm breasts perfectly. She smelled so wonderful, like rose-scented soap . . .'"

"What woman actually wears that? He's describing a Victoria Secret commercial."

"I *know*! And what's worse is that this sex scene is with his new *younger* partner, Emilia Wren. They've been chasing the Cardiff Strangler all day. She fell into a *gutter* two hours earlier in the pursuit. I'm sure she wouldn't have worn this scratchy, sexy bra for a workday like that and that she'd smell like roses. But here . . ." Chloe types something on her phone. "I just sent you a copy of the book. Take some time to breathe, enjoy a light guilty-pleasure read, and think about taking a trip with that cute son of yours."

We talk a little longer, my guilt and grief waning in Chloe's company. When I finally leave, riding my bike back through the quiet neighborhood streets home, I see a missed call and text from Henry. I finally look at it as I walk my bike to my garage.

Henry: Did you get home alright?

I send a thumbs-up, my stomach lurching all over again.

Henry: Let's talk tomorrow. Please.

I don't respond.

Two Days Later

"Yoo-hoo!" Mirabel coos through my front door screen just as I'm bribing Heathcliff to eat oatmeal and soy milk. Admittedly, it looks like *Oliver Twist* gruel.

At sixty, my mother-in-law is annoyingly beautiful. Her clingy jade-green dress and coiffed blond hair make her look like Jessica Lange.

"*Nana!*" Heathcliff yells, leaping up from the kitchen table.

"Mirabel, I'm running late."

But she's already inside hugging Heathcliff. Her cloying cigarettes-and-lavender scent hits my nose like a heavy brick. She's lied for years about smoking. Yet, Philip remembered her leaning out the den window in her bathrobe every morning with her cigarette.

"Now, listen to your mama, Heathie, and eat up your . . ." she wrinkles her nose at the bowl's contents ". . . breakfast."

She glances at the soy milk carton on the table.

"I see you're still not feeding him regular milk."

"As I've told you, he's lactose intolerant."

"We don't have any of *that* in our family. My mama always made us drink our milk every morning."

I clench my teeth as I follow her into the den, where she runs a finger along my dusty fireplace mantel.

"You should have called before driving up all this way this morning."

"Now, hush, Elizabeth. I'll cut to the chase."

I tighten my lips. Things between us have always been a bit cool. But she's never spoken to me this sharply.

She narrows her red-rimmed eyes. Like me, she's grieving. I'm sure losing Philip has almost broken her. But Mirabel likes secrets, not emotions. And that night of the accident hangs between us like a swinging scythe.

"Your *law-yer* called mine yesterday. Philip's old friend Henry Lawton's been prodding around about a trust I have all set up for Heathcliff. I need to know what your game is." She crosses her arms, gold bracelets clattering.

"Game?"

"Did Philip tell you anything that night?"

"He left a message that we needed to talk. It seems like there's something I needed to know."

She closes her eyes in relief.

"Are you going to tell me what it is?"

"It's a trifle. It doesn't matter."

"Then why did you drive all the way here to talk about it?"

She glares, tapping her manicured nails on the mantel, her mouth firming into a tight line. She's wishing for one of those cigarettes she doesn't smoke.

"Look, Mirabel, I have to get to work . . ."

She marches toward me, pointing her finger. "You should

stay *out* of this, Elizabeth. Just be happy that I have a bit of money set aside for my grandson's education."

"Henry's just protecting my son's interests."

"No *games*, Elizabeth."

"I'm not the one playing games here."

She scowls, picks up her purse and leaves, slamming the door hard behind her.

My fingers tremble as I brush Heathcliff's hair and pour coffee into a thermos. She's trying to rattle me, and it's best to let Henry deal with her at this point.

After Mirabel's unexpected visit, I realize Heathcliff missed the bus. I'm late dropping him off at school, and amid the scramble, I left my coffee thermos on the kitchen counter. I'm so shaken, I clench the steering wheel driving to work. My head pounds from lack of caffeine. And damn it, I stayed up too late reading *Blood Oath*. Chloe wasn't lying—it really is the most marvelous trash reading.

The headache hits hard as I'm walking through the department. As I pass her desk, Sandra lets me know she left a few letters for me.

How bad can it be? No one wants to actually write letters anymore.

Unfortunately, a small *pack* of envelopes lies at the foot of my office door.

Additionally, someone taped one torn, spiral-bound notebook sheet to my door. I tear off the sheet first.

> Miss Wells, can I have extra credit? This Austen chick is like so tough. —B

Furious, I scoop up the letters and unlock my office door.

There's four from Bill Rhodes. I only read the first one. Nothing else from him is worth reading.

> **We need the fucking humanities fall budget by 2:00 today. Your weird Amish experiment can't keep you from doing your job.**

Then there's a simpering note from Dean McGregor asking if I can cut Brad some slack in my seminar: *He's really looking forward to Cancún . . .*

There's one barely legible letter from the provost asking me to hire four more adjuncts for the fall.

Three students left handwritten requests for overrides for my fall classes.

I slump in my desk chair, staring at Everett Dane's smoldering gaze and then promptly send each letter through the shredder. I try to finish grading my latest batch of papers, but my mind can't stay anchored on my students' semicoherent thoughts. I head over to the library to try to start collecting sources for a Brontë conference I'm speaking at in October.

But by midmorning, I've had a full-blown panic attack—racing heart, sweaty palms, vertigo—when I briefly thought I left Philip's bird urn in the encyclopedia section. It turned out I stashed him in my bag when Bill Rhodes walked by. (I wasn't going to expose Philip to Bill's patriarchal toxicity.) After stowing the urn in my pocket, I hurry from the library toward my classroom building.

My phone dings.

Mirabel: Don't forget my advice. Stay out of this.

I still see her in that too-tight dress, reeking of cigarettes. Seriously, with all this drama she's drawing even more attention to whatever it is she's trying to cover up.

I chew my lip angrily, trying to forget my hundreds of small problems amid my big looming problem: Philip is gone, and I have to learn to live without him.

I cut across the main campus lawn, passing a large white events tent. There's a ribbon-cutting in an hour for the new glossy Student Support Services Center—a center we clearly cannot afford. Patrick told me that the new director is making three times what we do. I stare at the rows of empty folding chairs in the tent.

I'll skip it.

"Dr. Wells!" Professor Evie Caldwell, head of the art department, hurries down the pavement toward me. She never actually earned her doctorate. Instead, she was given an honorary doctorate in the '70s for walking around Berkeley wearing nothing but Post-it notes on her naked body and paper clips in her hair in what was supposed to be a profound artistic feminist statement. Something about women's bodily presence in the workplace.

She stands far too close to me, and on her clothes, I smell the burrito breakfast meal she eats during midmorning meetings. She's thin, and her thick, swoopy gray hair falls long around her shoulders.

"Did you attend the Fiscal Oversight Committee meeting this morning? The funding allocation for this Student Services Center is *unbelievable*."

She resembles a fairy-tale witch. I picture her luring children to a cottage with a trail of candies. I should keep Heathcliff away from her.

"Are you listening to me, Dr. Wells?"

"What? Yes."

She attempts to look empathetic. "I'm terribly sorry about Colin."

"Philip."

"*Philip*. I know you're in mourning." She glances distastefully over my black skirt and blouse. "But there are grave consequences if you can't convince the provost to stop taking money from the humanities to give six-figure salaries to consultants and Student Services Center workers. It's criminal."

"It actually isn't."

"Whose side are you *on*, Dr. Wells?" And then she *pokes* her finger into my chest for emphasis before storming off. "Oh, and I would suggest that you be careful. You're on Bill's shit list."

I realize how amazingly little I care that Dr. Bill Rhodes in philosophy continues to hate me and Patrick. I realize how little I care that Professor Caldwell also hates me.

I stand on the lawn, staring at the empty white tent, its sides rippling in the soft Carolina breeze.

For the first time in fifteen years, I don't want to teach class.

I walk into my seminar, where we're wrapping up *Pride and Prejudice* today.

"Jesus—she's still dressing like Morticia Addams," Brad snorts to Ryan next to him. Anger flares poker-hot inside me, that unedited letter burning in my satchel. Best to ignore Brad and focus on my twenty other students. As least two want to be here. Kayla is smiling and attentive in the front row as I arrange my notes on the lectern.

I try very hard to lose myself in the material. I try to remember why I tolerate campus politics and committees—it's because I love teaching these books. But I'm not feeling it today. I keep playing with the jet necklace at my throat as I lecture, but I can't block out Brad unashamedly texting and chewing on a Dum-Dums sucker, the stick hanging out the side of his mouth. I see Mirabel. I see Henry's handsome face too close to mine. And underneath it all, I feel the goddamn awful heartache.

"Is it a happily-ever-after for Lizzy Bennet by the end?"

"No?" Kayla offers hesitantly.

My phone lights up.

Mirabel: Your LAWYER tried to call me again. Now you both will be hearing from MINE, Elizabeth.

I see red.

"No! Despite what everyone tells you, there is no such thing as a happy ending. Ever, ever, *EVER*. Sure, Elizabeth Bennet's happy now—she's bagged Mr. Fucking Darcy. But it won't last. There's still that god-awful *dysfunctional* family. Lydia will always ask for money. Mrs. Bennet is always going to be a drama queen. And Lady Catherine de Bourgh is *always* going to be the rotten bitch who sticks her nose in everyone else's business."

Everyone's listening to me now. Even Brad.

"And *then* . . . one day, fifteen years from their wedding, Mr. Darcy, the perfect husband, father, and picture of health, dies in a stupid motherfucking carriage accident on the way home from Brighton. It's a dumb accident. Just a little rain, and the carriage slips clean off the road, killing him instantly. Lizzy doesn't know what to do except soldier on. But everyone hounds her: Her hot solicitor wants her to help settle estate questions instantly, like *right fucking now*. Lady Catherine de Bourgh shows up on her porch every goddamn week to micromanage her life. She's got this gaggle of silly scullery maids quibbling endlessly over the STUPIDEST things, and MEANWHILE Lizzie's just trying to take care of her children and put herself back together after she's been broken *into a million GODDAMN pieces*!"

I'm crying, sniffing, and shaking as one giant ball of rage and grief seizes up in my chest.

The tears won't stop flowing and all my students stare at me.

Kayla kindly brings me a little box of Kleenex.

As I blow my nose, Brad speaks up. "Miss Wells, did you get my note about the extra credit?"

"Oh, *Brad*. Indeed, I do have a response for you," I say icily.

The sucker stick stops mid-chew.

I pull out the envelope from my satchel, dramatically tear it open and read it loudly.

"Dear B—

In my fifteen years of teaching, you are the most entitled, sexist dodo to darken my classroom door. You smell like skunkweed, beer, and unwashed sheets. You strut about like you are God's gift to women. You park your red BMW in reserved faculty spaces without consequence. You call Jane Austen a 'chick,' but you are the classic insufferable fool who shows up in her pages again and again and again—boastful, ridiculous, and, above all, STUPID. You are fodder for novels and will end up as comic relief in a good many women's more relevant life stories.

I will never—in a MILLION years—give you extra credit.

If you want a good grade in my class, you put in the elbow grease and FUCKING EARN IT.

Sincerely,
DR. Wells"

"Whoa! Dr. Wells just roasted *Brad*!" Pauline yells from the back as all the women in the class cheer. Kayla high-fives Susanna next to her as Maddy yells, "*Burn!*"

Brad stands, red-faced, waves the middle finger at everyone, and storms out, classroom door slamming behind him.

"That was awesome, Dr. Wells," Kayla says.

Everyone's smiling, including Ryan.

I'm somewhat satisfied that I've finally given a voice to the universal female dislike for Brad McGregor. Although I'm still a hot mess, reading the letter was cathartic. Steam releasing from a screaming kettle. But obviously I can't teach now, so I dismiss class and head to my office.

I've stopped trembling, but I'm drained and sad, unable to do anything, even the smallest task, like unbending a paper clip.

I pick up the five-by-seven-inch silver-framed photo from my wedding day with Philip.

I wore a simple sleeveless ivory wedding dress, my light brown hair twisted back in a French knot. In the photo, Philip and I are kissing in front of our wedding cake, our cheeks youthfully round and flushed with champagne and joy. Philip had wanted us to take professional dancing lessons together before the wedding, but I never scheduled them. Still, we'd swayed to our favorite Beatles song, "If I Fell." Before dinner, painfully shy Dad broke out of his comfort zone to toast me with an eighth-century Japanese poem celebrating daughters. My unsentimental mom lifted her champagne flute to me, toasting to "the most beautiful daughter in the world, to the girl who has her grandma's strength and heart." I shed happy tears, and Philip squeezed my hand under the table.

Last summer, I'd remembered Mom's wedding toast as she withered away from breast cancer. Philip had taken the best care of Heathcliff while I went on leave and stayed in Indiana, brushing Mom's peppered hair as it fell out in clumps and feeding her broth. I loved Philip more than ever when he came to her funeral, stood beside me, and wept like she'd been his own mother.

Between losing Mom and then the film premiere, last year had been a lot. I'd felt devastated and thrilled and broken and grateful in so many short months. There hadn't been time to process any of it. For Christmas, Philip had bought us dance lessons, a gentle reminder that life is short and precious, and we should cash in now on the experience because there would be no better time or guaranteed tomorrows. But I'd never acted on it, and the gift card lay untouched on my jewelry box. In spite of his nudging, I hadn't really danced since high school show choir. Now he's gone, and we'll never take the lessons.

Someone knocks at my door. Quickly, I wipe a tear from my face and set the photo down as Patrick comes in.

He runs his hand through his beard. "I just got a call from Dean McGregor . . ."

"I'm fired."

"No," Patrick sighs. "You're too valuable. Unlike the rest of us, you write books people actually read."

"Well, Brad had it coming."

Patrick smirks. "Oh, your Dear John letter sounds fucking awesome."

"But . . ."

"You're to go on paid leave from now through the rest of the summer."

"Are you kidding? *That's* my punishment?"

He shrugs. "I'll take care of everything—I'll finish the class, give the final next week, get all the grading done, and keep Rhodes at bay. You just leave and forget about this place for a while."

I sit frozen at my desk.

"Go on, Lizzie. You deserve so much."

I GET IN MY CAR AND MAKE THE CALL BEFORE I'M EVEN off campus.

"Hey, Sarah—I'll take you up on the London town house offer."

From *Blood Oath* by A.D. Hemmings:

Chadwick Hall speeds along Wye Valley Road on the route to Tintern, autumn leaves rippling from the trees around him.

He needs this journey—not only to interview the latest victim's sister, but to reassess his love life.

He can't stop thinking about last night with Emilia Wren. Her scent, her stockings. She was bloody amazing. And she'd been so deft at that rooftop chase. Wren reminded him of the other partner Catherine (or was it Caitlin?) he'd shagged after one too many Irish whiskeys while they'd been on the heels of that sapphire jewel thief in Bangor.

Is yet another affair a good idea?

More importantly—will he ever be able to commit?

He runs his hand through his hair as his sleek olive Bentley picks up speed.

From *The Heathcliff Saga*:

"Where are we going?" Cathy asks Linwood as he leads her through the steep downhill path, heather brushing against her skirts.

"On a journey."

He smiles crookedly. Her heart seizes up. She loves Heathcliff. But she's not immune to Linwood's charm, his chiseled chin, the way his blond hair falls over his tall forehead.

But she stops at the narrow cave entrance, an almost invisible slit between towering gritstone rock. Goose bumps prickle her neck.

"Nelly said never to come here. It's the fairy bed . . ."

"Nelly doesn't want us to know about the magic. We can summon it for ourselves, Cathy."

He steps inside, reaches his hand out, beckoning her in.

She hesitates, peaty wind from the cave mouth blowing

softly against her cheeks. "I don't know, Linwood. Heathcliff inherited his powers—but the moor's magic. It's not to be messed with."

"You're afraid."

She tightens her lips. "Never."

That crooked smile again. He takes her hand, tugs. "Then come along."

5

....

Previous Year

New Year's Eve

That winter after Mom died, Ian and I made sure Dad wasn't alone for the holidays. After Christmas, while my bachelor-brother flew off to New York City with friends to guzzle champagne and watch the ball drop, I flew up to Indiana to be with Dad. Not that I was complaining. For introvert-me, New York City at this time of year seems like a special kind of hell, and if I were back in South Carolina, I'd be at Philip's law firm's party trying to keep a grip on my martini glass through satin opera gloves.

    Instead, Dad and I sit on the couch in flannel pajamas watching the Times Square crowd on television. We're like Bridget and her father in *Bridget Jones's Diary*, except instead of paper crowns, we sport beanies and heavy sweaters. The fire roars, but the 1915 farmhouse I grew up in still has its original windows. Although a little drafty, the house is cozy. Cedarwood paneling glows warm in the firelight while heavy pale green damask curtains help insulate against Midwest winds.

Earlier in the afternoon, I made rhubarb pies using Mom's canned fruits in the pantry. It's been years since I've had time to make a pie, and I enjoyed slicing through the butter and flour with the pastry blender, rolling out the dough to an eighth-of-an-inch thickness, and then pressing it carefully into one of Mom's blue glass pie dishes. It was a labor of love, as I knew with each step that nothing would reach her culinary perfection. My crust would be a little too thick or chewy and my fluting ruffles uneven. By the time I opened the canned rhubarb and poured it into the pie crust, I had to wipe away a tear. Her garden lies just beyond the window. There, dormant tomato, blueberry, and rhubarb bushes quiver, brown and stalky, under a dusting of snow. I doubt Dad will know how to tend them come spring.

Thirty minutes before the ball drops, I go into the kitchen to cut pie slices, hopeful that after all these years sugar-free, Dad might enjoy a piece. When I bring it back, he thanks me, but leaves his plate on the coffee table untouched.

"Still no sugar?" I ask, readjusting my beanie hat and reaching for my own piece. Dad has followed a strict no-sugar diet for years.

He shakes his head. "She used to make a few jars just for me with no added sugar. I finished the last one last month." He stares ahead numbly at the television. "It was her canned blueberries."

I wonder if he'll ever loosen up with his diet. Then again, perhaps his discipline is paying off. He might be pushing seventy, but his bloodwork always comes back excellent, and he takes a brisk five-mile walk outside every morning. Nothing stops him—even this Jack London–novel weather.

I take a bite of pie, sweetened rhubarb stalk pieces crunching in my mouth. Mom's filling is of course heavenly, and my from-scratch pie crust is, well . . . not bad. Still, I can almost hear Mary Berry's voice in my head primly telling me my dough is a little too crisp.

"We used to dance," Dad says suddenly.

"You and Mom?"

"Yes."

I stare up at my parents' framed wedding photo over the fireplace mantelpiece. Mom wears a simple white A-line dress with bell sleeves, her hair neatly sprayed in a modest beehive under a fingertip veil. Dad stands beside her sporting a '70s version of his tortoiseshell glasses. His hair is darker and thicker.

"I can't see Mom dancing."

"She danced."

I mute the television.

"You know that gala where we met back in college?"

I nod. I knew they met at a dance, but I've never heard the details.

"The school wasn't comfortable with the disco moves everyone was doing at the time, but they agreed to allow salsa dancing and hired a small conga band. She came up to me—I remember noticing her confidence, her perfectly smooth hair and her short buttercream dress—she was so *put together*. 'Hi, I'm Nora,' she'd said, putting her hand out. I told her my name was Gaylord, and she didn't laugh."

His voice tapers off as he stares down at his uneaten pie slice.

"And then you danced?"

He shakes his head. "Not yet. She told me I had punch dribbled on my tie, and she dabbed it off with a napkin. Then she asked me to dance. I told her I didn't know how to. She said I'd be fine, just to follow her."

I can see Mom taking charge, leading my awkward young

father away from the sidelines of the university ballroom and showing him all the right steps.

"She taught me to dance that evening. And then after we were married the next year and had a little extra money from her nursing job, we took some salsa dance lessons. She was as focused at the lessons as she was with everything else. She said the dancing was good for our hearts and our joints and that it would keep us young. I remember how she smiled when we danced, how she pressed her palms against mine during the lessons. She made it look like I led, but she did. She led all the steps and sent me in the right directions."

"Why'd you stop?"

He shrugs. "We had you and then Ian. Between my grad school and her hospital shifts, I think it just became too much. I have few regrets with her. But I wish we'd kept that up."

We sit there in silence, listening to the fire crackle and watching the muted partiers in Times Square. I try not to think about Philip's Christmas gift to me last week—a couple's dance lesson package at a local studio. He was so proud, so excited to give it to me. He had smiled like Heathcliff in a candy shop when I opened the envelope.

Well, what do you think? he'd asked.

Ummm . . . sure? I'd responded, clearly not as enthusiastic as he'd hoped. He still kissed me and then began to put batteries in Heathcliff's remote-controlled Batmobile.

Why am I so resistant? What am I afraid of? I think I'd just feel silly.

Philip would take lessons with me in a heartbeat. But then again—I'm pushing forty, on the wrong side of thirty-five. And with *The Heathcliff Saga* movie just coming out . . .

I'm just too busy.

Henry: Hey, Liz. I know things are pretty darn awkward after the other night. You might not want to talk to me, but we need to talk about Miss Mirabel. Just call or text. How about it?

Lizzie: I'm on my way to London. I'll call or text when I get there.

Henry: LONDON???

During the plane ride, Heathcliff alternates between sleep and his tablet. With the time change combined with the airport donuts and screens, he'll be a gremlin by the time we land. Meanwhile, I'm flying through *Blood Oath*. Sure, Chadwick Hall is a royal ass, but with his suave moves, fast car, and the lightning-speed plot, it's pretty hard to put down. As the cabin lights go out for the night, I reluctantly put it away, monitor

Heathcliff as he brushes his teeth in the closet-size bathroom, and give him a melatonin gummy.

I settle back in my seat and (perhaps unwisely) think about some of the problems I'm leaving at home.

Philip hadn't liked talking about his family. Did he have a *good* relationship with his parents? Yes, I suppose he did. I never saw him argue with them. But were they *close*? That's a different question. He never called Ted *Dad*—only Ted. He called Mirabel *Mama*. But there was something very formal about their relationship. In fact, there was something very formal about that whole sprawling *house*—The Azalea Dream.

Bordering the Ashley River, the white clapboard structure with painted black shutters looks like something from the pages of *Southern Living*. Azaleas, daylilies, and bold pink zinnias bloom in the surrounding gardens, while star jasmine wraps up along the tall porch columns. Ted himself always seemed more porch fixture than human, an accessory for Mirabel and her home. With his red bow tie, newspaper, little mint julep, he naps through weekend afternoons on one of Mirabel's many white wicker rockers. Mirabel tends the gardens herself—her yellow gardening gloves matching the large yellow bow of her sun hat. Everything always looks coordinated and picture-perfect in her world.

Years ago, Mirabel told Philip she'd never really loved Ted, and they weren't more than roommates. She'd confessed this after an evening of too much Chardonnay with the Methodist Women's League. He'd been twelve at the time.

"It was weird and confusing," Philip told me. "I asked her about it the next day, and she said she never said it. But I know what I heard."

Mirabel fights hard to keep everything perfect. I remember portraits lining the Azalea Dream halls—posed photographs of Philip in perfectly pressed sailor suits and pristine seersuckers, an oil painting of Mirabel as a young debutante. She lies about smoking; what else does she lie about? What did Philip want to tell me so badly on the night of the accident?

Heathcliff snores softly, and I tug his Batman blanket up under his chin.

I put my black satin sleep mask over my eyes and lean my seat back. I haven't had any weird widow dreams yet, but maybe due to the melatonin and two glasses of airplane Merlot, I slip into one now. It's nothing too gothic or Brontë-ish. I'm simply following Philip through Mirabel's big azalea garden at the back of the house. We're on a meandering path at the peak of spring; fat honeybees buzz lazily among the bright pink petals. Philip wears khakis and a light blue checkered pressed shirt, something he would wear to work when he's not in court. He walks ahead of me, sunlight glaring on his neatly cut blond hair. The distance between us grows with each step. I can never quite catch up. I call out to him, but he never turns around. The garden melts away to Parliament Square on a sunny morning. Jostling against picture-taking tourists and people on their way to work, I follow him, calling his name, but he never looks back. Again, the distance between us increases until he's lost in the crowd.

I wake up, a sick feeling of separation and loss spreading through my gut. The cabin lights are still off, but early twilight peeks over the clouds outside my window. We'll land in London before long, and I'll take an Uber with Heathcliff to the Bloomsbury row house. We'll eat whatever delicious meal Sarah's housekeeper has waiting for us.

Meanwhile, no matter what happens around me or wherever I am, in my heart, I'm always chasing Philip.

MS. FERNSBY STANDS IN THE DOOR OF THE ROW HOUSE, and I almost drop my third Starbucks coffee of the day.

Around sixty, she looks like she stepped out of a Masterpiece Mystery! episode, one of those cozy murder mysteries where she's the sweet, pink-cheeked hobby-investigator who gets villagers to spill the beans over tea and scones. Gray hair pulled back in a neat knot, she wears a flower-print dress down past her knees with gray tights and loafers. Everything about her is warm and inviting. I want to tell her all my secrets.

"Oh, *hullo*, dearie," she coos at Heathcliff, kneeling down and hugging him tightly. He grins dopily. For all his Batman-toughness, he loves to be babied. "You're a cute one. I've heard your tummy doesn't like cheese and milk, so I've been baking you dairy-free treats all morning."

"And you, luv." She stands, hugs me tightly now.

God, she even *smells* warm and inviting—like garden roses and baking chocolate. "Sarah told me about your loss. I'm so sorry. I hope you can breathe a bit here."

She leads us into the house. The front door opens into a sizable parlor with damask curtains, a little fireplace with a cuckoo clock on the mantel, a comfortable vintage love seat and sofa, and polished walnut floors. Except for outlets tucked into the whitewashed wall beams, the room looks unchanged for the past two hundred years.

A large tabby lingers on the sofa.

"*Cat!*" Heathcliff yells.

The cat hisses and runs from the room. Heathcliff follows in hot pursuit.

"And don't mind Lucy," Ms. Fernsby says as she fluffs up a sofa pillow. "She'll warm up to him in no time."

"And he won't hurt her," I promise. "He just wants to cross-examine her a bit."

As we leave the parlor, we pass through a small dining room. An antique table takes up most of the space, with classic touches everywhere—a simple, elegant chandelier, long peony-print curtains framing the windows. The dining room opens into a small but adorable kitchen where light blue painted cabinets display crystal glassware and antique plates. The only modern furnishing is the large high-end gas stove taking up half a wall. At the opposite end of the kitchen, I follow her up narrow wooden stairs, the wall lined with framed pressed flowers and pinned butterflies.

Sarah's silver-haired House of Lords father stares imposingly from a portrait at the top. I've always assumed she wasn't particularly close to him. She talks more about Ms. Fernsby and her serial nannies than her parents.

"This is young Heathie's room," Ms. Fernsby says when we walk by a little room with a twin trundle bed.

"Hey, Mama," Heathcliff says from where he's sitting on the area rug making a LEGO building. Poor Lucy must be hiding somewhere.

"I knew he'd take to LEGO. They were my daughter's years ago."

"Oh," I murmur, wondering about Ms. Fernsby's backstory.

She shows me her cozy bedroom. A well-worn Harlequin, *The Governess and the Duke*, lies open on the bed's pink rose-patterned coverlet. "It's been my place for the past forty years, and then . . . here is where you'll be staying." She opens a door at the end of the short hall. The room is pleasant with a large, canopied bed, a comfortable sitting area with more antique chairs, and a bathroom. The bathroom has a large garden tub and a new sink embedded in an old walnut vanity lined with scented soaps, lotions, and candles. A plush marigold-colored robe hangs from a hook on the back of the door. This *must* have been Sarah's parents' room. I picture her politician father shaving, stern-faced, in the bathroom mirror as Ms. Fernsby calls him to breakfast.

"You'll make yourself at home here, I hope. I've left some

books on the nightstand." Her blue eyes suddenly sparkle as she nods to *The Heathcliff Saga* atop the stack. "It was such a pleasure reading your book. I love a steamy romance, and I flew through it in three days!"

She leans forward as if to whisper a juicy piece of gossip. "Is it true that Bella Patel was dating *both* of them?"

I feel my mouth twitch as I remember all the romantic drama between the actors. Bella Patel (Cathy) dated both Harry Waters (Linwood) and Everett Dane. I still remember how she'd confided in me with all her angst last fall after the premiere. Still, I want to maintain her privacy.

"I'm not really clear on the timelines."

"Well, I say good for her!" Ms. Fernsby says, tightening her apron strings. "You're only young once, and if she has a chance with both of those handsome men, she should take it." She heads toward the door. "Get some rest, luv."

"I should get Heathcliff settled."

"Now, don't you worry about him! I'll put him down myself if he gets tired. I'm about to pour myself a cuppa, and I'm sure he'll want a treat."

She winks and shuts the door.

I open my suitcase, staring at the folded black leggings, blouses, and dresses. Philip's bird urn lies nestled within the fabrics. What am I doing here? As I stare at my Victorian-ish widow styles, touch gently the jet necklace at my throat, a strange mix of fear and anticipation swirls in my chest like a whirling dervish.

My brain is too foggy to sort through it all, so I brush my teeth, and sink into the bed. I clutch the bird urn and fall into a deliciously deep sleep.

I wake up groggy, pillow imprint on my cheek, my hand still tight around the bird urn.

Hazy late-afternoon sunlight streams through the curtains. Except for some traffic noise from the street below, all is quiet.

I feel low feline purring and a warm weight on the bedcovers.

Lucy. I'm so glad she found a Heathcliff-free zone for napping. Gently, I rub her back, and she stretches languidly, peering at me through one half-open green eye.

I stretch as well, suddenly remembering I forgot to text Henry. Drat. I do have to start talking to him. There's an ocean between us now, so things can't be that awkward, right?

Setting the urn on the nightstand, I reach down to where my suitcase lies open on the floor and feel around for my phone.

Instead, I accidentally grab Philip's phone. For his screen saver, he has a photo of us holding chopsticks up dramatically over a large platter of sushi. I've seen this image a million times, and during sleepless nights, I like to scroll through his social media—his last Instagram post from the weekend before he died is of Heathcliff jumping inside his kiddie pool wearing a Batman mask. His last Facebook post was of me sitting across from him at our favorite café. I'm wearing a teal sundress and smiling wryly over an espresso. He captioned it "I'm the luckiest."

Most people lie about how great their lives are on social media. But not us.

We really were that damn happy.

Sad and numb, I just want to keep scrolling. After looking through his social media feeds, I jump over to his saved photos. There are a million of us. Buried amid the shots of Heathcliff and me is one from the week before he died. It's a picture he took with his phone of a photo from the '70s.

I make the image larger: it's a bunch of people at a party on the banks of the Ashley River. Steam rises from roasting oysters, and people stand around sipping beer under dripping Spanish moss. I spot Mirabel, and she looks *amazing*—sporting Farrah Fawcett blond layers and a hot-pink trapeze dress with white leather booties. She's laughing with a couple—the man tall and blond in a blue seersucker suit, the woman red-haired in a fitted Jackie O. blue dress. The man, woman, and Mirabel are dressed very sharp and look a thousand times more interesting than Ted. In fact, Ted stands near the large grill contemplating the oysters. He looks the same as he does now, only a little less gray.

Ted and Mirabel would have been married around this time. (He came from an old moneyed family with a large trust fund.) And Philip would come along about three years later. But who is this handsome couple? Something tickles in the back of my head. Philip saving the photo, so close to that night he went to Mirabel's for dinner . . .

My phone rings, jolting me from my thoughts.

"Ian?"

"Hey, Lizzie. I'll keep this short because my international phone plan sucks. I'm worried about Dad."

"Is he ok?" I ask, alarmed.

"Oh, yeah, sorry I should have clarified. Physically, he's fine. But you know he's never been super-talkative. Lately he's been downright withdrawn. Like he just wants to sit in his study and read articles about Ralph Waldo Emerson."

"How isn't that normal?"

"He's not hanging out with people. He's stopped giving guest lectures at the university or doing any of his morning nature walks. Also, when I stopped by to check on him the other day, he was eating a *Twinkie*."

"Okay, that is weird." Dad didn't even eat the cake at my wedding reception.

"Yeah. Anyway, I just wanted it to be on your radar."

He asks me how I'm holding up, and I give him a brief update.

"Good. Just please, continue to take care of yourself, sis."

After the call, I slump back on my pillows, half-heartedly stroking Lucy. Perhaps I should have gone back home to Indiana. Guilt washes over me. Dad might need me.

Why didn't I think of him?

Dad was a distinguished English professor specializing in American transcendentalism. And not at a little failing college like Willoughby, but at Notre Dame. He published only in the most prestigious American literature journals. If his colleagues were as terrible as mine, he never complained.

He wasn't particularly emotional or affectionate. And yet, I knew he loved me.

How did I know?

On the fourth-grade playground, I accidentally hit Janice Falls in the face with a dodgeball, and like a banshee from hell, she pummeled me. I came home humiliated because the whole class saw my underwear in the scuffle. Dad took me out for ice cream. Of course, he never bought ice cream for himself, and he said very little as I cried and retold the whole story and licked my cone. But he sat by me, and he listened, and I felt better.

Dad and Mom were a pair. She was a no-nonsense hospital nurse. She cleaned all the time. Like, you could *eat* off our bathroom tiles. She loved us, but she was a "tough love" sort of parent. There was no babying. Resilience was everything. We had to drink a full glass of milk every morning. No exceptions. Good strong bones and all that.

Obviously, Dad and Mom weren't the romantic types, but they loved each other like crazy. Mom would pull something out of the oven, like her lasagna—cheese, noodles, and tomatoes put together with perfect precision. Dad would walk up behind her and put his hands on her shoulders, his nose close to her neck. It wasn't a hug. He just seemed in wonder at her scent, and Mom's lips would curve into a soft, happy smile.

In graduate school, when I returned from Haworth heartbroken, Mom listened, letting me cry on her shoulder for a full five minutes before telling me that Wes was a "stupid weasel," and I should never cry for more than five minutes over such a person. Shamefully, I couldn't keep my tears to the allotted time, so I wept softly in my bedroom until Dad knocked on the door: *Do you want to go out for ice cream?*

Mom and Dad couldn't have been more different and yet they were perfect for each other.

I realize now how much she grounded my academic Dad in so many ways. Underneath my preoccupation with my own grief and widowhood, I've worried about him and what he's doing without her. Her constant cleaning, her perfectly arranged lasagnas, her scent—it all anchored him.

I stare at my phone. Dad doesn't text out of principle. He prides himself on staying "technologically disconnected," as he puts it. I think it's a transcendentalist thing. Emerson didn't text.

I call him, but it goes to voicemail. I leave a message telling him even though I'm in London, he's on my mind, and I love him. I tell him my neighbor, Edith, is caring for the pretty orchid.

Henry: Are ya'll there yet?

Me: Yes, but jet-lagged. Can we talk tomorrow?

Henry: Holy hell, have I hit some walls with your MIL. Piece. Of. Work. Will 6:00PM London time work?

Me: Sure

The dots start like he's typing something, then stop. I hope we can dial back the awkwardness and wrap up this strange trust business.

Blushing, I remember how nice that almost-kiss was.

Maybe we can just pretend the almost-kiss didn't happen.

Lucy purrs into my side through the covers, and I rub her back.

I might be wearing nineteenth-century widow's weeds, but even I'm not that delusional.

AFTER A HOT BATH, I VENTURE OUT WEARING MY FAVORite black silk pajamas.

Pausing at Heathcliff's bedroom door, I watch him snoring softly. He has Philip's hair color and face shape. I tug the covers up and kiss him, inhaling that wonderful little-boy smell of sweat and cotton Batman pajamas.

Downstairs, Ms. Fernsby sits at the kitchen table with a scrapbook. "You took a good nap, luv."

"It was nice. As was the bath afterward."

She puts a red teakettle on one of the gas burners, turning it on with a few loud clicks.

"Have some biscuits while I reheat dinner," she says, pushing a cookie plate toward me.

I realize how hungry I am. Soft and delicious, the shortbread cookies have a subtle maple flavor. After three, I remind myself that well-behaved widows probably didn't binge on baked goods. While Ms. Fernsby puts a platter of roast beef and asparagus into the oven, I hesitate, then go ahead and reach for a fourth cookie. Widowed Queen Victoria certainly looked like she gave up on squeezing into corsets.

I start flipping through the open scrapbooks. Most of the photos are polaroids with what is undoubtedly a younger Ms. Fernsby and a look-alike girl.

"That's my Mabel. She's your age, and she's trying to go back to school. She didn't do so well her first time at uni. But she's a good girl and tired of working in the coffee shop."

I stare at the little girl cuddling a Cabbage Patch doll.

"You're probably wondering who her father is."

"Oh . . . uh . . . *no?*"

"Lord Archibald Routledge—Sarah's father."

I almost choke on the cookie. Sarah never said anything about *that*.

"It happened soon after I started working here. His wife stayed married to him on account of his money, but she never fancied me. I hadn't wanted to hurt her. But . . ." Ms. Fernsby shrugs. "He felt badly and kept me employed. He was also always afraid of it leaking out—that someone with the newspapers would learn he had a daughter with his young housekeeper. I had mixed feelings about staying here, but I had nothing—no schooling, no money. He could give Mabel a life I thought I couldn't. It's his money she's using to go back to school."

The teakettle screams. She steeps our teas and brings the mugs to the table with a little porcelain dish of sugar.

"It hasn't been a bad life." She spoons a teaspoon into hers and then nudges the sugar bowl to me. "But it never felt like mine."

I swallow a sip of the lavender tea, warm and comforting.

"*He* never belonged to me. The house never belonged to me. Mabel's the only thing that's truly mine, and I needed him to support us. Strangely, I still often feel like I'm keeping the house nice for Lord Routledge even though he's gone now. If it all hadn't happened, I would have wanted my own proper family."

She leans forward like she's whispering a scandalous secret. "You know, I tried one of those dating apps last year. I had no luck at all. They were all thrice divorced solicitors or perverts."

I chuckle.

"And you should get yourself on one of those sites when you're ready. It's an experience."

I imagine myself scrolling through profiles, "swiping right," as the young singles say. And then, troublesome grief comes out of nowhere. I want Philip back. I don't want to spend my evenings on dating apps.

I start ugly-crying over the plate of shortbread cookies.

"Awww . . . I'm so sorry, Lizzie. I didn't mean . . ." She hands me a handkerchief and holds me while I wipe my eyes. Again, her smell of gardens and baking chocolate comforts me.

"It'll get better," she says, rubbing my back soothingly. "I'm talking in platitudes, luv, but you'll put one foot in front of the other. Soldier on. You'll be surprised one day when you wake up not so miserable."

WHEN I FINALLY SINK INTO THE BEDCOVERS, I TAKE A look at the nightstand books.

Under *The Heathcliff Saga*, I'm delighted to find *Blood Oath* and *Blood Ties*. With only three more chapters to go, I crack open *Blood Oath*. Chadwick Hall is a grade A asshole. I don't like how he slept with the suspect's sister two days after his night with Emilia Wren. But I'm sure the suspect's sister is the Cardiff Strangler. This book better not end with a cliffhanger, or I'll have to start *Blood Ties* tonight.

Just as I settle back to read, my phone dings with an Instagram alert.

It's a photo of Bella Patel and me from the film set. She's in full costume, long, muddied tweed skirt and boots, loosened white blouse open and soiled after a romantic tussle with Everett Dane in the last scene. She's sipping an iced coffee and sharing a joke with me as a makeup artist fluffs her dark curls.

> Heading back to England for Heathcliff Saga business (stay tuned, peeps!!!). I can't stop thinking of this woman who started it all!!!

I smile, remembering how much I enjoyed hanging out with Bella, Everett, and Harry on the set and at the film premiere after-parties. Although young, beautiful, and on the cusp of stardom, all three were delightful. Just really fun early twentysomethings.

> Lovely to hear from you @bellapatel! Actually, *she* started it all!

I reply back with the famous portrait of the Brontë siblings as a GIF with flashing stars around Emily's face.

Bella hearts my reply within seconds.

Sarah hadn't said anything about the actors having to be in London. She's been hesitant to bother me about anything nonurgent since Philip's passing, and I'm more than fine with that. Still, I'm curious about what's going on . . .

I think fondly of my time with the actors—Philip and I flew out to visit the LA set for a week during filming, while Mom drove down from Indiana to our house to watch Heathcliff. It had been shortly before her advanced breast cancer diagnosis, and I've been beyond grateful that she had that special time with Heathcliff. Somehow, someway, she convinced my then four-year-old that green vegetables are delicious and would give him superpowers. Meanwhile, Philip and I spent time with Bella, Everett, and Harry, and they made us feel wonderful and young again. Over the course of the next year, I joined the three on a few podcasts, and the weekend before the movie premiered, I flew up for an interview with Bella on a flashy New York City morning show.

It had only been a few months since Mom passed away, and I'd walked onto the studio set nervous, with a hammering heartbeat and sweaty palms. I'd been wearing one of Mom's Jackie O.–style dresses, clingy but feminine and tailored. The dress was mid-length and pale green with an angled neckline and classic belt. Of course, Mom was never "trendy." Her clothes were timeless, simple, and economical—as fashionable in 1960 as they are today. Dad gave me several of her favorite dresses before I flew back to South Carolina after the funeral. Wherever she is in eternity, I hope she saw me that morning onstage wearing her dress and trying to channel her nerves of steel.

Bella had smiled at me from the studio's red couch, and I instantly felt like a schoolmarm. I hadn't seen her since the LA film set visit. She was wearing a cropped red sequined shirt with long, wide-legged trousers and the spikiest spiked gold heels I'd ever seen. And *geez* . . . whose skin looks that spectacular under studio lights? She tossed back one of her beautiful black locks, smiled warmly, and got up to hug me. "Hey, Lizzie!"

Although the show's host, Jenna McGathery, had prepped us ahead of time, I'd worried my IQ would plummet two minutes before the interview. Fortunately, Bella was more seasoned with these interviews and helped me feel at ease. Then Jenna asked me why I chose the *Wuthering Heights* story in which to infuse my tale. I still remember my response: *It couldn't be any other backdrop. Unlike so many other romantic stories, Emily Brontë's characters get beyond the warm fuzzies and happily-ever-afters to the raw, aching nature of love that if left unchecked has the potential to ruin us. I think that's why after all these years so many still connect with the book. We all know that love can be wonderful, and we'll go to desperate lengths to find it. But even for the lucky ones of us who find our soulmates, there's always that risk of loss.*

My chest clenches while I stare at the silly Brontë GIF I just posted as I recall those words. I never imagined that this loss would play out for me so soon. Additionally, I think what I said resonated with Bella, because after the interview, she started confiding her romantic woes to me like I was her relationship therapist. I'd felt flattered, but woefully inadequate. I mean, yes, I had my soulmate, but I'd always felt that was just splendidly dumb luck. My previous experience in the romance department had been misreading a textbook cad and fantasizing about meeting the cravat-wearing man of my dreams in a Victorian tearoom.

Immediately after the interview, in a back studio dressing room, Bella started weeping on my shoulder, mascara streaking down her cheeks. I soothed her, holding her in a hug and giving her a Kleenex. I realized that out-of-this-world beauty and a chic Brooklyn brownstone couldn't make anyone immune from heartbreak.

"He's just not that into me!" she'd wailed about Harry into the shoulder of Mom's dress. Between what I'd gleaned from the set and the paparazzi magazines I'd followed, my head spun from the drama between these three. After a whirlwind romance, she'd recently broken up with Everett to be with Harry.

"Of course he is . . ." I muttered, not knowing what else to say. Still, I remembered how on set he'd stared a little too longingly at the hot Australian actor playing Dr. Kenneth.

"I left Everett for him—but he just doesn't seem that attracted to me! I could strut around in a string bikini, and he still wouldn't pull himself away from watching *Dance Moms*."

I smoothed her now mussed locks and handed her another Kleenex.

"Bella, so I don't know everything that's going on, but as your nerdy, much-older sister-figure, I want you to know that if it doesn't work out between you and Harry, all of this will pass, and you'll feel better one day. Trust me, I know. After my first heartbreak, I thought the bottom would drop out."

"Do you mind me asking what happened?"

"It involved a contorted sex position and an antique icebox."

"Huh?"

"Never mind. My point is that you will weather this. These things all have a way of working out in the end."

I remember how she nodded and then profusely apologized for the mascara on my dress. I reassured her it was fine. Mom would have liked knowing that her sensible dress's shoulder fabric kept this young woman's mascara from running on the extravagantly glam and ridiculously expensive crop top.

I wonder how Bella is doing and who she's dating now. I wonder why she's heading back to England. I send her a quick Instagram private message, letting her know I'm in London for a few weeks and if it works out, it would be wonderful to meet for lunch or coffee. I then send Sarah a quick text asking if she knows why the actors are making their way here.

Turning off my phone for the night, I dive back into *Blood Oath*.

8

By morning, I learn Ms. Fernsby makes a to-die-for English breakfast.

I've never cared for beans, but there's something special about Ms. Fernsby's not-too-sweet, smoky baked ones. So flavorful and stewed to perfection. While eating the beans and bacon, I watch Heathcliff chatter to Ms. Fernsby about his Batman comic book. I zone out, remembering Philip and me making marvelous weekend breakfasts—quiches, specialty pancakes, hash brown casseroles, and French toast. For the French toast, Philip would make a sourdough bread starter a few days earlier, allowing the yeast to properly ferment. Then by Saturday, we'd make thick cinnamon French toast, sprinkled with dark brown sugar. Working next to each other in our tight, warm kitchen was like a type of foreplay. We felt especially close while cooking together, and we both agreed that post-cooking weekend sex was the best sex.

I haven't used my stove since Philip's death and instead heat up all the frozen casseroles in the microwave. The stove sits untouched like a sacred relic.

I glance up, meeting Ms. Fernsby's sympathetic gaze.

"Why don't you and Heathie start exploring things today? The weather is supposed to be lovely."

"How does that sound, Heathcliff?"

"Good, I guess," he says, mouthful of toast.

On my way upstairs to get ready, I turn on my phone and check my messages. Bella had replied almost immediately to mine from last night: Hey Lizzie! Yes, we're heading to London! Getting ready to board a red-eye in a few minutes. Our agents want us to be seen at some events before the sequel news is announced! So freaking exciting! And YES—I'd love to meet up!

Sequel? I haven't written a sequel yet, so this is curious.

I jump over to my texts and see a quick response from Sarah: Good news, and it's all happened at lightning speed. We MIGHT have a sequel deal (book and film!). I'm up to my eyeballs in conference calls regarding offer details this morning, but I'll be in touch very soon!

I blink, unbelieving, trying not to pinch myself. Writing a sequel would be amazing, but between Mom's illness and then losing her and then Philip, my brain has felt like mush. Still, if my audience is hungry for more Cathy-Heathcliff-Linton windswept angst, I can provide it.

WE START WITH THE BRITISH MUSEUM. BY MIDMORNING, Heathcliff and I find ourselves in the Egyptian gallery featuring mummies. "These are *real* dead people?" he exclaims, running up to the exhibit.

"Very real. They once lived and breathed and ate like us."

Staring into the glass, I tell him about how the Egyptians removed the organs and placed them in jars and this had to do with beliefs about the afterlife.

"Was Daddy made into a mummy?"

"No, we found other ways to honor him."

Gently, I explain cremation. I tell him how we put Daddy's ashes in different places to memorialize him, and how when we hold the little bird urn, we think of Daddy. Heathcliff's eyes glaze over soon, and he starts shaking his longish hair from side to side to watch the blond locks fly.

Philip's little bird urn weighs heavily in my satchel as I stare at the beautiful inner coffin of an ancient priest. I'm mesmerized by the gilded mask, the intricate designs and bold colors. After losing Philip, I agonized over where to place his ashes. Now, as I neurotically keep some of his ashes with me, a piece of his hair in the jet brooch around my neck, I realize the Egyptians and the Victorians understood that the care and placement of bodies, arms, limbs, and organs matters. The Victorians were quite romantic when it came to death: Thomas Hardy's heart rests with his wife, Emma. Writer Radclyffe Hall lies buried at the foot of the vault belonging to her lover, Mabel Batten. Famously, Robbie Ross wanted his ashes placed in the modernist tomb of his lover, Oscar Wilde. The final resting places signified fidelity and eternal intimacy.

Mom hadn't been cremated. She'd been buried in a peaceful corner in the cemetery of the little Methodist church I'd grown up in. As we walked away from the site after the funeral, I looked back and saw Dad lingering in front of her open grave. His name had been engraved next to hers on the stone. He didn't cry. Dad just stared at the stone blankly, hands in his trouser pockets. I felt sorry for him then and even more so now. I understand the weight of separation. It had been strange the first time I saw my name next to Philip's on the niche—me on one side and him the other.

A child bumps into me, knocking me into the glass.

"Careful, Heath . . ." But it's a little blonde girl in a cap. She murmurs an apology and runs back to her mother.

"Heathcliff?" I look around me. There's a moderate crowd in the gallery, but I don't see him anywhere.

He's probably just looking for a bathroom.

Quickly, I walk through the gallery. All the glass cases look the same with mummies, jars, hangings and exhibit descriptions. I approach a middle-aged security guard who looks like he wants to be anywhere but here. "Did you see a blond-haired child run by?"

"We have many blond-haired children here."

"He's wearing a Batman shirt and worn white tennis shoes."

The guard audibly sighs and motions for me to follow him.

"You're taking me to him?"

"I'm helping you find him."

He says something into his walkie-talkie about locating a missing child.

I'm not in a full-blown panic yet, but I'm getting anxious. Children must get lost here all the time, and surely all museums have organized systems for finding them. Still, my maternal reptile brain fires up. My son isn't in my sight. He's lost, away from me and in danger of predators . . .

"Mom! Hey! Over here!"

I whip around and see Heathcliff on the shoulders of a ridiculously handsome British man.

"Here you go, Mum," the man says, swinging Heathcliff down and into my arms. I hug him hard as he squirms away excitedly.

"There was this room with *giant gold statues* and *creepy art* and it was so *big* . . . and . . . *cool* . . . a little scary, and I couldn't find you, and I only got a little scared, and I tried to stay where I was like you told me to when I was lost but you didn't come and my eyes watered a little . . ."

"He was a brave chap when I found him," the man says, winking at me.

"So we're all okay now? Happy reunion and all that?" the bored guard asks.

"Yes, fine. You've been very helpful," I snap irritably.

Now that I have Heathcliff, I can't stop looking at this dashingly beautiful man. There's something vaguely familiar about him. Did I meet him at a conference?

"August Dansworth," he says, extending a hand. Tall, with blue eyes, dark hair, and a dimple, August is about my age and sports a jaunty Hugh Grant–like demeanor. I hope Philip can't see me right now, how my palm sweats as I shake August's hand. He squeezes mine warmly, and I accidentally happen to notice he's not wearing a wedding ring.

"Lizzie Wells." I'm glad I wore my nicest black sundress and cardigan. Nervously, I tighten my grip on my satchel and play with my jet necklace. My mouth dries, and I'm not sure what to do. What did proper widows do with this kind of excitement?

He lingers. He's wearing a nice tweed suit and looks like the type of dashing college professor I always imagined myself working with in graduate school. Not porky, sexist short men like Bill Rhodes.

"Guess what, Mom? August knows Batman!"

"Guilty," August says, dimple deepening. "I told him I'm Alfred Pennyworth's long-lost son and pop in often for tea."

"Isn't that the *coolest*?"

"The very coolest. Thank you, Mr. Dansworth."

"August, please. Mr. Dansworth is my father." He lingers. "Your blood sugar must be ghastly low after that fright. The least you can let me do is take you and Heathcliff to my favorite pub."

"Oh, I don't know . . ."

"They have fabulous sausages and cake." He smiles at Heathcliff.

"*Please*, Mama! I want cake!"

WITHIN AN HOUR, I'M SQUASHED INTO A PUB BOOTH too close to August Dansworth as Heathcliff makes paper shapes out of the children's menu. I'm pretty sure this *isn't* proper Victorian widow behavior, but it also seemed rude to turn down his lunch offer. And it would have disappointed Heathcliff.

"So what brought you to London?"

Grief. Asshat colleagues. Asshat Brad McGregor. An embarrassing public meltdown.

"I'm a writer and professor, so I've been here to research a lot. This time, though, Heathcliff and I are just on summer vacation."

"There is something saucy professor about your style." He glances over my jet necklace and black clothes. I squirm, self-conscious about my weird widow fashion.

Our drinks arrive. He sips his cider while I put Heathcliff's straw in his lemonade cup and then he screams at me that he wanted to do it, pulls it out, splashes lemonade on my cheek and does it himself.

I take a long sip of wine.

"What do you write?" August asks.

"It was a young adult book. You might not have heard of it—*The Heathcliff Saga*."

"You're bloody kidding."

"You have heard of it?"

"I *love* it. I thought your name sounded familiar. And the movie—it's like the new *Twilight*." He smiles, revealing nice straight teeth.

"You're not exactly the target audience."

"I'm not young, cool, *hip*, as you Americans say?" Rakishly, he raises an eyebrow.

"I didn't say that," I mutter, blushing.

"I do a bit of writing myself."

"Really?"

"Really. I write murder mysteries. Have you heard of A.D. Hemmings?"

"You're fucking kidding me." Guiltily, I glance over at Heathcliff, but he's concentrating on shaping an origami piece of poop. "I *love* your books. I just finished *Blood Oath*. I'll say—you had me on the Cardiff Strangler. I didn't see that end coming."

He beams. I can't believe I didn't make the connection before. He'd been wearing tortoiseshell glasses in the black-and-white headshot at the end of the book. That must have thrown me off.

He scoots a little closer. He smells nice—like cider and floral aftershave. "What a fortuitous meeting, then. Right?"

"Ummm . . . yeah."

I'm a little lightheaded, like I'm back on the couch with Henry Lawton. What's *wrong* with me?

I straighten my back. Time to sound professional. This is fine, actually. We're two writers. It's just a business meeting. Networking. Nothing more.

"So does your writing research bring you often to the museum?"

He points outside. "I live just around the corner, in a flat near Bedford Gardens. When the writer's block hits, I take a stroll through the galleries."

"Sorry my son interrupted your creative flow."

He smiles at me over his pint rim. "No, not at all. I love all the galler . . ."

"I have to *potty*!!!"

"Oh god," I murmur, scrambling to get myself and Heathcliff out of the booth. In my rush, I knock over my satchel.

The bird urn propels out across the pub floor.

"No, no, *no* . . ." I whimper, horrified as a server almost trips over the urn, accidentally kicking it farther away. Customers stare as I dive out of the booth and scramble on all fours across the sticky floor. The urn slides straight toward a large intake chute.

Then August is suddenly beside me, deftly catching the urn just before it falls through the grate.

"Thank you," I whisper through tears of relief as we stand. My heart pounds, and my fingers tremble as I take the urn from August. Philip's ashes were almost lost for good in the bowels of this stupid crowded pub.

August watches me quizzically.

I carry the little urn like an actual baby bird back to the table where Heathcliff waits.

"Special paperweight?" August's blue eyes search mine as we slide back into the booth.

"Yes." I wipe the dust off the urn with my black cardigan sleeve.

"It's Daddy's ashes," Heathcliff says. "Mama says I can hold it and think of Daddy."

August stares at me as he sips his cider, his expression both horrified and (possibly?) turned-on. He might be a bit of a flirt, but I'm drawn to him. He's like a Pandora's box of wit and delight rather than curses and woe.

"Can I hold Daddy now?"

"Don't you have to go to the bathroom?" I hiss, dropping the urn safely back into my satchel. I feel like a complete weirdo.

By the time Heathcliff and I return to the table, our meals have arrived. I squirt ketchup onto Heathcliff's sausage to meet his specifications and then squeeze a lemon wedge over my calamari salad.

Heathcliff stabs the little side dish of steamed spinach with his fork. "Grandma Nora said to *always* eat my vegetables first. She said they'll make me like Batman."

"Your grandmum sounds like a wise woman." He turns to me. "So you're a widow." He thoughtfully takes a bite of kidney pie.

"I'm a rather recent one. His name was Philip and we were very close, married fifteen years."

"I'm sorry. That must have been difficult."

"It's been awful." I stare into my now-empty wineglass. "We had one of those rare friendship marriages."

"I can't even imagine."

"I'll be alright. This trip was actually much-needed." I tell him about our adorable town house and housekeeper. "We're in good hands."

After a minute, August asks Heathcliff about his favorite superhero, and my son's ensuing monologue carries us through the remainder of lunch.

When we leave the pub, I thank August, telling him that this really was a lovely treat.

"Will we see you again?" Heathcliff asks pleadingly.

"Heath . . ."

"Actually, Lizzie, I wouldn't mind seeing both of you again, or perhaps just *you*? Would you fancy a little tour of the area and dinner? Perhaps your lovely Ms. Fernsby could give you a well-deserved night off? I promise, I'm going to do everything possible to get you out of your brilliant mind while you're here."

My words won't work.

"Lizzie?"

"Ummm, yes, sure. Why not?"

"Excellent!" We put one another in our phone contacts.

As Heathcliff and I walk away, I feel like I'm getting the vapors again, kind of lightheaded and trembly. If I had a corset, I'd loosen it to breathe.

9

That afternoon, I sink into a deliciously hot, sudsy bath of floating pink rose petals from Ms. Fernsby's garden. I listen to a Norah Jones playlist and ruminate over the surreal meeting and pub lunch with August Dansworth. I'm still reeling from his suggestion that we meet up again but *without* Heathcliff.

Would a meetup qualify as a date? A *romantic* date?

No. My insides roil at the thought.

There's definitely something about August that smells like trouble. But it would be perfectly fine to meet up as two creative *professionals* brainstorming and networking together. That's all it is. Sarah would be thrilled to know I've cultivated a *professional* relationship with the famous A.D. Hemmings.

I massage eucalyptus oil onto my legs. The scent soothes my muscles, sore from walking for half the day. As I start shaving, I wonder when I'll feel like I'll be ready to even consider dating again. This is a place I never expected or wanted to be in—I can't imagine going out with someone at my age. The thought of sifting through online profiles makes me queasy.

Middle age is a weird time to lose a soulmate. I had the happy Jane Austen ending, but the story was cut short. Even my friends who are still married don't love their husbands like I loved Philip. I was a lucky duck. Not long before my grandma died five years ago at the ripe old age of ninety-five, I visited her in her nursing home. Her mind had been lost for some time to dementia, and it worsened after Grandpa died the year before. I told her about my recent research trip to England and answered her question three times: *Did you have tea with the Queen?* (I said yes, because that really would have been so much fun.) Then she settled back, a vague smile on her face. Her rheumy blue eyes looked out the window at shaded bird feeders and the Midwest's sprawling hostas. I tried to get another bite of pudding into her mouth, but she shook her head faintly, lost in a memory.

"I had a man once."

"Really, Grandma?" I smiled, leaned forward. She'd married at age twenty-three, and I was hoping for something juicy, a tidbit about a past love before Grandpa.

"Yes. I had a man once."

I'm quiet, spoon poised.

"And . . . *Oh how he loved me!*"

Of course. The man was Grandpa.

I remember thinking how if I'd inherited the family Alzheimer gene and would eventually find myself in a nursing home with Heathcliff spooning pudding into my mouth, I wanted this moment—where my love with Philip would break through the fog. Where I could be certain that Philip had loved me even when I thought I'd had tea with the Queen every Tuesday.

After a bit, I let the water out, and I dry off, wrapping myself in the fluffy marigold robe. Although it's only about five thirty in the evening, I slip on my cozy black pajamas. The house is unusually quiet. When I reach the kitchen, I find a simmering creamy watercress soup on the stove. Ms. Fernsby left a note on the island telling me that she and Heathcliff popped down the street to pick up a fresh baguette.

I pour a glass of wine and return to my room, settling in one of the sitting chairs to start *Blood Ties*. I was so mad that Emilia Wren turned out to be the Cardiff Strangler. I didn't see that coming. I was sure the killer was the suspect's sister, Penny Bledsoe. Chadwick Hall slept with Penny the first night they met in Tintern after an evening of too much gin.

A copycat strangler strikes in the first chapter. I'm hooked right away—twenty pages in and I jump when my FaceTime rings.

Henry.

Drat. I forgot we were supposed to talk tonight. I wanted to put more thought into what I would say after our awkward evening the other night. But between August, possible book news, London sights, and Ms. Fernsby's cooking, I guess I pushed aside my little problem with Henry.

"Henry?" I set my book down and prop up the phone.

"Is this still a good time?"

"Ummm . . . yes?"

Henry works from his den office this afternoon. Bonnie paces in the background, shaking a chew toy. He smiles kindly, thoughtfully rubbing his beard. "*Ummm . . . yes*, this is a good time? Or *ummm . . . yes*, we're stalling, tiptoeing around a big darn elephant in the room?"

"Both."

"Look, Lizzie, I was Philip's friend, but you've been in the picture too. I can't forget your kindness throughout the years—even on my wedding day."

I smile at *that* memory.

"My point is that I don't want the other night to come between us. There were a lot of emotions. We were both feeling a lot."

I nod.

I'm waiting for him to say it shouldn't have happened. Because we *should not* have almost-kissed. But he doesn't say it. I try to say it. But I can't.

"Let's just . . ." Even through my small phone screen, I see his face reddening. "Let's just . . ."

"Pretend it didn't happen," I say quickly.

"Sure."

But he winces. It was the wrong thing to say.

The downstairs front door crashes open, and I hear Heathcliff chattering excitedly.

Henry rustles the paperwork on his desk, puts on his reading glasses. "So I asked Mirabel some simple questions about the trust, and she shut me down, referred me to her lawyer. I called her Summerville lawyer, and *she* refused to tell me anything."

He shakes his head.

"I'm going to subpoena the trust documents, but it's all bizarre. Never in my fifteen years of practice have I seen such fuss and secrecy about a *trust fund*."

"Ted? He's from old money. Could he have set it up?"

"It would make sense for him to set that up for his grandson—but *why* the secrecy? We have to pursue this. There's something mighty fishy."

"Speaking of fishy, I was going through Philip's phone the other night, and I found this oyster roast pic from the late '70s."

I text him the photo of Mirabel at the party. "It might be nothing, but Philip had it saved in his phone shortly before he died."

Henry's phone dings, and he opens the text. "She sure was a looker. Hasn't changed much."

"It's because she's a witch."

Henry glances up, lopsided grin. "Maybe. That hair's the same damn color. Impressive. I wonder—" he peers down, making the image larger on his phone "—who the couple is . . ."

"You think there's something important here?"

"Maybe. It looks like Philip did."

He leans back, taking off his reading glasses. Bonnie plops her toy in his lap, and he rubs her head. "Look, I'll do some more digging on my end. Meanwhile, you enjoy London and think back on if Philip said anything that could shed light on this."

"I will."

An awkward pause. "So London, heh?"

"Heathcliff and I needed to get away. It was kind of spur-of-the-moment. It's hard at home."

"I get it." He clears his throat. "How long do you think you'll stay?"

I shrug. "Probably for at least a few weeks."

"Well, you and that poor little hurricane of yours take care. Bring me back one of those Big Ben tower souvenirs."

We say goodbye, and I settle back in the chair, sipping my wine.

Lucy leaps up onto my lap, and I rub her back. That went about as well as I could have hoped. We just needed to get past the other night. Even if we're both a little attracted or curious, too much could go wrong. Henry's not just any man—he was Philip's best friend. Losing his friendship would be like losing yet another piece of Philip. I touch the little jet necklace, only the stone separating my fingers from Philip's hair. I just can't lose anything else now.

I refocus my thoughts on Mirabel, digging hard into memories from the weeks before the accident.

It's a blur of our beautiful routine. Saturday morning pancakes and cartoons with Heathcliff. Reading the *New York Times* with coffee on Sunday mornings. A long afternoon at Edisto Island. We chattered about where we'd go out to eat on our next date night. What movie we'd see. But something had been *off*. It was so subtle, I'd barely noticed it. Philip had unusual moments of quietness. One morning, as he rinsed out his oatmeal bowl in the sink, he stared out the window, thick blond brows furrowed, stuck in some kind of daydream. *Everything ok?* I'd asked. *Oh yeah*. And he snapped out of it.

He was preoccupied with something, and he hadn't wanted to trouble me with it.

Why?

Heathcliff yells up the stairwell that it's time to eat. Lucy leaps off my lap, running for cover under the bed.

I stand, brushing the cat hair off my pajama bottoms before going downstairs for dinner. It might take some time to find these answers, but I'm determined. I owe it to Philip to uncover what he wanted me to know so badly that night.

Ten Years Earlier

"TRY TO LOOK A LITTLE HAPPY. IT'S YOUR WEDDING day," I say, sitting next to Henry at the bar. "Or is it the music you're bummed about?"

"Summer of '69" blares from the dance floor behind us.

Henry smiles sideways. "Hey, aren't wedding reception songs supposed to suck?"

"Sure. It wouldn't be a wedding otherwise. I'm not even sure you'd officially be married."

He chuckles.

The bartender hands me a hard cider, and I clink my bottle against Henry's.

"To bad wedding songs."

"To bad wedding songs."

I've only talked to Henry a handful of times, but there's something sad about seeing the groom drinking alone. Not that it isn't easy to get lost at this wedding reception. It's ridiculously expensive and crowded, and we're in a century-old factory building remodeled into an art gallery, niche office building, and reception hall. The enormous room has worn brick walls and gaudy chandeliers; string lights dangle from the high ceiling. Little offshoot corridors and quirky unused rooms jut out from the space with plenty of vintage nooks and crannies for hookups. Three minutes ago, I saw Ginger's maid of honor slip into a side room with Gabe, an old law school friend of Philip and Henry's.

"But seriously, is everything okay?"

I glance back to the dance floor, where Ginger and her former sorority sisters rock out to "Material Girl." Ginger's blond hair twirls as she holds up bunches of her tulle skirt. Her Pekingese, Zoie, yips at the corner of the dance floor in a matching gown. Zoie was actually the wedding ceremony star, carrying the rings up the aisle in a special rhinestone pouch.

"Yeah, everything's great. We both thought it was time to make it legal."

He stares down into the bottle, only a third full now. I search his expression and wait for him to say something else. But he doesn't.

Oh no. He knows she's not right for him.

I take a big sip of cider, staring at the wet ring of condensation my bottle leaves on the knotty wood counter.

He rubs his eyes. "We just see how happy you and Philip are, so we took the plunge."

I glance over at Philip at the grits bar. He's talking to Henry's law partners and layering shredded cheese over his grits. I frown. He's lactose intolerant and will regret that later. But even now, watching my husband eat something he shouldn't, knowing he'll be gassy and bloated tonight, my heart pumps harder at just *seeing* him. What we have is special, and I feel a sick lump in my stomach that Henry "took the plunge" with someone he's not madly in love with.

"Well . . . best wishes to both of you," I stammer, pressing the right toe of my taupe high heel into the metal bar stool's base.

"Thanks."

We both sit in silence. I want to go join Philip over at the grits bar, but I can't leave Henry alone here. Not like this. Not after this well-disguised confession.

A string of 90s Madonna songs ends, and James Blunt's "You're Beautiful" blares.

I grimace, catch his eye, and we both chuckle. But then Ginger suddenly grabs his shoulder., "Come on, *babe*, it's our song!"

No way . . . I mouth.

He reddens, grins, and heads back to the dance floor.

Finishing my cider, I tug my pink shawl around my shoulders and walk over to Philip.

I hug him, wrapping my arms around his waist tightly. Not caring about who sees, I kiss his cheek, leaving a light rose lipstick imprint. "I love you," I whisper.

"I love you too." He sets his empty plate down and returns the kiss. Then he smiles against my forehead. "What's that for?"

I shrug, keeping my arms tight around him. The stuffy law partners look away, uncomfortable.

"I just *really* want you to know, because it's fucking true." I look up at him. "Hey, there's this really cute gallery just down the hall I want to see."

"You don't want to slow-dance to James Blunt? We can pretend its prom and awkward-dance. *Or* better yet you can show off some of your old show-choir moves."

"Ha! You know I'm, like, fifteen years too old for that."

"Oh come on." He pulls me closer to his chest. "When are we going to take those dancing lessons, Lizzie?"

"Sometime, I suppose. Eventually. When I get up the guts again. But *now* I want to check out the gallery."

"Why . . . ? Oh . . ."

Then, holding hands, we slip out of the loud, crowded hall.

10

"Will you look at *this*?"

Ms. Fernsby sits with the tabloid open at the kitchen island in the morning. She's sipping coffee, and Heathcliff wolfs down a giant stack of blueberry pancakes. He mutters good morning as I tousle his blond locks, pour a large mug of coffee, and peer over Ms. Fernsby's shoulder.

My *Heathcliff Saga* actors pose on the red carpet somewhere. From between Everett and Harry, Bella is looking snatched. (At least I think that's what all the kids are saying now.) She's wearing a clingy sequined dress, so short, I'm not sure it covers her rump. The guys wear brightly colored tuxedos, shirts unbuttoned down their chests. The outfits would look silly on anyone who isn't young and ridiculously hot. I hope everything's alright between them. Hats off to them for keeping their drama private. Not many young actors can do that.

"This happened last night right here in London!" She looks closer at the image through her reading glasses.

"What were they doing here?" I ask, stacking pancakes onto my plate.

"Why, I thought you'd know! Is there another book in the works?"

I wipe syrup off Heathcliff's mouth before he runs into the living room to watch cartoons.

I lean forward conspiratorially and smile. "Sarah said there is a potential sequel brewing. Everything is very hush-hush now, but she said she'll be in touch soon."

"Oh *my stars*! Book or movie?"

"It seems like both!" I say excitedly, slathering butter and syrup on my pancakes.

"How marvelous! As soon as she calls, let me know. There's so much exciting telly news! Did you see your American actor Brad Pitt is playing Chadwick Hall in the *Blood Oath* series? He certainly looks the part, but he'll need a good accent coach. That Welsh accent isn't easy to pick up."

I blush and take a bite of fluffy pancake, a hot blueberry popping in my mouth. I haven't told Ms. Fernsby yet about meeting the real A.D. Hemmings. Based on her reading interests, I get the feeling that she loves romance and happy endings, and I'm uncomfortable with the routes her imagination might take.

My pragmatic late mother would advise changing the subject.

"These pancakes are amazing. What kind of buttermilk do you use?"

THAT AFTERNOON, I BUY SANDWICHES AND LEMONADE for Heathcliff and me as we wander about Kensington Gardens. The day is sunny and beautiful, the park grounds crowded with young families and couples lolling about on picnic blankets. We sit on a bench near the Peter Pan statue to eat our lunch.

"We never did read *Peter Pan*, did we?" I ask him.

"Who's Peter Pan?"

"He's a character in a book, a magical boy from another world who flies and fights pirates."

"Oh." He's unimpressed. His blond brows furrow like when he's deep in thought.

"Did we fly here to see Daddy? Because we haven't seen him yet."

A sick feeling spreads through my gut. I worry that Heathcliff can't really understand the concept of death. Chloe tried to talk to him after the funeral, but it's hard to know how a six-year-old brain thinks. It pains me that he thought we'd see Philip on this trip.

"No, Heathcliff. We're not going to see Daddy again. But remember what I told you lives on about Daddy?"

"His love."

"That's right."

I thought my mini-lecture about mummies at the British Museum might have helped Heathcliff understand the finality. Obviously, it didn't. I've worked with college students for years now, but young children, even my own, bewilder me. Maybe I'm turning into my sweet but stiff professor-Dad.

"Do you have any more questions about Daddy?"

"No." He swallows and takes a long swig of lemonade. "I wonder if Daddy can see Batman from where he is."

"I sure hope so."

Soon Heathcliff starts playing ball with four other children, and after a few minutes, my phone rings.

"Dad?"

"Hi, Lizzie."

As I ask him how he's doing, I hear kitchen appliances rattling, the oven door opening, and a timer beeping. It would be about 11:00 there, so an early lunch?

"I'm trying to bake your mother's lasagna."

"Oh . . . how's it going?"

"I can't. It's not going well."

"Dad, I'm so sorry about Mom."

"The cheese, the meat layers. They're uneven. The noodle edges burned."

We're quiet. It's all too heavy for words.

"Do you want me to come home? Because I will, Dad. I'll fly back if you need me."

"No, Lizzie. I don't want to cut your trip short. And Ian stops by often."

"But I will."

"I know."

Through tears, I watch Heathcliff kicking a ball around. I take a deep breath and swallow. "London's been wonderful so far, Dad. We went to the British Museum. I told Heathcliff I'd take him to Westminster Abbey tomorrow. Sarah's row house is adorable, and she has the kindest housekeeper—Annabel Fernsby. She makes these lavender scones like nobody's business . . ."

"I'm sorry about Philip, Lizzie."

I swallow hard. "I know you are, Dad."

We talk a little longer. His back is feeling better, the physical therapy helping. He's thinking about teaching a class just for fun at the university this fall.

"I think I'm going to try to redo this lasagna."

"Are you sure you're up for it?"

"I think I can get it right this time."

We say goodbye, and the grief—losing Mom, losing Philip, seeing Dad lost like this—sinks like an uncomfortable stone in my chest.

"I'm ready to go back now!" Heathcliff shouts in my ear, jolting me back from my thoughts.

He waves goodbye to the other children and starts chattering about his playtime.

"Mama, they have names I've never heard of—Archie and Matilda. And they call cookies 'biscuits.' I told them you put gravy on biscuits, and they laughed at me. But a cookie looks like a cookie and not a biscuit."

"They think a cookie is a biscuit. We learn these things when we travel."

He sighs. "Can I watch *Batman* when we get home?"

"Sure."

Soon after I turn on a cartoon Batman episode for Heathcliff, Sarah calls.

"We have offers!" she exclaims breathlessly.

I scream, nearly dropping the phone.

"Hey!" Heathcliff barks grouchily. "I can't hear!"

"Sorry . . ."

I hurry into the kitchen, where Ms. Fernsby is putting together the most amazing cottage pie. She's sautéing copious amounts of fresh rosemary and sage from her garden with the chopped leeks. She turns around, wiping her hands on her apron. "Well, you look excited, luv!"

"You're on speaker, Sarah," I say smiling and let her know that it's just Ms. Fernsby in the room.

"Oh, wonderful!" Sarah says quickly as she greets her old housekeeper warmly. As usual, she sounds like she's hurrying on her way to catch a meeting or a flight or an Uber. "So, I'm trying to catch a quick flight to Dublin for a conference, but it's all good news. We have an offer on a sequel and film rights."

Ms. Fernsby claps her hands in the air before pulling me into a tight hug. "Oh, I knew it! I *knew it!* This calls for some bubbly! I bought this last week just knowing something exciting was coming!" She scurries over to the fridge for the bottle.

"Yes, drink up and celebrate!" Sarah exclaims over the phone. She quickly gives me the basic offer details and tells me we'd be crazy to turn them down. "But let's meet as soon as I get back, Lizzie. There are some requests that I want to make sure you're okay with before we agree. You're the creator, and you need to be happy with it all."

"Yes, of course."

"Wonderful! My shuttle is here, but more soon, you fabulous author!"

Beaming, Ms. Fernsby pops the cork and pours champagne into two vintage blush-colored coupe glasses. We lightly clink glasses and take a celebratory sip before I wash my hands and help her with the pie.

By evening, after indulging in a large portion of Ms. Fernsby's cottage pie, along with steamed vegetables and two glasses of champagne, I tuck Heathcliff into bed and slip my pajamas on early. The good meal and long Kensington Park playtime must have made him sleepy because he's snoring within ten minutes.

I curl up in my bedroom's sitting area with Lucy to read *Blood Ties*. I'm deep into the book now, and the suspect's sister, Penny Bledsoe, stays on as Chadwick Hall's love interest. But he's hot on the heels of the Copycat Strangler, and I'm sensing an Indiana Jones archetype here—during the masculine, adrenaline-fueled chase, he's tired of being romantically tied to one woman. So cliché and misogynistic, yet here I am page-turning. Damn you, August Dansworth.

My phone dings with a screenshot from Chloe of a toy wooden maze with little metal balls that roll around.

Chloe: Hey! Thought I'd send you something more priest-appropriate than trashy book recs and wine😊 I just can't stop thinking of you as I'm playing around on this tonight. Remember the importance of labyrinths! Blessings, friend.

I smile. Chloe *loves* labyrinths. Last year, for her sabbatical, she studied spiritual mindfulness practices in Tibet, concentrating on monastic garden patterns and sand labyrinths. Upon coming home, she created one in our church garden. She personally maintains the boxwood shrub hedges, ensuring weeds and overgrowth don't mar the overall shape.

When she returned from Tibet, she had told me: *It's about uncertainties. You walk the path, trying to find the center. You have to trust the path. You walk purposely without knowing exactly where you are going. You hit dead ends and twists, but you just keep moving forward.*

Me: Thank you, Chloe. I needed this reminder.

I pause, wondering if I should tell her about Dansworth. Oh, why not?

Me: I met the real A.D. Hemmings yesterday in the British Museum.

Chloe: No way! Are you serious?

Me: Yes! It was surreal.

I linger over the phone, wondering if I should tell her he suggested meeting up again. I really can't tell anyone this now.

Besides, I likely won't hear from him again. As a Victorian widow, I'm supposed to do *this* in the evenings—curl up and read with a cat on my lap. I decide to frame it as if it was only a brief fangirl encounter.

@ADHemmings *selfie having a shot with Brad Pitt*:

Just celebrating with *Brad Fucking Pitt* as we wrap up filming. Sometimes I still pinch myself. #authorlife #goals

11

....

Heathcliff and I spend the next three days sightseeing.

For some reason, Chloe's labyrinth text inspired me to explore ancient religious sites. With my widow's fashion and attempt to find my way in my post-Philip world, I suppose I'm on a pilgrimage. To my knowledge, there aren't any sacred labyrinths around me, so walking about a church gallery seems to be the next best thing.

First, we tour Westminster Abbey. Heathcliff is rather underwhelmed by the arches and stained glass. "This is BORING. Are we going to be in here FOREVER?" But he does perk up when I show him the coronation chair and explain that everyone has to sit in it when they become king or queen.

"Did the Joker ever try to bomb it?"

"Not to my knowledge. Some suffragettes did once."

"Do they work for the Joker?"

"No." I almost pee my pants giggling. "They were women who stirred up trouble so they could vote."

"Oh."

The next day, we take the train to Stonehenge. The sun and wind beat down on the Salisbury Plain. A strong breeze ripples the grasses, but not enough to drown out the surrounding native starlings' songs. Fortunately, there are plenty of places here for Heathcliff to run about and no stuffy museum guards to glare at me. I tell Heathcliff a bit about the history, that this was a sort of *very* old church. Heathcliff asks why we can't go to a "church like this" where we can run around "old giant stones."

I see his point.

On the third day, we take the train to Canterbury. I text Chloe a photo of the cathedral. For centuries, pilgrims came here seeking health, peace, war, or love. Like me, they probably didn't even know exactly what they sought. Canterbury Cathedral just seems like the logical place to be when unraveling a very tight knot. I can't take my eyes off the indentations in the altar's stone steps from countless pilgrims who found themselves kneeling here since the twelfth century.

Heathcliff found Canterbury more to his liking than Westminster Abbey. We had a lively tour guide who dramatically retold the gruesome murder of Thomas Becket and how one knight stirred the archbishop's brains with his sword. Heathcliff was delighted when I bought him some miniature knight figurines from the cathedral gift shop on our way out.

I decide to grab an early dinner before taking the train back to London. We slide into the pub booth, and Heathcliff spreads the little knights out on the table. I'm just looking at the menu when August texts me.

> Hullo Elizabeth! Sorry for the delay. I've had a helluva few days on an Inspector Hall deadline! If you're still interested, I would love to take you out for a drink at the Hotel Café Royal. (I'm sure you of all people know

what a literary gem it is!) Anyway, let me know if you're interested, and I can meet you there around 3:00 Friday.

My heartbeat picks up as I stare at the text. I half-expected not to hear from dashing August again. I'm not even pissed that he's calling me by Elizabeth even though that usually drives me *nuts*. Dansworth gets a pass since he's British and charming.

I privately acknowledge that meeting a handsome man at a café within the same year that my husband has passed away goes beyond riding alone with him in a carriage or flashing him my ankle. I can't go. It's too improper. Realizing I'm dangerously close to rejecting this intriguing man, I go ahead and respond before overthinking it.

Sure thing, August! I'll see you then!

"Who ya' texting?" Heathcliff asks, as his plastic knights battle it out.

"No one." Sweat breaks out on my forehead. I'm not doing anything wrong, right? Why do I feel so funny about this?

By the time we get back on the train, I realize how exhausted I am. My feet ache inside my black walking shoes. It's been a wonderful but very busy three days. Heathcliff falls asleep pretty quickly on the ride home. I'm looking forward to a couple of quieter days at the row house with time spent reading and sipping cups of hot tea.

Pretty soon, like Heathcliff, I fall asleep. I'm in the Azalea Dream's sprawling backyard practicing archery with Mirabel. We're in a clearing behind the gardens; it's an ideal summer day—a gentle breeze rippling through the pines, bluebirds clustering around her wooden feeders. A little iron-wrought stand with a glass pitcher of lemonade and glasses rests between us.

I shoot first, my arrow bouncing off the edge of the canvas target.

"Drat!" I mutter lightly.

Mirabel, under the shade of her giant, yellow-bowed sun hat, nocks her arrow.

"I hope your aim's better than mine," I say, pouring myself a glass of lemonade.

"Most definitely."

I glance up to see her smiling maniacally, her arrow pointed straight at me.

I wake up with a jolt, Heathcliff still asleep on my shoulder.

Yikes. Mirabel aiming an arrow straight at me on a sunny day has to be one of the scariest nightmares I've had in my life. Just under the one where I'm giving my dissertation defense in my underwear. I shake my head, take a few deep breaths, and check my phone. We're about twenty minutes from London.

There's also a cheery text from August: Excellent! I'll see you then!

Hmmm. Well, I suppose I'm meeting A.D. Hemmings at the glamorous Café Royal on Friday afternoon for drinks.

From *Blood Ties*:

Hall downs two pints within half an hour. The pub's growing crowded as uni students start pouring in. But he's not about to give up his large booth. He needs space and drink right now. He orders another pint.

Why is he always messing up with women? He didn't even see that his own bloody partner, Wren, had been the Cardiff Strangler the entire time. And Penny Bledsoe is fit, with her long blond locks and silk stockings—she's bewitching him. But it's at that critical point where she wants more. Sure, she ignites him in the bedroom. But in her longing dark eyes, he sees her need. He takes a slow draw of his diminishing third pint and grimaces.

She wants a relationship.

He signals the server for another drink.

Love never goes smoothly for him. Will it always be about the hunt? Why does it have to be so fucking complicated all the time? He's after the Copycat now. Maybe it's just in his blood to pursue women like he pursues criminals and then not know what to do with himself when the chase is up . . .

He sighs. He's starting to feel a little pissed. Good. He heads to the loo.

When he returns to the table, there's a fresh amber pint waiting.

But right next to it is a tiny, miniature rope, fashioned like a noose.

The Copycat.

He takes a long sip, puts his hat on and stands to leave.

It's a cat-and-mouse game now.

But he'll be the bloody tomcat. Always.

Excerpt from *The Heathcliff Saga*:

"If you ask, me, Cathy, you'd do best to leave the both of them alone."

Nelly narrows her eyes at Cathy while churning butter.

"But, Nelly, that's impossible. Heathcliff stirs my blood, and Linwood . . ."

"Oh, that Linwood boy!" Nelly plunges the dasher violently through the lid. "He's all charm, with his smooth, high cheekbones and gentleman's clothes. He's been mollycoddled his whole life, and it's done 'im no good."

"But he's smart and handsome . . ."

"And *rich*," Nelly spats.

"I'm going out."

"You've been going out a lot."

Furious, Cathy looks away at the mince pie Nelly left to cool on the windowsill. Steam rises through the crust's slits. Beyond the window, a sea of blooming heather ripples.

"On my way to the Grange, I saw 'im disappearing into Penistone Crags," Nelly adds. "If he's summoning the magic himself, it will be disastrous for us all."

Cathy tightens her lips. "I've got it under control, Nelly."

"Do ye, now? You don't even have control over your own heart. This 'ere's magic, luv. You don't know what yer messing with."

12

....

The next day is wonderfully slow.

We stay inside. I wear my black pajamas all day. I read tabloid news on my phone, checking in on Everett's, Bella's, and Harry's social media pages. From the looks of it, they've been cavorting around London. I try to get caught up on their love lives. It looks like Everett and Bella are back together again. Harry has come out as gay and is dating a fellow hunky young actor in a new werewolf drama series. I search for August and find his handle—*@ADHemmings: Writer, Sex God, Chadwick Hall's Boss. But not in that order.* (Fine. So he's a little cheeky. Tomorrow afternoon should be interesting if nothing else.) It's all mostly book news, teasers for the upcoming Netflix series, noir-filtered photos of his bar drinks. No women.

Guiltily, I leave his pages. I'm not actually breaking any rules. Victorian women didn't even have Instagram. I'm doing nothing other than keeping tabs on a friend.

Henry texts me an image.

I open it. *Oh my god.*

It's a fuzzy mug shot of a much younger Mirabel. It must be the early eighties from the looks of it. She has the heavy dark eye shadow and liner. Her now-coiffed blond hair was permed with four-inch-high puffed bangs sprayed heavily into shape. Best of all, though, is the workout headband, slipped down at an awkward angle. She's scowling, shiny pink lipstick smeared as she holds up the ID card—weight 120 pounds. Those Jane Fonda workouts paid off.

Me: WTF!

Henry: Running into court. Four hearings in a row. Give you a call at 9:00 your time tonight? Got some serious shit-tea to spill. 😊

I keep staring at the mug shot, disbelieving. Did Philip know his mom had been arrested?

No, because he would have told me. What would *Mirabel* have done to end up in handcuffs? Steal from the Methodist Women's League's garden fund?

Heathcliff runs up behind me in a superhero cape, and I put down my phone before he can see his grandmama's mug shot. We eat sandwiches in front of cartoons for a while before he goes up to his bedroom to play LEGO. I sit at the kitchen island sipping more coffee and watching Ms. Fernsby put together an apple mincemeat pie. She's beaming with pride as she tells me about her daughter going back to school. Apparently, there's still some funds left over in the education fund Lord Routledge set aside for Mabel.

"She says if she makes it through, she might go straight on to law school. I told her it's never too late," Ms. Fernsby says as she cuts steam vents into the dough top. "It's really never too late for anything. At least, that's what I tell myself . . ."

For a second, her expression darkens as she wipes her fingers on her apron. I wonder what Ms. Fernsby would have done if she hadn't felt tied to Lord Routledge's house and money for Mabel's sake. She leads a comfortable life here. But on cozy evenings, when she sips her brandy over a novel, does she think of what else the world might hold for her?

After dinner, Heathcliff Zooms with Mirabel from my bedroom's sitting area. She looks great even on my grainy laptop screen—her teeth white as anything, blond hair coiffed around her shoulders, freshly applied peach lipstick. So different from the disheveled mug shot.

I stay off camera as Heathcliff chatters about Lucy, his "new best friend" (even though she still hisses at him every time he enters a room). He tells her about Batman. He tells her about the "nice man" who found him when he got lost at the museum and then took him and Mama out to lunch and bought him hot dogs and cake.

"And then do you know what?"

"What, darling?"

"He asked Mama for her number and said he wants to see her again."

"Oh *really*? Well, your mama seems to be enjoying herself." My cheeks burn.

"She is!" Heathcliff says happily. "She really is. We both are."

"Well, that's wonderful, darling. Your granddaddy and I miss you so much—do you hear me? Hey, if your mama's there, can I talk to her for a minute?"

"Mama!" Heathcliff yells even though I'm right beside him.

"Hi." I scoot over in front of the laptop camera as Heathcliff makes a beeline out of the room.

"Hello, Elizabeth." Mirabel pushes on the cuticles of her

freshly painted nails. "Well, it sounds like you and Heathie are having yourselves a grand time there. Museums, cake, British *gentlemen*."

"We are, Mirabel." I ignore the insinuation.

"You know, Elizabeth, Henry Lawton keeps calling my Summerville attorney with personal questions about my background. You have your money for Heathcliff's college, so why *the hell* is he poking around, digging into matters best left alone?"

"Those are questions for him. He's just doing his job, Mirabel."

She glares at me through the screen and taps her long nails loudly.

"You know, I had a problem earlier this week. A little groundhog family took up residence under my garden. They created all sorts of chaos, tunneling, messing up my beauties' roots. If they'd been anywhere else in my yard, I would have played nice—set out some live cages, some herbal repellants. But they were in my *azaleas*, Elizabeth."

"I'm sorry, Mira . . ."

"Anyway, I was so put out yesterday, I took out my granddaddy's Colt Navy pistol. I loaded it and waited for three hours—luring Mama Groundhog, Daddy Groundhog, and Baby Groundhog out of their home with bait. I was so patient, sitting there in my favorite chair in the shade of my favorite sun hat. As soon as each one poked their head out of the ground—" Mirabel deftly holds an imaginary pistol "—I shot their furry little skull."

She smiles. "I don't like anyone nosing around my gardens. I've taken great pains, Elizabeth, damn great pains, to grow and flourish my blooms, establish and keep my gardens' boundaries, and nothing will disrupt that. Do you understand?"

"Yes."

"Good. Then I'd better let you go . . ."

"Mirabel, I've got some precious blooms myself, and I'm making sure mine are just as safe."

She raises an eyebrow. "You really want to do this?"

"I just want to protect my own."

"Well then, you've just set a pretty little fire in your garden."

"Goodbye, Mirabel."

I slam my laptop shut, fingers trembling in rage.

Why does she think she has the right to keep secrets that might affect my son's inheritance? It's not even about the trust money. I'll have more than enough to pay for Heathcliff's education. It's about the lies and secrets surrounding the whole affair. It's also incredibly strange that she's being aggressive and threatening when we're both in mourning.

I won't drop this.

When I lost Philip, I worried I might also lose myself.

Theoretically, I shouldn't lose my *self* even when I lose my soulmate. I should be more independent than that. But when you live with a partner for so many years with our kind of intimacy, it's just fucking impossible not to feel unanchored. We were such a team, and I'm struggling to know how to play alone. I'm chasing Philip in my dreams for connection, but also for help and affirmation. Still, little by little, I'm finding I have an untapped reservoir of strengths. I'm pretty good with hunches. When I've ignored my gut, as I did in grad school by keeping serial-cheater Wes as a boyfriend, it's never turned out well. When I listen to my gut, as I did by marrying Philip, things turn out wonderfully. Ever since Philip's death, I've had a hunch there's something Mirabel never wanted him to know. It's all connected to that awful evening. Now I've seen the mug shot, and she just tried to intimidate me with the story about murdering her garden family of groundhogs.

What could she have done that was so bad Philip left that urgent voicemail wanting to talk?

Why now, amid her grief, does she still feel the need to protect it?

You've just set a pretty little fire in your garden.

She's trying hard.

And yet I remember the hollow look in her eyes since we lost Philip. I'm angry, but I also feel sorry for her. Since losing Mom and Philip, I've learned grief does strange things to everyone involved. Mirabel's guarding her secret more fiercely than ever.

I'm worried if she keeps this up, she'll devastate herself in the end.

"Hey there!" Henry says as we FaceTime.

He's sitting in his backyard just in front of his garden boxes, sipping a bourbon on the rocks. Bonnie rolls happily in the grass at his feet, collar and tags jingling.

"Happy hour?"

He smiles. "You bet. Court was a downright boxing match today. Four contested wills between folks with too much money. Your case is much more interesting. I'm just scratching the surface, but Mirabel's 1982 arrest was something else. Seems she got into a fistfight with the mayor's wife at a Piggly Wiggly."

"What?"

"Yep. Mirabel Wells started taking swings at Lila Mae Dubose one fine Tuesday afternoon smack-dab in the middle of the produce section. According to the police report, they sent apples and avocados flying everywhere. Lila Mae's high heel smashed through a ripe tomato. And here . . . look at this."

My phone dings with the image of Lila Mae's mug shot. She's got a bloody nose, and her permed ponytail tumbles out of the banana clip.

"Whoa," I mutter. "Gives new meaning to the saying 'You should have seen the other guy.'"

"It sure as hell does. Your mother-in-law can pack a punch."

"Why does she look familiar?" I say, making the photo larger.

"Because she's the woman in Philip's photo."

"My god, she is!"

"Listen, I'm still piecing things together, but Lila Mae's husband, Frank Dubose, the other man in the photo, was the town's mayor for a good while. Lila Mae and Mirabel started a gardening business in 1980. All seemed to be going well, but the downtown shop closed abruptly just before the fight. They were arrested but only booked for a couple hours. Frank, being the mayor, and Ted, being . . . well, old money, bailed them out and got the charges dropped. I'd like to know what happened. I've got a gut feeling that Miss Lila Mae and Miss Mirabel, both being strong-willed women, couldn't run the shop together. But I'm having a dickens of a time getting information."

"What do you think this has to do with Heathcliff's trust fund?"

He takes a sip of bourbon and rubs his beard. The quirk is cute.

"Curiously, the trust was set up shortly after the arrest. I'm thinking an arrangement was made between the couples. It was perhaps some kind of settlement money from the Duboses to the Wells over the business."

"But why would they pay Mirabel?"

He shrugs. "That's the million-dollar question."

"Where are the Duboses now?"

"Frank and Lila Mae retired and are living out on Edisto Island. He started a lucrative real estate business after his tenure as mayor. They never had children, and she continues to garden. Her roses won first place at the state fair three years in a row. I've tried to contact them, but they hung up on me. Their lawyer sent me a cease and desist letter. No one wants to talk about this. And Miss Mirabel's lawyer isn't being any more cooperative. She sent the scantiest legal document, nothing more than a notarized note with the date the trust was set up. I'm going to have to keep subpoenaing."

I tell him about my call with Mirabel.

He chuckles, shakes his head. "Again, that woman's a piece of work. I get that a tanked garden business and ladies' fistfight would be embarrassing to all parties involved, but the secrecy about something that happened forty years ago—it's wild."

"I'm just trying to swallow all this. I mean, I've been in this family for fifteen years. I've never heard of these people or these stories, and I'm sure Philip hadn't."

"I get it. Welcome to the South, where batshit families like to keep their secrets close to their chests. Don't worry, though, Lizzie, I'm going to keep digging."

We're quiet. I'm suddenly self-conscious. I'm still wearing my black pajama set, hair pulled up in a messy bun. I'm propped up in my bed with pillows, the lamplight not exactly flattering my image on the screen. Also, I should have thought this through more. Is FaceTiming from bed provocative? Awkwardly, I play with the jet necklace.

He clears his throat. "How're you doing, Lizzie?"

We're back at the wedding reception bar. But this time he's checking in on me.

The grief bubbles up, and I can barely speak.

"Not well. It's not just that Philip's dead. It's that he's—just *not here*. Heathcliff lost another baby tooth. The *Heathcliff Saga* actors are here in London. I had the best homemade lavender scones the other morning. My agent called and there's another movie and book deal on the table. But Philip . . . he's missing it all."

And then I have to stop because I'm crying.

"I know, Lizzie. I know." He sighs. "I think of him every day. I went fishing last weekend—just sitting in the boat without him. The silence is the worst."

He stops, wipes his eyes. Bonnie, sensing his need, lays her head on his lap. I like that he doesn't immediately pivot to the good things: Heathcliff growing up, the book deal. He's here, just sitting with me in my grief.

"You know, I always envied what you two had. But Ginger and I—we could never make it work. I kept trying—year after year."

"I'm sorry, Henry."

He shrugs. "It had to happen. We just had to rip off the Band-Aid at some point. It is what it is."

He throws Bonnie's toy; her collar jangles as she chases after it. "I miss you, Lizzie."

I stop playing with the necklace. After several seconds of awkward silence, he clears his throat. "Did I hear you right? Do you have another book and movie in the works?"

"Not quite officially, but yes. A sequel to *The Heathcliff Saga*."

"You don't say. That's pretty darn impressive."

"A PhD in Victorian literature put to good use," I joke.

He finishes the bourbon. "When you get back—do you think you can come over?"

"I . . . I'm not sure that's a good idea, Henry."

"You could bring Heathcliff over too. He'd love to play with Bonnie. I'll throw something on the grill. It's just I'd like to spend more time with you . . . with both of you."

"I . . ."

"Think about it, Lizzie."

"Alright."

After the call, I sink back into my pillows. Henry and I can talk about Philip seamlessly. He overshadows everything between us. I'm feeling more attached and comfortable with Henry, particularly as we dig into these secrets Philip pursued before his death. But underneath it all, I'm scared by all the connections.

13

Six Years Earlier

My derriere aches as my meds wear off exactly two hours after giving birth to Heathcliff Ian Wells. I hope the nurse (What was her name? Kara? Karen?) comes back soon with more painkillers because—*ouch*.

I've been binge-reading *Wuthering Heights* and the *Twilight* series, and maybe it's the drugs, but I'm getting obsessed with the idea of writing my own steamy Victorian teen romance. Lots of heaving bosoms, passionate kissing in damp Yorkshire caves and windswept moors. I'll throw a little supernatural into the mix—maybe even give Cathy a happy ending . . .

"Henry says congratulations," Philip says after his phone dings.

Philip stands near the hospital room window holding Heathcliff, swaddled tight, the little hospital cap over his head. It's our first quiet moment as a family. Mom and Dad left a little while ago. Mom had counted and recounted Heathcliff's fingers and toes, checked his neck strength and reflexes, looked him over with her keen nurse eyes. She drove Kara/Karen nuts asking when the hospital lactation consultant would be available.

Dad held Heathcliff before handing him back to me with care and fear, as if my newborn was a grenade. In old photos, Dad always looked bewildered by baby Ian and me. He just never knew what to do with babies. He can't handle one like he can a paper on American transcendentalists. He knows the procedure there. But there's no procedure with a squalling, squirming petty-tyrant newborn. It's all another reason Mom was such a good match for him. As a nurse, she had been *paid* to keep babies alive for years.

Ted and Mirabel will be up this afternoon. They didn't have to fly in like Mom and Dad. They only live an hour and a half away and yet they're running late. She called once, congratulating us before growing quiet when Philip told her our newborn's name. Then she gave Philip a piece of her mind.

"Why is this such a big fucking deal to her?" I mutter, whimpering as I adjust my rear and put another ice pack between my legs. "My ass hurts like a mother . . ."

Philip smiles crookedly. "You know, you're cute when you swear."

"Ha."

He pats Heathcliff's back gently and sits down.

"You know all the hints she dropped about naming him *Philip*. Mama says every oldest son for the last five generations is named Philip, and I'm squandering that by using a frivolous, romantic name like Heathcliff. 'This is Elizabeth's doing,' she said." He rolls his eyes. He's always been able to take his mother's drama tongue-in-cheek.

"Way to welcome her first grandchild to the world."

He shrugs. "She'll get over it. But you know her. Everything has to be her way. Her garden, her house, her grandchildren's names. She'll cool off when she's here holding him, when she sees how perfect he is."

"Humph. I like the name Heathcliff. And it's not like we can name him after Dad—*Gaylord*." I push the call button: "Can I please have more Vicodin?"

"It's not time for your next dose," the nurse says through the intercom.

"It should be."

"I want to do things differently," Philip says, a soft expression on his face as he looks down at our son.

"Huh?"

"I mean, Mama always had to dress me up in sailor suits or seersuckers for church. Her routines were always more important to her than just being my mom. I always wanted a mom who could just eat a peanut butter and jelly sandwich with me and listen to me talk about comic books. I wanted her to be more down-to-earth. And Ted—he's not bad, but he never felt like a real dad, just a pretty ornament for Mama's front porch. I want to be a different kind of parent than them, and I want you to help me live up to it."

@BellaPatel *coy smile selfie*:

Fingers crossed about some possible good news for *Heathcliff Saga* fans! 😊

Sarah: Long London layover tomorrow. Let's talk! Tea or wine at Monmouth tomorrow late afternoon? 5:00-ish?

Lizzie: Sure, but I might be running a little late. I'm meeting A.D. Hemming for a drink.

Sarah: Lol

Lizzie: No, really, I am.

Sarah texts back a surprised emoji.

Lizzie: Stay tuned—I'll send you a selfie

MS. FERNSBY NEARLY DROPS THE CHICKEN SHE'S BRINging when I tell her I'm meeting up with August Dansworth (aka A.D. Hemmings) at the Café Royal.

"Why, of *course* I'll watch Heathie for you! You can't miss an opportunity like this!"

"We're just talking about writing..."

"Ohhh... He really threw me with that *Blood Oath* end reveal that the inspector's own partner, Emilia Wren, was the murderer. And now I'll have *Blood Ties* finished almost any day." She frowns. "I think the inspector's going to dump that sweet Penny Bledsoe for some silly tart. It's just the way he is. But I can't even imagine who the Copycat Strangler is in this one! Can you?"

"Not at all!"

"Well, I'm wagering anything it's the inspector's half sister. She's always in the background, and there's something not quite right about her. Add to that the inspector is rubbish at reading women."

She washes her hands and dries them on her apron. "Mark my words, a child will pop up in the next book or two. He can't go around tupping all those women without *that* twist."

She clips some rosemary pieces over the chicken, and blushes. "Is he really as handsome as he is in the photos?"

"He's not *bad*-looking."

"Well, you have yourself a wonderful time and tell me all the details when you get back. Oh, and here..." She runs to the parlor and pulls *Blood Oath* off a shelf. "Please ask him to sign it for me. Tell him to write it out to Annabel—*A-n-n-a-bel*—Fernsby."

"Do you want to meet him?"

"Oh no, I'd never impose. You go enjoy your date, you lucky girl!"

"It's not a date . . ."

But she's distracted by Heathcliff as he clambers down the stairs in a Batman cape, asking her to turn on the television.

A date . . .

My armpits sweat like crazy as I walk toward the Hotel Café Royal entrance.

I suppose I took extra care with my hygiene and appearance. I didn't eat anything that would make me gassy, and I slathered on extra deodorant. But I'm still properly wearing all black—black leggings, an attractive black tunic. As an afterthought, I applied red lipstick before leaving my bedroom—just because as a writer meeting up with another writer, I should look my best. Right? There are absolutely no expectations here, and this is *not a date* in the traditional sense.

Intentionally, I carry Philip's urn in my satchel, and I'm wearing not only the jet locket, but a fingerprint necklace with Philip's signature on the back. I'm not sure where the lines are, but I feel like the extra widow symbols will protect me in the next few hours. Like talismans, all three pieces will remind me how I'm supposed to feel when I'm feeling all the wrong things.

For some reason, I'm thinking of a grad school friend, Heather. She was blonde, pretty, and from a religiously conservative background. We went out for coffee after class once, and as we talked about dating, she held out her finger to show me the wide gold purity ring her parents gave her when she was a teenager. She told me it was her tangible reminder that when she went out on a date with a man, she wasn't supposed to have premarital sex or even think lustful thoughts.

Does it work? I asked her.

She giggled. *Not really. It kind of burns into my finger when I'm out with a hot guy, so I just stick it in my pocket. Still, I try, right? It's the gesture.*

Are all these widowhood trinkets, fashions, and rituals the same for me? Maybe they simply remind me of how I'm *supposed* to live even though I wobble and stray?

I walk in and find the place fairly crowded. I tell the hostess I'm meeting someone and give her both names. She nods at *Hemmings*, and I don't think I'm imagining a slight blush.

I follow her to some cushioned seating in a lounge area near the bar.

August stands when he sees me, and, oh god, he's still as handsome as I remember. Maybe even more so.

I sit down across from him, hoping he can't see how much my hands shake as I set my purse down. It's a ridiculous thought, but I wonder if Philip can see me somewhere, see me on this date (?) with another man. I hope he knows I still love him. I finger the jet necklace, panic rising in my throat.

"What are you thinking about getting?"

"I don't know. I'll probably just go with a nice, chilled glass of Pinot Grigio since it's afternoon and so hot . . ."

"No, I won't hear of it. You can't come all the way to England for bloody *Pinot Grigio*. Let me order for you."

He calls the server over, asking for two double shots of Irish whiskey.

He leans forward. "This single malt is best to drink neat, and it can get us in a lot of trouble."

I chuckle, remembering how years ago I once had a double Irish whiskey at a women writers conference at the University of Virginia. I'd tested the old theory that Emily Dickinson's poems can be sung to the *Gilligan's Island* theme song with a delightful older scholar named Edna.

"How's your book coming along?" I ask as our drinks arrive, and we both take a sip.

"Ahhh, swimmingly. Really great. I met my deadline on the last one, and it's full speed ahead on the new one now. As you know from reading *Blood Oath*, Inspector Hall tups Penny Bledsoe after getting pissed on too much gin. It was a mistake and . . . take care, I'm about to give you privy writer information . . ." He leans toward me a little, his breath smelling like the pear-and-spice-heavy whiskey we're drinking. "If you've been reading the sequel, *Blood Ties*, you see it's not a great love match. He stays with her for a while before learning that she's not all that—all fur coat and no knickers—nothing close to an Irene Adler. But there's a baby and that will all come to light in *Blood Offspring*, so stay tuned."

Ahhh . . . good call, Ms. Fernsby!

He takes another sip. "Now, enough about my books, I want to hear more of your story—not the fantastic *Heathcliff Saga*, but *you*. To be honest, I'm fascinated. I've literally never, ever been on a date with a widow. I snogged one at uni years ago. She was a bit older, and her name was Brenda . . . no, it was Barbara. But it wasn't a date—she was my best friend's mum."

I arch my brow. "Are you really this much of a cad, or is it all smoke and mirrors?"

He puts his hand over his chest and gasps in mock-hurt then recovers and leans forward. "Elizabeth, you've been through a lot, and I promised you from day one I was going to get you outside of your mind while you're here, and that's what I intend to do."

"You didn't answer my question."

"Cad, I am not. Free spirit, I am."

Hmmm. I take another sip. "So, as a writer, what do you do to get outside of your mind?"

"Burlesque. I'm a burlesque dancer on the side."

I laugh.

"Really! You should see me in a corset." He smiles, little laugh lines crinkling around his eyes.

Whatever else he may be, August Dansworth is good company.

"But back to you. Please tell me more about you. You've been through so much . . . emotionally . . . enough to give you depth and you're . . . so . . . so . . . ?"

Sexually needy. The phrase hangs in the air because it's so cliché and true, and the whiskey makes me almost say it out loud. But I'm still not too buzzed, so I don't.

"Tragic. And tragic women are interesting. Right?" I quip.

"Well . . . no, that's not how I'd put it."

I finish my drink in another gulp. August smirks, and motions for the server to bring us a second round of doubles.

"We widows are terribly tragic. Real downers. I met my husband, Philip, fifteen years ago while we were both students. We married quickly and had a fucking happily-ever-after. It was the real deal. Wonderful. All our friends envied us. We had our Heathcliff and then his car ran off the road during a rainstorm and it was all over." I snap my fingers. "Just like that. He's gone. I wear black all the time now and carry around his ashes in a bird urn."

"So I've noticed."

I stare into my second drink.

"I'm intrigued by why you do it. Why the black? Why carry around the urn?"

I see Queen Victoria in my mind, black taffeta skirt, bodice embellished with carefully arranged black grosgrain ribbons.

"Lizzie?"

"I don't know. I guess it provides structure to my big, sad feelings."

He nods. "And *that* is what makes you so delightful."

"What?"

"Those big, sad feelings. That's what I was getting at. Not that I like it that you're sad at all. But your experience makes you more compelling to me."

"Please don't tell me I'm going to end up in one of your novels."

"Oh bloody hell, yes. Chadwick needs a new love interest and I'm afraid you're the inspector's next affair. He's going to be snogging the mysterious Widow Wells by the third chapter."

I kind of like the idea of my sexier alter ego ending up in his book. Maybe she can put Chadwick Hall in his place.

"What does a typical writing day look like for you, August?"

"It's really quite dull."

"You live in Bedford Gardens and take breaks at the British Museum. That hardly sounds dull."

"But you see, it really is. I get up. I drink loads of coffee and sit in my study and think about murderers and people who solve murders and then I write about murders and people who solve murders. I take breaks, walk around the museum. Or I sit in here. I usually teach at least one writing class a year as a guest lecturer at the University of London, where the girls write *I love you* on their eyelids like they do for Indiana Jones in that god-*awful* American film you all love. I love what I do. It's just everything that happens in my head is so much more bloody interesting than what happens in my real life."

Even amid my Irish whiskey buzz, I'm a little miffed that his writing day looks so very different from mine. I don't have time to meander around museums when the writer's block hits. It's hard enough to wrangle Heathcliff into his school clothes and not murder Bill Rhodes at faculty meetings.

August sighs, raps his knuckles quickly on the coffee table in front of us. "I suppose you could say I'm chronically bored."

"Boring isn't bad. I'd give anything to have my happily boring life back," I mutter, my tone darker than I intend.

"Right," he replies carefully.

I shift in my seat. "Do they really write *I love you* on their eyelids?"

"No, but they do leave their numbers on their papers."

He looks over the jet and fingerprint necklaces. "So what happens if you take it all off?"

A blush burns like a flame on my cheeks.

"I mean the necklaces, the . . . the sad trinkets."

Why does everything he says sound so goddamn sexy?

Then August's actual question sinks in.

What *would* I do if I stopped wearing black, took off the jet locket?

The vapors hit hard, like a corset squeezing my chest.

My ears ring.

Ribs compressing, I can't breathe.

I'm about to fall into a void.

"I'm sorry . . ." August says suddenly. "I'm so sorry."

I take deep belly breaths, something my mom taught me to do once when I fell and got the wind knocked out of me. I remember Chloe's instructions on breaths.

"Forget it, Elizabeth. Let's talk instead about my great-great-great-uncle Albert. Ran an opium den in Shoreditch with a wooden leg. Interesting chap. He . . ."

With each breath, the corset loosens. I gradually pull myself away from the void and listen to August's story. My breathing and heartbeat slow until I'm rooted again. August is a great storyteller. After his tale, I share my much more mundane family history—Midwest farmers descended from rather severe Swiss nonconformists—and eventually forget that terrifying moment a bit earlier.

After we finish our drinks, he signs Ms. Fernsby's book for me.

"Obligatory author photo selfie?" he suggests, smiling rakishly as he pulls out his phone.

And then before I know it, I'm leaning into him as he snaps our picture.

August insists on paying and escorting me back to the row house. I protest as we step out onto Regent Street, but he won't listen.

"Now, I'd be a bloody bad chap if I don't see you back."

I can't argue with that. Admittedly, I'm a little tipsy after the drinks.

We talk easily and freely on the way back. Even if I weren't attracted to him, I'm sure we'd be friends.

He doesn't seem keen to leave me when we get to the front door.

"Quaint house," he says, admiring Ms. Fernsby's roses. "It's very storybook-ish."

We linger for a minute at the front door. The sunshine, roses, lingering whiskey, and August make me forget that I'm supposed to be sad now. My widow's jewelry works for me about as well as Heather's purity ring worked for her. Drat.

"Shall we do this a second time? Can you endure me again?" he asks.

"Maybe. You do know, though, that I'm only here for a few weeks."

"Let's just worry about the time you're here, shall we?"

@ADHemmings *Lizzie and August's selfie*:

Drinks with the lovely @LizzieWells at Café Royal. Plotting and general debauchery.

14

"You weren't kidding!" Sarah says, staring at her phone.

I sit across from her at Monmouth and order a very strong tea as the post-whiskey headache spreads across my temples.

She shows me her screen. It's August and me. For a selfie, it's not bad, particularly with the flattering brightening filter. I'm smiling, looking less tense than usual, my cheeks flushed from the drinks. August looks rakish, dimple showing more with the filter, one eyebrow raised roguishly.

"God, is that bad?" I groan.

"Not at all! He's just a notch above you sales-wise—more weeks on the bestseller list. The publicity is marvelous. And look—it already has over 700 likes!"

She always looks so well put together. The upper-crust British accent only accentuates this. Even after a long flight from the States, her red hair remains smoothed back in a chic ponytail, her printed blouse tucked French style into her jeans. Sarah wraps her fingers around her mug, nails manicured with a soft teal polish.

"As you know, we have offers for a film and book sequel. I'm afraid Bella got ahead of herself, but they're on the table. The actors' agents have been notified and want them out and about to keep *The Heathcliff Saga* momentum going. Timing is crucial."

"Absolutely."

She leans across the table. "So here's what I wanted to talk with you about: there are some caveats. You gave Cathy and Heathcliff their happy ending. They want this one to take place in the next generation. Cathy, Heathcliff, and Linton are immortals thanks to the moor's magic, so they're still young and beautiful, but the stakes are higher. They want Heathcliff and Cathy to break up again—create some sort of complication. They want intrigue—maybe a war or high-profile murder. This one needs to be darker but not depressing. You can hammer it out in the proposal. The nonnegotiable, though, is another happy ending."

I take a long sip of the tea, noting hints of pepper and cardamom in the flavoring. "We're getting further away from Brontë territory by the second."

"But you'll do it?"

"Of course I'll do it. The happy ending too."

She smiles, relieved, as she texts our film agent and publisher.

"Ironic, isn't it?"

She glances up, arching one carefully waxed eyebrow.

"Of all people, *I'm* contracted to write happy endings."

"Oh, Lizzie . . ."

"Sorry, I wasn't seeking sympathy. It's just . . ."

Sarah straightens. In her expression, I see whatever Mary Poppins nanny told her to keep a stiff upper lip throughout her childhood. "You—Lizzie Wells—have more control over your happiness than you think."

I stare down into my tea, unsure what to think about that one.

"Ooof . . . I have to run," she says, glancing down at her Apple Watch.

She slings her taupe designer bag over her shoulder as she stands to leave and walks out. Struggling to keep up with her pace, I tell her about how much I'm enjoying the row house and Ms. Fernsby.

"I knew you would. And I'm sure she told you about my half sister, Mabel."

"Uh . . . maybe?"

Sarah holds the door for me. "Father's affair was the most open secret on our side of London. Behind closed doors, my parents argued. But Mum mostly looked the other way, you know—the good politician's wife avoiding scandal. I put it all together pretty early on, and I didn't mind having a girl around my age in the house. Mabel was fun, really. I just thought of her as family. We played Barbies and popped leftover Christmas crackers in the patio garden after the holidays. Does this all shock you?"

"Not really."

With all that's coming out from Philip's family, how can it? I'm learning some families really like to keep their skeletons in the closet. Or, as in Sarah's case, they make the skeletons dance, as the old saying goes.

"I'll be in touch about the contract when it comes in." She smiles, kissing my cheek as her Uber pulls up. "And, Lizzie, remember what I said. I can't have you not believing in happy endings—especially for yourself."

AS I WALK BACK INTO THE ROW HOUSE, IAN TEXTS ME.

> **Ian:** Hey Sis, SOS. Check out Dad's Match app profile.

> **Me:** Dad's on Match????

> **Ian:** I suggested it because he kept serial baking lasagnas.

He texts me a screenshot of Dad's Match page.

For his profile picture, he's sitting at a desk in his den sporting a gray sweater vest, tortoiseshell glasses perched on his nose. He's not smiling, his expression very . . . professor emeritus. In terms of interests, he lists: *Neoromantic, American Transcendentalism with a specialization in Emerson.* Although I know he's a caring person, the entire profile gives off Hannibal Lecter vibes.

Me: Yikes! Any sane woman is going to swipe left before he eats her liver. But it's good that he's getting out there! What can we do?

Ian: I'm working with him this evening. I'm telling him to stick to long morning walks as interests. Can't find a photo of him smiling, but I did find one of him at a barbecue last year looking not-scary.

I wish Ian luck and tell him to let me know if he needs any input.

I still picture Dad struggling over and over to get the lasagna just right. I'm glad he's trying to move forward again. But I know all too well how hard it is. My Victorian widow's rituals keep me rooted. I wonder what might help Dad.

Lucy yowls loudly from upstairs.

"Oh dear!" Ms. Fernsby exclaims from the kitchen, before storming up the stairs. "You do *not* dump the cat in the bathwater! Ever! That was naughty! You'll have your bath tomorrow. Now you're going straight to bed."

From the look of the row house, Heathcliff's been a terror. LEGO and puzzle pieces cover the parlor floor. Crayons and superhero coloring books clutter the dining room table. As I hurry through the kitchen to go upstairs, I see Heathcliff somehow managed to get our British housekeeper to buy him a microwaveable corn dog and potato chips. The stick and leftover crumbs lie in a pool of ketchup on his plate, and an empty orange soda sits nearby.

On the second floor, I find him wearing his Batman cape and mask and struggling against Ms. Fernsby's tight grip. A wet Lucy flies into my bedroom.

"But she works for the *Joker*!" he shouts as Ms. Fernsby and I wrangle him out of the costume and into his pajamas.

"You're getting a nice, *quiet* story tonight, Heathie. You've had enough of these superheroes." She pats her mussed hair, and I tell Ms. Fernsby I'll finish putting him to bed. I can't even begin to imagine what her day's been like as I've been cavorting with a dashing British writer and my agent.

After Heathcliff brushes his teeth, I read him a nice, boring picture book about a boy and his rabbit where literally nothing happens. He's fast asleep before the end. Then I help Ms. Fernsby clean up, putting the ketchup-covered plates in the dishwasher and picking up every LEGO and crayon. I give Ms. Fernsby the signed copy of *Blood Oath*.

By the time I head upstairs, she has her feet up in the parlor and a snifter of brandy as she reads the last chapters of *Blood Ties*.

When I reach my room, I plop into the cushioned chair. Maybe it's the alcohol waning in my system, but I need to talk to a friend to wind down. So much exciting stuff has happened in the last several hours. I find myself fighting a random and strange urge: *I want to talk to Henry.*

Calling him is a ridiculous idea. I just talked to him last night. Besides, he was more Philip's friend than my own. But he's still a friend. It's early evening in South Carolina and of everyone I know, Henry is the most predictable. Right now, he'll be hanging out in his backyard with Bonnie or in his den daydreaming about his weekend fishing trip. He's a known world to me, and I'm craving his stability and warmth.

I pause over the FaceTime button. What will I say? Oh gosh . . . I'll look stupid. I had qualms when he suggested we hang out. It seemed like a terrible idea. So why does calling him seem like such a good idea now?

Before I can overthink it anymore, I hit FaceTime, and he picks up immediately.

"Ouch!" I exclaim at a spreading purple bruise above his temple.

"Does it look that bad?"

He reddens sheepishly, leaning back on the den couch to press a small pouch of frozen vegetables on the bruise.

"What happened? Did Bonnie sucker punch you?"

"Nah . . . I just got it when I was out."

"Out doing what?"

"Working out. CrossFit." But his face deepens to a cranberry red.

I smirk. "You know, you're a terrible liar. Come on . . . how'd you really get it?"

"Okay . . . okay . . . it's a *yoga* injury." With an endearing grin, he pulls the pouch off. "Ginger always wanted me to join her in yoga class. She used to complain that I never did anything *new* with her. She'd been pestering me about it for some time saying that I wasn't interested in anything other than lawyering, hunting, and fishing. She bought me a yoga mat last year, but I never even took it out of the package."

"What was holding you back?" I ask, feeling every bit the hypocrite as I never took those dance lessons.

He shrugs. "Cowardice, maybe. Like what if I pass wind when I'm in downward dog?"

"Everybody does that at least once."

"Or what if I fall on my butt doing one of those eagle poses? I feel like a dang fool standing there with my knee bent up that way. But I suppose Ginger was right that I am a little set in my ways. Tonight was my first class, and ten minutes in, I pitched forward during some leg-up forward bend."

I'm laughing at that point, unable to see Henry in yoga leggings, flowing through all those movements.

He grins again. Bonnie comes up, wagging her tail, and he hands her a chewy treat.

"Are you going to go back?" I ask.

"Yeah—I guess so. It can't get much worse, right?"

"Unless you loudly pass wind during Savasana."

He grins again. "What's going on with you?"

I'm still a little giddy from the afternoon with Dansworth, but for reasons I don't completely understand (or want to admit), I don't want to talk about him with Henry.

"It looks like the book and movie sequels are a go."

"Well, that's fantastic, Lizzie!"

"I'm still in shock. It's been . . . well, it's just been an exciting and unusual day."

"You know what this means?"

"What?"

"I'm going to have to read the book. I never read anything but legal crap—briefs and case histories. Now I'm doing yoga, so why not add good old *Wuthering Heights*? I probably need to dive into that one before I read your book. At least I'll get to know the characters, like your little hurricane's namesake."

I chuckle, unable to see Henry reading *Wuthering Heights* out on his fishing boat.

We chat a bit more about lighter topics. A new fishing pole he bought, Ms. Fernsby's amazing cooking. We don't mention Philip, but I feel him on the margins of everything between us. We both know Philip would be ridiculously proud of me. We know we wouldn't even be friends now if it weren't for him.

I'm attracted to Henry, and I love his company. But I'm also confused. Where can this possibly go?

SOON AFTER THE PHONE CALL, I GO TO SLEEP.

I'm in the front hall of the Azalea Dream at dusk. The hall glows with hazy twilight, the long, damask drapes drawn over the windows. Waning light slips in, streaking across Mirabel's polished hardwood floors, her pricey oriental vases and the portraits lining the hall.

"Philip?"

He stands at hall's end, looking up at his baby portrait. I've seen it a million times—a one-year-old Philip holding a stuffed Winnie-the-Pooh. Baby Philip wears a pressed sailor suit; wispy blond curls spiral out from his head, and he smiles widely, showing off two brand-new lower baby teeth.

Philip doesn't seem to hear me, and I can only make out his silhouette.

In that frustrating way dreams work, the hall seems to be getting longer. Space doesn't make sense. Also, I can't move quickly—the sensation is like walking through water.

"Philip?"

He keeps his gaze glued to the baby portrait. *What are you trying to tell me?*

And I wake up, asking the question out loud in my room, my heart pounding in my chest.

As always, that heavy longing hits me hard after these dreams. He's always just beyond my fingertips, just out of reach, and I miss him—the desire something like pain.

According to my phone, it's one o'clock in the morning. The house is quiet and dark.

What would Philip think of me and how I'm living now?

At once, the previous days fall on me like a crushing weight.

He's only been dead a little over two months, and I've already almost-kissed his best friend. In spite of all my excuses and justifications, I'm attracted to August Dansworth. Yet I'm wearing Philip's hair in the jet necklace, his fingerprint on another chain. I'm wearing mostly black widow's clothes. But I text, and I wear red lipstick, and I lust after insouciant rakes.

I'm a widow failure.

I toss and turn in the bedsheets, trying to go back to sleep. Annoyed, Lucy leaps off the bed and onto one of the room's upholstered chairs.

I was a neurotic child and often had trouble sleeping. Mom always told me that middle-of-the-night worries appear bigger than they actually are. She explained that they're like monsters under the bed, an utterly ridiculous fear that rears only at night. She told me that when night worries hit, I might as well get up and do something else until I'm tired again. *Warm milk is the antidote to worry*, she'd say, and I'd sip her microwaved milk from my favorite cat mug until my anxious brain cooled.

Since Philip's death, the middle-of-the-night-worries have grown tenfold, and I've tossed and turned, but never actually come back to her advice until now.

Tiptoeing downstairs, I microwave some milk, and sip at the kitchen island. Filtered street light streams through the window above the sink, and I stare at the shadow of quivering ivy through the curtains.

Soon Ms. Fernsby walks softly down the stairs, hair up in pins. She tightens her robe belt when she sees me and makes a motherly tsk-tsk sound with her tongue.

"It's too late or too early for you to be up. Do you mind me asking what's troubling you?"

"Monsters."

"What?"

"Sorry, worries—middle-of-the-night worries. They're just as silly as monsters under the bed. At least, that's what my mom always said. But she's not here anymore."

She shakes her head sympathetically. "Was that Grandma Nora?"

"Yes," I mutter.

"Even with his corn dog, Heathie asked for broccoli tonight. He told me his Grandma Nora said superheroes always eat vegetables."

"That was her. She was wonderful. Dad hasn't been doing too well since her death. I lost her last year and then Philip this year. It's been too much."

She pulls out a plate of her shortbread cookies, removing the Saran Wrap.

"You know, luv, my mum read myths to me as a child, and Sleep and Death were brothers in the underworld. I've always thought when Death pays a visit, Sleep gets out of sorts and can't figure out his place in a household. Of course, I didn't have the same relationship with old Lord Routledge that you had with Philip." She chuckles, "God knows, he was my employer, a married man, and even though he could be such a grumpy old codger, I did love him. When he died, I felt grief like never before, and I couldn't sleep through the night for a year."

"It's just awful, isn't it?" My vision blurs with tears. "The separation, I mean. I just don't know what to do with myself. I miss him so much."

She hands me a napkin when I can't hold back the tears. "Heathcliff doesn't get it. He thought we'd see Philip here when we got to London even though I regularly show him this." I pull the bird urn from my pajama pocket, setting it by the cookie plate. "He asks if his daddy can see Batman from where he is. But *I* don't know where Philip is. None of us can.

I don't even know if he *is*. Like maybe he is just in that urn. Maybe it really is the end. And that's—*awful*."

Ms. Fernsby sips her milk, staring at the urn.

Prince Albert died at about the same age as Philip. In addition to wearing widow's weeds the rest of her life, Queen Victoria slept with a plaster cast of Albert's hand nightly. Most scholars believe she and Albert had an affectionate marriage. As a widow, she lived under far more pressure than I do. I just have to keep it together for Heathcliff. She had to keep it together for all of England. Surely, *she* fell apart sometimes? In those sleepless early hours of the morning, I can't imagine she didn't scream into her pillow and clutch that plaster cast. Surely, she chewed out at least one poor lady-in-waiting for misplacing the plaster hand.

"You're right, Lizzie."

"About what?"

"That the separation is awful, and you never—at least on this side—will know for certain where your Philip is. But you'll feel a little better each day. You'll realize you like a song you haven't liked since losing him. You'll remember how much you loved your favorite cake. You will, gradually, in spits and starts, come back to life."

Come back to life.

"I really think, Lizzie, that's why you're here. You think Philip took a bit of you to the grave. Your heart's broken and lying to you about that part. But you're fully alive. Your heart just needs to catch up and realize that grief doesn't mean you're not still living."

"I really do want to come back to life."

"I know, Lizzie."

We're quiet for a few seconds; I chew a shortbread cookie and stare at the urn.

"I have someone I want you to meet," Ms. Fernsby says carefully.

"Thank you, but no. I'm in mourning, and I'm really not supposed to date yet . . ."

"What? Who says there's a proper time frame? Well . . . we can talk about that another time. This isn't a date. I want you to meet a friend who I think could help you."

"A therapist?"

"I suppose you could say that, luv. She works in the same way. I don't want to say too much else about her now. And don't worry about Heathie. My Mabel will take good care of him while we're out."

@ADHemming's Social Media Poll:

Hullo, Chadwick Hall fans!!! Getting ready to write the third book, and who should his next love interest be?

- Ⓐ A Femme Fatale
- Ⓑ Another Hot Partner
- Ⓒ A Sexy Widow

RESULTS: 113 for Femme Fatale; 115 for Hot Partner; and 150 for Sexy Widow

@ADHemmings: Thank you, fans! Sexy Widow it is! Now back to writing 😊

@BluestockingBadass: Forgive me if I'm underwhelmed @ADHemmings. Brainy women everywhere can't wait for another string of poorly written misogynistic love scenes where all sexual pleasure will be for and about Chadwick Hall. #misogyny #blah

15

The next morning, I'm finishing up my coffee and eating a piece of Ms. Fernsby's steaming mushroom quiche when my phone dings.

Chloe: Can I stop being a priest for one minute?

Me: Go for it

Chloe: Is this FUCKING REAL??? *Lizzie and August's selfie*

Me: Guilty 😊

Chloe: Wow! If I didn't have to clean baby poo off my blouse and plan out my Sunday sermon, I'd call you now. Promise you'll spill all the tea when you get back.

Me: I promise.

Chloe: 😊 And don't forget about the labyrinth. Trust the path, friend.

I smile, send her a few selfies of me and Heathcliff from the park the other day, and ask her about baby Asher. I sip my coffee—I have a full day planned with Heathcliff, and Ms. Fernsby says her "friend" can meet with us this evening.

Over my second cup of coffee, I let out a breath of gratitude. Between Henry and Chloe and my department chair, Patrick, I have so many good friends supporting me from abroad.

AFTER A FULL DAY OF CHASING HEATHCLIFF, I COLLAPSE onto the parlor couch the second we walk through the door.

Why had I thought bringing him to the National Portrait Gallery was a good idea? He constantly wondered why "nobody smiles in their picture," and he said their ruffled outfits looked "stupid." By noon, I gave up and just let him run like a wild thing around a pocket park playground. Then we did some shopping, and I spent too much money on him for souvenirs, including a British edition of *Harry Potter*. We'll start reading a chapter every night because I'm not about to raise a Muggle.

I'm relaxing with some lavender tea and *Blood Ties*, my sore feet up on the parlor coffee table, when August texts me to see if I want to go on a Jack the Ripper tour tomorrow evening. I shush my Victorian widow's brain as I text back agreeing to go. She whispers advice in my ear like a fusty great-aunt, and sometimes I just really want to ignore her.

I'm flattered by August's continuing attention, but I do wonder why he likes me. Maybe it's just our writer's connection. Or maybe there's just a strange novelty to cheering up a weepy widow.

I can't think too much about all the whys of our friendship. Instead, I drum my fingers on my teacup, scouring my mind for something else to worry about. Mirabel is of course at the top of the list.

It's been a few days since I've heard from her. I wonder if Henry's getting anywhere with the subpoenas and how long they take. I grip my teacup more tightly, as I'm suddenly nervous about what Steel Magnolia hurricane might be brewing in South Carolina.

I can't stop thinking about Mirabel sitting in that chair with a big sun hat, cigarette clenched between her teeth, pistol poised to shoot another groundhog. She doesn't give up. She's fiercely guarding a piece of her past, and she's a fighter.

I hope Henry knows what he's dealing with.

BY EVENING, I'M RIDING IN AN UBER WITH MS. FERNSBY toward Peckham to meet her friend.

Ms. Fernsby looks very cute with peach lipstick and a little red cap on her head. She's excited, speaking breathlessly and fidgeting with her floral-patterned purse during the ride. "Now, Darcie's lived in this neighborhood for three decades. It was quite dodgy for a good while, but now these young people moved in with their expensive coffees and little toy dogs and wine bars."

After passing a string of the pricey wine bars, we're dropped off near a tall, very old row house covered in ivy.

"She's a bit eccentric," Ms. Fernsby whispers, opening a low wrought iron gate for me, "but she can help you now."

"How?"

"You'll see what I mean."

Darcie opens the door and briskly kisses Ms. Fernsby on the cheek.

She's a short, heavyset woman in a drapey floral dress with

black boots, hair dyed an unnatural but interesting shade of red. Very Raggedy Ann. About Ms. Fernsby's age, she looks like an eccentric great-aunt.

Darcie takes my hands in hers, but not in a kindly manner. She maintains her grip while scrutinizing me over tortoiseshell readers. She says nothing while I mutter an awkward greeting, squirming under her gaze.

Ms. Fernsby and I follow her into a drawing room worthy of any Anthony Trollope novel. A large, quirky antique chandelier hangs from the ceiling. Dark mahogany bookshelves line the walls. Leafy William Morris wallpaper patterns cover every square inch of exposed wall, and I count no less than five senior cats lounging about the room. Darcie shoos them off the furniture before Ms. Fernsby and I sit down. One glares and hisses at me as Darcie leaves the room.

She returns soon with a slightly tarnished silver tray of brandies and hands us each a snifter.

"Now, Annabel told me nothing about you, Lizzie, except that you're a widow."

"That's correct," Ms. Fernsby says. "And I've told her nothing of *you*, Darcie."

"Oh!" Darcie smiles proudly, settling back in her creaky chair and pushing her glasses farther up on her nose. She takes a sip from her snifter. As I take a sip from mine, I notice it's antique Waterford. I'd doubt anything in this room is less than one hundred years old, including, maybe, the persnickety cats.

"By *day*, I input data for the National Health Service. But Ms. Fernsby brought you here because I have a gift for communicating with the dead."

"I don't understand. You're a psychic?"

"I never advertise it. I'm not one of those tarts you pay by the hour. I never take money. It's only a gift I offer some of my friends for closure or peace or whatever it is they need."

"And she's the *real thing*," Ms. Fernsby says, leaning over to me. She smells like lavender powder and brandy. "Last time she summoned my grandmother Doris here and we heard things that no one except family could have known. She even knew about Uncle Christopher's syphilis infection. We *never* talked about that."

"Acquired it in the navy, Doris told me," Darcie says, topping off Ms. Fernsby's brandy. She nods in tipsy affirmation.

I'm speechless. I've always thought the psychic stuff was silly, but the Victorians were obsessed with spiritualism. Ghost photographers like William H. Mumler tricked many a grieving widow into believing that her beloved late husband could materialize in an image. Other intelligent late-Victorians like Sir Arthur Conan Doyle fell deeply into the spiritualism and ghost photography trend while grappling with loss. My chest tightens even now as I think of Doyle seeking out psychics to connect him to his beloved son Kingsley, who died after the Battle of the Somme in World War I.

"If you're not comfortable with it . . ." Ms. Fernsby mutters weakly.

"No . . ." I hesitate.

I stare at a geriatric Siamese cat on the carpet licking her fur. If I was an authentic Victorian widow, I'd be sitting in a room like this, trusting someone like Darcie to summon Philip's spirit. Obviously, this isn't the kind of thing I would have sought out on my own. But there just isn't a good reason *not* to do this.

"Alright, I'm game. Let's do it." I finish my brandy in a gulp.

Darcie closes the heavy dark red curtains and takes us to an Edwardian-era table in the corner of the room. Ms. Fernsby trips lightly over one of the ancient hissing cats.

"Are *they* staying?' she asks irritably.

"Yes, their moods often change with the entry of spirits. The Egyptians were well aware of this."

After dimming the drawing room, Darcie lights a large, heavy candelabra and sets it in the middle of the table. She refills our snifters and settles herself in her seat, then takes in a deep breath through her nose and exhales.

"This really is like a séance," I admit, rather excited now. "Very atmospheric."

"It's not actually necessary. I could sense the spirits if we were sitting in Starbucks over milky coffees. But incense, candlelight—the ambience helps."

We're quiet as Darcie closes her eyes.

Ms. Fernsby's lipsticked mouth twitches excitedly.

As much as I try, I can't believe in ghosts. I can't believe that Philip's spirit is pressing on the veil somewhere close. Nonetheless, I try to stay open-minded and surrender to this exercise.

Outside, lamplight breaks through drapery cracks, casting long shadows across the old books and patterned wallpaper. The cats grow restless; a fluffy Persian walks across the frayed floral area rug and bats at the tabby resting on the floor. The calico leaps back up onto the sofa, clawing at the worn upholstery, and stares back at me in the semidarkness. The room smells like dry rose petals, stale dust, and musty pages. With only the candelabra and antique glasses on the table before us, I'm transported to a time of corsets and tarot cards, where, despite new steam engines and phonographs, there's a yearning for the unknown.

"Hmmm . . ." Darcie murmurs.

"What?" Ms. Fernsby whispers.

Darcie silences her with a hand wave.

For a brief second, I think—I desperately *want* Philip to surprise me and break through my unbelief. Can he please surprise me? My mouth dries, and my heartbeat races. My head swims a little from the brandy.

Philip.

"Hmmm..." Darcie mutters again.

She frowns. "I don't like this gent."

"Who?" I whisper hoarsely. There's *no way* she wouldn't like ghost-Philip.

Her penciled eyebrows furrow behind her glasses.

"Annabel, he says he appreciates the way you're taking care of the house."

Ms. Fernsby gasps. "Archibald... Lord Routledge!"

"Yes," Darcie says irritably.

The Persian hisses from behind me.

A chill zips up my spine. Oh god. If this vintage balderdash is real, maybe this is the moment where we've opened a door to something evil. It seems like a crucial moment in a typical PBS period drama. Agatha Christie's *The Sittaford Mystery* comes to mind. Shit. We're going to end up dead. Victorian twins resembling those little girls in *The Shining* are going to appear to Heathcliff back at the row house. They're going to ask him to play with them and lure him someplace dark and dangerous.

"Should we be afraid?" I whisper, a little panicky.

"Of old Lord Routledge? Goodness no, don't be daft!" Darcie scoffs.

Ms. Fernsby tears up as she speaks. "If you are there, I do wish you could see our Mabel. You'd be so proud. She's doing so well. She's making good grades this second time at uni. She's working so hard at the coffee bar. She wants to be a solicitor, and she will even if she's a bit late in the game. She'll make an extraordinary one."

It's quiet again. The Persian cat relaxes, settles on the rug. And yet all the cats glare at a fixed point in the room. The candelabra flames flicker. Admittedly, it's a little strange.

"Did he hear me?" Ms. Fernsby asks desperately.

Darcie wrinkles her nose, pushes up her glasses. "He did. He's glad for all that. But he does want you to know that he would like his old upstairs suite repainted butterscotch yellow and to use a new draper for the room. This time, Buford and Sons."

Ms. Fernsby grips the pearl necklace around her throat. "I don't understand."

Darcie sighs, waves her hand in the air. "Get away from here. You've said enough and my cats don't like you."

I'm not sure if it's the second glass of brandy, but I feel the air loosening like a relaxed cord. We're quiet, staring at each other as a clock chimes from somewhere in the house.

"Was he like that when he was alive?" Darcie asks.

"Like what?"

"Like a bloody twat."

"No . . . well . . . he was particular about how I kept the house."

Darcie shakes her head. "You don't work for him anymore, luv. You don't keep that house for him anymore. You don't *need* him anymore. If you want to stay in the house because you enjoy taking care of it, fine. But don't do it or *anything* else for him." She shivers. "Good heavens, I'm glad he's out of my house."

A tear slides down Ms. Fernsby's powdered cheek. She might be employed by the Routledge estate, but all the scrubbing, dusting, and cleaning she does is for him.

She's still in love with him.

Darcie sighs, refilling our snifters before settling back in her chair heavily. "Give him up, Annabel. He was never worth it."

Ms. Fernsby's hand trembles as she lifts the glass to her lips.

Although admittedly, some weird Victorian shit just went down, I'm still struggling to believe that Mr. Routledge was here in this room with us. But Ms. Fernsby looks shaken, as if she's been touched by a ghost.

"You know," Ms. Fernsby says softly, "my first day at the

row house, thirty years ago, he did give me an entire day of training for how his shoes were supposed to be arranged in the closet. He had a closetful and was meticulous about the order in which the pairs were organized. And although he would send the most extravagant gifts, he didn't come to a single one of Mabel's birthdays."

"Be done with him, Annabel. He's dead."

We're all quiet. Ms. Fernsby dabs her eyes with a handkerchief.

Darcie kindly places her hand over Ms. Fernsby's on the table. "Do you think, after all these years, you can finally give him up?"

"Maybe."

"I think you can, Annabel. I think you *should*."

Ms. Fernsby nods. "And what about her Philip? He's the one I was hoping we'd see."

Darcie looks at me, a strange expression on her face. "We'll give it a try."

Once Ms. Fernsby calms, Darcie closes her eyes, and we wait.

My heart speeds up. If Philip could come back to me, he would.

I wait, watch for the cats to start getting restless. I stare at the candelabra, willing it to start flickering. Please, *please* flicker . . . Do *something* unexpected . . .

"Nothing," Darcie says, sighing.

"*Nothing?*" I ask.

She shrugs. "Sometimes they don't show up."

What did I expect?

If I hadn't downed the two brandies, I'd have realized that Darcie likely had this whole séance event staged to help her friend move on from a long-dead asshat. Still, privately I desperately hoped Philip would appear. I realize how much I wanted it to happen. I ached for it.

"Can you try again?" I ask pathetically.

"Let's see."

She closes her eyes, and collectively we hold our breath in silence. Then she snaps her eyes open and shakes her head.

"Sorry, luv. He's not coming."

"Well, why ever not?" Ms. Fernsby implores.

"Sometimes, they choose for us not to see them. It can be a kindness."

Really, Philip?

"Lizzie, we can always come back here," Ms. Fernsby says gently. "He might just not be up to it tonight. It uses up a lot of energy, right, Darcie?"

Darcie shakes her head. "It's not that. Sometimes the spirits know it's not good for us to see them."

"Why wouldn't it be good for me to see Philip?"

"I've encountered this before. Sometimes, the love is so strong it continues uninterrupted, steady as it was in life. You don't need me to bring him here."

"You didn't answer my question. Why wouldn't it be *good* for me to see him?"

Darcie speaks slowly, choosing her words carefully. "There are dangers with this type of love, Lizzie. Because the love is sturdy, when one partner dies, the other one remains actively attached in such a way that they are unable to move on. The good spirits know this about their living loves. You don't *need* Philip to show up to you tonight. And he won't—because he knows it's not good for you."

"I HOPE YOU'RE NOT TOO DISAPPOINTED," MS. FERNSBY says as we ride back to the row house. "These séances—they rarely turn out as expected."

I stare out the Uber car window at the passing streetlamps.

I'll probably feel embarrassed in the morning, silly that something in me wanted to believe Philip could return to me. But I think part of being warm and human is holding out hope in the fantastic—that we can be surprised in our ordinary, known world.

"How do *you* feel about what happened?" I ask.

She sighs. "Released."

BACK AT THE HOUSE, WE FIND MABEL SIPPING HOT TEA at the kitchen island. Everything is clean and quiet, with Heathcliff safely tucked in and asleep upstairs. Ms. Fernsby has settled into a distracted mood since we left the séance, and after chatting a bit with her daughter, she heads up to bed. I sit across from Mabel. I'd only met her briefly before we left for Darcie's, and here in the kitchen light, I see immediately her resemblance to Lord Routledge—the high cheekbones, the long nose. Although not much younger than Sarah and me, she could pass for a college student. Sporting an oversize sweatshirt with floral yoga pants and hair up in a high ponytail, she looks fun, like someone who hares off backpacking to Switzerland on a long weekend.

"Love that little boy of yours," she says, her eyes a warm blue like her mother's.

We make small talk for a bit. She tells me about how she and Heathcliff built a LEGO Gotham City and how he managed to negotiate three books before bedtime. (Fiercely negotiating beyond one book at bedtime has been Heathcliff's longtime MO with babysitters.) When we hear Ms. Fernsby's bedroom door shut upstairs, Mabel leans forward, lowering her voice.

"Mum seemed a bit off. Is everything okay?"

I tell her about the séance and Ms. Fernsby's response in the car.

"Released," Mabel says thoughtfully, taking another sip of tea. I stare at the tea bag, wet and limp on a nearby floral saucer. "It's about bloody time."

"She's loved him for all these years," I murmur. "I could tell that by the way she talked about him during the séance."

"And he never deserved it. He provided for me, but that was it. He never considered himself anything more to her or me. Don't misunderstand me—I'm not bitter. I have Sarah, and she's every bit a sis to me. But Mum, she's pined after Lord Routledge for all these years, never really ready to move on."

"Maybe after tonight?" I say hopefully.

Mabel nods vigorously. "If *anyone* can convince her to move on, it's Darcie. They've been friends for years, and I've sat in on many of her 'events.' She convinces people about what's good for them far beyond what any therapist can do. Whatever ghost gobbledygook happens in her parlor, Darcie works magic. Trust me."

As I'm pulling back the bedcovers, Henry texts me a screenshot of a paperback copy of *Wuthering Heights*.

Henry: Diving in!

I text back a smiley face, strangely tickled that he's trying yoga and reading *Wuthering Heights* in the same week. I suppose he should inspire me.

I wonder if I'll ever have the courage to dance again.

16

A few hours before the evening Jack the Ripper tour, Mirabel calls as I'm bathing Heathcliff.

"Hi, Mirabel," I say, drying off my hands.

"Your lawyer friend won't stay out of my garden."

Ms. Fernsby comes up the stairs with some towels and takes over drying Heathcliff as the water drains loudly from the tub. I take my phone into my room and shut the door.

"What are you talking about?"

"Henry *Law*ton sent another subpoena to my lawyer today. He wants all legal documents related to the trust and other things that don't matter one iota. Trust me, Elizabeth, he's chasing after family matters that are better left alone!"

"Mirabel, if this has anything to do with what upset Philip that night, it would serve you well to tell me and Henry the truth. We'll find out one way or another. Philip was upset for a reason, and I need to protect Heathcliff's interests."

There's a very long, scary silence.

"Mirabel..."

"Elizabeth, I had a consultation with my attorney today over some concerns Ted and I both have. Your behavior since Philip died has been peculiar and erratic. You wear black all the time and all that morbid *jewelry*. And now you've made this wild quick trip to London. Heathcliff mentioned something about men, and, well, I don't know what you're exposing our grandson to."

"What the hell are you talking about?"

"Language, Elizabeth. I know grief drives people to do crazy things, but it's Heathcliff we're concerned about. My Summerville lawyer suggested that given our concerns perhaps we should order a toxicology report on you and apply for guardianship of Heathcliff. Then the court can determine if you're a fit parent."

Nausea seeps through my gut.

She can't do that.

Can she?

I haven't done anything to warrant losing custody of Heathcliff. But this stabs at some deep fears of mine. My meltdown in front of my class. My Victorian compulsions lately. Of course, I haven't been in my normal state of mind since Philip died. But I'm definitely not crazy.

I take a deep breath, reminding myself that this is a woman who wears oversize sun hats and shoots groundhogs point-blank in her garden.

"You can't do that."

"You have your lawyer. I have mine. And mine says that depending on how our own investigation goes, we have a chance to take guardianship of Heathcliff. Perhaps we could even return him to you after your behavior is more... regulated."

"I'm a perfectly fit mother," I say through clenched teeth.

"I sure hope so, sweetie."

She hangs up.

She's never called me "sweetie" in all the years I've known her. I don't think she has any grounds whatsoever to take my son, but I'm terrified. People lie about parents' actions to get guardianship all the time, and I *know* Mirabel lies about more than cigarettes.

If anything reeks of a nineteenth-century novel plot, it's *this*. Gaslighting women into thinking they're mentally unstable in order to take their money, or their freedom, or their children. Even Charles Dickens tried to convince professionals his estranged wife needed to be committed. Thank god it's not the 1800s. Here, in the twenty-first century, I'm pretty sure I'm more protected now. At least I hope so . . .

Just to make sure, I try to call Henry, but he doesn't pick up.

I don't leave a message. After all, I'd be crazy to take her threats seriously.

Sarah: Whelp! Book contract came in already, but I got the automatic email reply that you're only sending and receiving letters. Huh?

Me: It's a weird widow ritual. I've had a lot less heartburn.

Sarah: Hmmm . . . well then, I'll just overnight it. Sign, return, and be proud!☺

WISPY CLOUDS STREAK ACROSS THE EVENING SKY AS I walk through the East End.

Tonight I'm wearing a black cardigan over my black eyelet dress, black tights, and buckled leather walking shoes. In my previous happily married life, the eyelet dress was for casual dates out with Philip. But I'd wear an elegant wrap instead of the sweater, and pink flats instead of walking shoes. I'd show off bare legs and arms and sport cute chunky bracelets on my wrists. Currently, I suppose the widow accessories make me look more like a dowdy Audrey Hepburn.

Since getting off at the Aldgate East tube station, I remember how lively the East End of London becomes at nightfall. With the crowded Spitalfields Market and the colorful street art of Brick Lane and Hanbury Street, the neighborhoods are a hodgepodge of bohemia, grad student culture, pub shenanigans, and pickpockets. I keep my purse strap tight across my shoulders. When I'm almost to our meeting place in front of the Whitechapel Gallery, I pass a tipsy man in a cap tap-dancing on a slow-moving taxi roof. He salutes me, and I automatically curtsy. It's a strange and delightful interaction.

August stands near the back of our walking tour group. He smiles wolfishly, sexy as always as he hands me my ticket. "Have I told you how stunning you are in widow's black?"

"Widow's weeds are just my style?"

"Without a doubt."

"Hey," August whispers, tugging me away from the loitering group toward a streetlamp. He continues with the magnetic smile, his dimple deepening. "Do you want to try something?"

He holds out a little packet of gummies.

I giggle. Back in grad school, I tried marijuana once. Wes, a few department friends, and I shared a joint through all six hours of the 1997 *Pride and Prejudice* miniseries. My muscles stopped working, and I couldn't move off the faded couch sectional. Yet I'd been very bothered by Colin Firth's sideburns. *Does anyone see how they're crawling down his face? My god, they're MOVING. They're really MOVING.* I called Ian: *We have to do something about Colin Firth's sideburns!*

"Come on, don't tell me you've never indulged before?"

"Sure. But it was years ago, and I had kind of a weird reaction."

"How bloody fun! Come on, then."

"I don't know . . ."

"Oh . . . come on—all the cool kids are doing it."

Taking the gummy certainly doesn't seem appropriate for high mourning. Then again, Victorian widows loved their laudanum. That's the nineteenth-century equivalent of a grape-flavored gummy, right?

"Sure, why not?" I accept the gummy and swallow, not overthinking this one.

"That a girl!" August says proudly, popping one into his mouth.

I suddenly remember Mirabel's threat.

"Oh my god!"

I run over to a trash can and stick my finger down my throat.

"Elizabeth, what are you doing?" August asks, alarmed.

I'm gagging, but even though the trash smells like rancid fried fish, I can't cough the gummy up. My throat just burns and feels scratchy.

I pull my head out of the trash can and start googling. "How long does this stay in your system, August?"

"I suppose a few days."

"This site says it can be detected in the hair for up to three months!"

He glances around nervously.

"Elizabeth, I think you need to calm down. Surely, your school doesn't *drug test* you. And your publisher won't for sure." He chuckles. "Besides, absinthe, marijuana—it's all bloody par for the course in our business. Do you think Hemingway ever cared about drug tests?"

"It's not that. There's so much more at stake." I call Henry, but he's still not picking up.

"Elizabeth . . ." He puts his hands gently on my arms and makes me look at him. "I don't know what's going on here exactly. But one gummy will be flushed out of your system by the time you get back to the US."

"But the hair sample . . ."

I raise my phone.

"Stop googling. You're just going to upset yourself more."

"But . . ."

I'm about to argue, but I see his point. This panic is only a bridge to nowhere. I need to wait until I hear back from Henry. I slow my breathing while August watches me carefully.

"Better?" he asks.

"I think so."

We wait around a few more minutes until our guide shows up. I'm sorely disappointed that he's an anemic grad student who looks like he leads this tour with about as much gusto as his DoorDash gig.

After collecting everyone's ticket, the guide stands on a wobbly stool so our tour group of about twenty can see him and begins in a monotone, "So here we are about ready to start our tour about the notorious serial killer Jack the Ripper, who went on his murderous killing spree one hundred and thirty years ago . . ."

"I can't believe he's reading from a *card*," I whisper in August's ear. I'm still not quite feeling the gummy, but I anticipate it kicking in soon. My stomach still churns a little with worry over taking it. But I try to push it from my mind and enjoy the tour.

"Bloody hell. This wanker is rubbish," August groans.

We follow along near the back of the group until we reach Mitre Square.

The guide stands on his stool and fumbles with the cards. "Now here we are at the scene of the murder of Catherine Eddowes. This was the night of the double murders. Scotland Yard..."

"Never mind this was one of the more *gruesome* of the murders!" August interjects. He describes dramatically the postmortem examination of Eddowes and how the Ripper taunted Scotland Yard by keeping one step ahead of vigilante policemen.

"It all happened against the background of the late Victorian period, the approaching fin de siècle, with glorious rebels like Virginia Woolf and Oscar Wilde. It was a time of rapid change and progress, where the world lurched and whirled forward! It was a time of phonographs, railroads. Industries burgeoned all over, and *London* was the center of it all. But the change was too fast for some. And *here*..." August waves dramatically around us. "Here was a forgotten place of gritty cobblestone streets, shadowy brickyards, and gaslight. It was a hardscrabble life in these parts, terribly easy to fall through the cracks or slip away, never to be found..."

"Wait!" an older woman interrupts. "Are you A.D. Hemmings?"

"Who?" her heavily mustached male companion asks in a thick Cockney accent.

"You know, Ralph—*A.D. Hemmings*, the gent who writes those slash-'em-up murder mysteries. I love that Inspector Hall." She pauses and giggles. "That inspector. He can get into my knickers anytime."

"Oh my *god*," a young attractive woman wearing a lavender cardigan exclaims, staring at her phone and then at August. "Yes, he looks just like him. Are you really him?" she asks, blue eyes sparkling.

"Guilty," August admits, trying hard to look modest.

"Well, he's doing a bloody good job, 'ere," the woman says.

"Can't he just finish the tour? Ee's got more flair than *you*." She stares rudely at the student-guide.

The guide shrugs. "Sure. As long as I get the gratuity."

"It's a deal!" August says, leaping onto the stool.

Only I can tell in the courtyard shadows that he's a touch high, blue eyes darkening and a blush spreading on his cheeks.

As for me, I'm feeling pleasantly stimulated, like I've had sufficient caffeine and vitamins and can tackle a new project.

The guide hangs back playing Pokémon GO on his phone while August takes over. The women in the group range from twenties to about seventy, but they all push past each other to stand near August. As I walk along in the little crowd, I suspect August must have taken these Jack the Ripper tours dozens of times, memorizing details and brainstorming his own next Inspector Hall scenes.

We continue through Mitre Square as August describes with gusto the mad police rush on the night of the double murders. He tells us the Ripper goaded the police by mailing in pieces of the victims' organs and handwritten notes. Sparing no detail, he paints a gruesome and chaotic series of events as skillfully as he writes an Inspector Hall scene.

My thoughts become a little more raw and uncensored.

I'm finding it harder than usual to take my eyes off August. I wonder what he looks like naked.

Will I ever see him naked? My mind slows and then races, "sticking" on random thoughts that grow as big as a universe in my mind: Will I ever see August Dansworth naked? Will I forget what Philip looked like naked? Thinking of Philip naked segues to Oedipal-like stream-of-consciousness thoughts about Mirabel. Weird. I see Mirabel's lipsticked face as clear as a photograph in my mind. I hear her threats as if she's shouting them in my ear now. "Peculiar," she called me.

I stare down at my dark clothes, the jet necklace. Philip's urn weighs heavily in my bag.

I'm not *peculiar*.

Or maybe I am, and Mirabel will get my son.

What if I am mentally unfit?

I'm fucking high, walking about on a Jack the Ripper tour. Panic and paranoia flutter again as I start ruminating once more about how long marijuana stays in the system.

We're near the end of the tour at Fournier Street in Spitalfields, just in front of The Ten Bells pub. The women crowd about August, who basks in the attention. They all vie to ask him questions while their husbands tip the student-guide and head into the pub for a drink. One by one, the women take selfies with August and flirt, begging for tidbits from the next Chadwick Hall book.

I lean against a lamppost and fumble in my purse for my phone.

"Henry?"

"Lizzie! Sorry I couldn't call you back earlier." Traffic sounds in the background. "I had the longest goddamn court . . ."

"Henry, I'm fucked."

"Hey—what's going on?"

"I'm in London."

"Yeah? I *know*. You don't sound right. Are you safe?"

"He just gave me a gummy."

"Who gave you a gummy?"

"You know, A.D. Hemmings."

"The author? Lizzie, you're talking gibberish. *Who* gave you something? Where are you? Wait, don't move. I'm going to call Ms. Fernsby. Don't go off alone with anyone."

"I'm fine! I really am hanging out with Hemmings. His real name is August. Look . . ." I text him our selfie.

"That sure does look like him."

"It *is* him. We're writer buddies now. But that's not the *point*, Henry. I called you because Mirabel is threatening to fight for custody of Heathcliff. She told me so on the phone tonight. I'm fucked if she does. She'll dress him up in little bow ties like Ted. She'll teach him how to shoot innocent garden groundhogs. She'll have him sipping mint juleps . . ."

Henry laughs loudly as he shuts his car door and turns on the ignition.

"This isn't *funny*! Why are you laughing?"

"Because, Lizzie, trust me, with all the crap I'm finding, no judge is going to give Mirabel Wells custody of a hedgehog. And I think that gummy's playing with your head and you're getting paranoid. Right now, I'm not worried about your piece-of-work mother-in-law, but I am worried that you're safe."

"She couldn't be bloody safer!" August says suddenly into the phone, from over my shoulder.

"That's him."

"*Who?* Lizzie, I don't feel good about this."

"God, stop being such a bossy *big brother*, Henry."

"Alright. Alright. Just make sure to text me when you get back. Or I could stay on the phone until . . ."

"I'll text you!" I snap, hanging up, weirdly annoyed and flattered he's so concerned.

"Henry?" August asks, checking his Uber app.

I glance around. It looks like our tour group is gone.

"Just an old friend."

"Hmmm . . ." He raises one eyebrow as he holds the car door open for me. I get in, noticing the paranoia easing away. Instead, I start to feel more in my skin. Everything seems sharper, *brighter*. Stringed lights drape from a nearby pub, glowing as warm as fairy orbs. Our taxi passes the flower market, and I'm mesmerized by the wooden crates of pink and red roses, yellow rhododendrons, the hues resplendent even at night. I still feel caffeinated and very alive.

Interesting.

"What's in this gummy, August?"

"No idea," he says, head leaning back in the seat beside me. "I bought it from one of my students this afternoon."

"You *what*?"

But his phone rings with Madonna's "Die Another Day."

"Hullo, Gertie!" August exclaims.

I glance sideways, but the taxi's maneuvering through loud Spitalfields Market traffic, and I can't hear the voice on the other end.

"Uh-huh . . . Uh-huh. Yep, sure. Be right there. In fact, I'm feeling good—kind of high, not quite ready for the night to end, and truth be told I was kind of hoping you'd call. This time I'm bringing my friend Elizabeth. She's a real gem."

"Huh?"

As soon as the call ends, he glances over at me with that irresistible smirk. Maybe it's the waning gummy, but his dimple seems deeper and my stomach lurches.

"So, Elizabeth, are you up for a bit more fun?"

"What kind of fun?"

"The worst kind. Deliciously wicked."

He leans forward, redirecting the driver to Soho.

"What kind of *fun*?"

"Bur*lesque*."

"I thought you were joking when you said you danced burlesque."

"No, I was joking about wearing the corset."

"I don't understand."

"It's very simple," August says as we pass by Soho's backstreets of brightly painted storefronts and cafés. "I told you I work hard to have a life outside the mind. My cousin Gertie manages the performances at The Fin de Siècle, and when she's short-staffed, or when I'm just *bloody bored*, I work there. I'm wearing loads of makeup, a bowler hat, and a very naughty vest—and no one knows who I am. It's marvelous. And tonight, *you* are joining me onstage."

"You can't expect me to *perform*!"

"Come on, now. I promised from day one I was going to break you out of your mind, so here we are."

"No."

"Gertie's in a real pinch tonight—down three dancers."

"Absolutely not."

"You've never performed before? *Ever?* Even in your high school's *Little Women* production? I bet you played the perfect Meg."

"Well . . . there was show choir."

"There you go!"

Show choir. My mother, concerned that I was far too shy for my age, urged me to audition my sophomore year of high school. No one was more surprised than me when I made the cut. It was a year of swirling tulle skirts and red sequined bodices. Amid my fear and hesitation, that year I let go in a way I haven't since. My contributing solo to Destiny's Child's "Survivor" helped win us first place in the Midwest Regionals. I felt glamorous, confident, and at-home in my skin in a way I haven't since.

But I was sixteen. Now I'm thirty-nine with a son, a PhD, stretchmarks, and real heartbreak. I'm too old and weighted to ever be that girl again.

Amid some weak protesting, I let August pull me out of the cab and through the back door of Fin de Siècle. I find myself in a dimly lit dressing room surrounded by beautiful women in full makeup and flouncy, short burlesque costumes. All are about ten years younger than me. Heavy curtains cover dressing rooms while cosmetics, glittery combs, and colorful fans clutter the vanities. Ribbon chokers with bright silk flowers dangle from mirrors, and everything smells like sweat, perfume, gin, and cigarette smoke.

"Gertie!"

"Oh, Auggie! Thank god you're here!" A young woman hurries to us, lightly kissing "Auggie" on both cheeks. She's wearing a cranberry corset with a garter belt, tights, and silver dancing heels; her black curls twist elegantly around her head. "Both Maud and Penny called in an hour ago, and my replacements are all booked! I'm starting the show tonight and we need more bloody dancers . . . Elizabeth?" She looks me over.

"I'm not dancing . . ."

"She's marvelous! American show choir circa early 2000s," August quips, slinging his arm around me.

"Don't worry, luv, you'll be fine," Gertie says. "I'm going to have Tyler fix you up and get you started. We're on in an hour!"

She hurries away, giving August costume instructions. He winks at me before disappearing behind a dressing room curtain. Yes, it's unusual that they'd take someone last-minute. But perhaps they aren't the most *high*-production-value place, and they're desperate and it's just a chorus role. Fear bubbles up as I contemplate making a complete fool of myself on a stage in front of strangers. I can run out now. I can leave and catch a taxi back to the row house. I'm under no obligation here. Yet I stay rooted to the floor, frozen with peculiar yearning as bustling performers hurry past me, brushing against my elbows with warm bare arms.

"Elizabeth!"

I turn around as Tyler introduces himself. He's wearing the same outfit as Gertie, with a silk pink rose choker around his throat, and he sports a long blond wig.

I ask him to call me Lizzie as he leads me to a makeup chair. Tyler's ease and American accent relaxes me as he slips a makeup cape around my shoulders and pulls out the drawers for hairbrushes and beauty products.

Gertie sets a tall pink cocktail with a black straw on the vanity. "Our most popular house specialty after the absinthe fountain. It's a sloe gin fizz. Not too strong, but just enough to take the edge off before the show." She pats my shoulder reassuringly and then raises an eyebrow, pulling my chin toward her. "Add some sparkles to those eyelids, Ty, to make her eyes really pop."

"On it," he says, handing me the drink as she hurries away to check on a quick skirt alteration. I take a sip, the flavor sweet, light, and tart all at once.

"So we have eyelid sparkles, and we're going to rouge you up a bit for under those lights." He holds an eye shadow palette against my skin, cocking his head one way and then the other. Then he starts to prime and powder, skillfully and quickly covering my face before he works on my eye area.

"What is this place exactly?" I ask as he darkens my eyebrows, narrowing his heavily lined eyes while concentrating with the brow pencil.

"Sweetie, when it comes to Fin de Siècle, this is the real deal. Best vintage bohemia outside of old Montmartre. We're everything granny and modern all at once: these sweet floral drinks, old-fashioned costumes, but we perform with all the fabulous pop culture fluff. You'll see and hear it all tonight."

"Oh."

He applies plum-colored lipstick and then gently blots my lips with a tissue.

"Show choir, huh?"

"That was years ago. I'm about to make a complete fool of myself . . ."

"*Stop*. It's the same concept, different moves."

"I won't have to strip, will I? I don't do that."

"No, not really. Maybe some peekaboo."

"What?"

"It'll make sense when we're out there. It's all very organic. And I'm going to give you a quick crash course."

As he sprays and twists, piling my hair on my head like Gertie's, he leans in to secure a lock on my scalp with a bobby pin. I notice a tiny tattoo on his inner wrist, a delicate broken heart surrounding the initials *F. W. R.* Solidarity swells in me like a curling beach wave.

Gently, I take his wrist and meet his eyes.

He freezes, three bobby pins sticking out between his pressed lips.

"My loss was Philip. He was my husband. I wear his hair around my neck."

I pull the jet locket out from under the makeup cape.

He swallows hard, removes the bobby pins from his lips. "My loss was Frederick William Roth. My husband."

He continues pinning and spraying, tackling some loose locks with a curling iron.

"I met Freddy ten years ago, when I was auditioning and waiting tables in New York City. I was sad and lonely, recently moved from my small life in the Dakota suburbs. But I knew I was in the right place. He ordered sushi at my table and had this adorable Cockney accent. He left his number on the receipt with a smiley face."

"I'm sorry," I say, as he tucks the last piece of hair up with a rhinestone comb.

"Thank you." He pats the back of my head, making sure everything stays in place.

"I met my Philip in a coffee shop fifteen years ago. And I lost him about two months ago."

"God. I'm so sorry." He blinks hard, his eyes dewy. "We're part of that strange little club no one wants join."

"Indeed," I answer.

Gertie walks through, reminding everyone there's only forty-five minutes until showtime.

After asking for my sizes, Tyler sends me into a dressing room with one of the cranberry corset costumes and a silky black, taupe, and silver strapless bra. (I gulp, afraid to ask why I need such a fancy bra.) Through the curtain, he passes me fishnet tights, a garter belt, a white silk flower choker, and heeled silver dancing shoes. In the darkness, I scramble to get dressed, trying not to think about what I'm doing—basically wearing my undies in front of a crowd of strangers and dancing to who-knows-what.

How did August drag me into this? And where the hell is he? I haven't seen him since he disappeared into the dressing room.

"Ready?" Tyler asks from behind the curtain.

"Yes."

He steps in, one hand behind his back, and flips on the light. I catch my breath at the sight of myself in the mirror. The corset fits perfectly, the seams, ruffles, and ribbons lined up in all the right places, the bust accentuating my modest assets. As I changed, I learned that the corset doesn't go on like an actual corset—no front busk with little metal tabs and loops. Rather, it stays together with a vertical strip of Velcro hidden carefully under a ribbon running down my chest. A dark lace-and-tulle bustle sticks out from my rear suggestively. I worried the makeup, particularly the eye sparkles, would be garish. But it all looks ethereal and dramatic now that I'm in full costume. I'm like an alter ego of my restrained, daytime widow-self, obsessed with propriety and everything black.

Although I left Philip's urn in my satchel in one of the lockers, I kept the locket at my throat, the choker holding it in place. I stare at my reflection, and I touch the cool jet surface. I remind myself that I'm the same woman who wore the modest black eyelet dress with tights and loafers earlier this evening.

"Perfect!" Tyler says, pulling out two full ostrich feather fans from behind his back.

"I don't look like me."

"Lizzie, you are more you now than ever before. Now, come on," he thrusts one of the fans into my hands. "We've got thirty minutes."

The playlist begins with Christina Aguilera's "Express."

"How familiar are you with these?" he asks, as he connects his phone to the room's stereo.

I smirk. "I know I *never* listen to pop culture singers when I run."

Tyler smirks back. "And I *know* you never lie. I'm loving the sass!"

He ticks off the essential burlesque rules and basic choreography of the three songs. He reminds me that like show choir, it's about sync and rhythm, except this time I'm supposed to let my body follow the fabric curves of my dress.

"*This* . . ." he says, gesturing to my bustle with his fan, "blooms out for a reason. Follow it. And when in doubt, stick it out."

I giggle.

He plays "Express," bringing out a chair to show me how to kick up in the air and spin my rear amid the beats. (Me: *Whee!*) During Michael Bublé's "Feeling Good," he leads, telling me at what points I'll be spinning in someone's arms. (Tyler: *But it's burlesque, so the women are really in charge. Men are YOUR props!*) Little by little, I feel an inner humming, and my body follows. And by the time we get to Britney Spears's "Circus," I'm singing. (Tyler: *Now we know who's listened to this fifty million times when no one else is in the car!*) Pieces of me I haven't felt in twenty years awaken. August never pressured me into performing tonight. He opened a door, but I willingly chose to walk through.

"I just might be able to do this . . ." I mutter as I mimic Tyler's sexy straddling of a chair before stomping my heel on the seat and twirling a long red ribbon.

"*Might?* You've got it. Just go with everything. And that pretty bra . . ."

I cock my eyebrow.

"It's your show. No one's going to make you do anything

you don't want to. But I'm *just saying*, if it feels right to rip off that thing and show your fierce beauty to the world—you fucking do it!"

WE'RE STANDING ON THE STAGE IN THE DARKNESS. I'M poised with my ostrich fan flared out across my chest. There's about twelve of us onstage, half in cranberry corsets and half in vests and bowler caps. One of the vested dancers positions himself beside me, where we'll do a little waltzy thing when the music starts.

I try not to look at the crowd. It's an old nerve-calming technique from my show choir days—don't look, just focus on my world up here. Nonetheless, my heart pounds.

"Looking good, Dr. Wells," August whispers from beside me with a wink.

I do a double take in the shadows. Black liner accentuates his eyes, and a bowler cap covers his hair. He sure was spot-on about the naughty vest. Black with sparkly silver rivulets threaded throughout the fabric like a night sky, its one and only purpose is to accentuate August Dansworth's bare, beautiful, toned arms.

I gawk like a fish.

The "Feeling Good" melody starts and a soloist in a vest costume belts out the first stanza.

August takes me in his arms as I try to remember the steps. But I stumble, then move against him when I should move back, move back too early as he pulls me in. The fan feels heavy and awkward in my right hand. We're wildly out of sync and it's Philip's voice I hear in my head.

When are we going to take those dancing lessons, Lizzie?

I freeze with sad regret.

"We're swaying now," August whispers against my ear as the beat picks up, and I'm pulled back to the present. He dips me dramatically over his bent leg, then I rise, swinging my fan over his shoulder before I melt into him and then back again.

Sure, Philip and I swayed at some wedding receptions, but we never *really* danced. Not like this. That was a world I left behind after high school.

Again, I try to refocus as we dance past the soloist, all the couples forming a wide circle.

Follow your curves, Tyler mouths to me as he sways gracefully past with his vested partner.

I close my eyes, inhaling August's fabric and faint floral cologne as he grips my hand, twirling me away from him. I twirl back, delightfully like a yo-yo. I push away all thoughts except the present, feeling the weight of the bustle, my breasts under the fancy bra.

As the song ends, August and I twirl and spin and dip into a strong finish.

"Bravo!" he whispers as we bow breathlessly onstage.

I'M DEFINITELY WARMED UP BY THE NEXT SONG.

Gertie sings, and the corsets mostly perform with chairs while the vests dance and twirl around us like a spinning constellation. I stomp my sparkly heel on the chair seat, swinging my hips, catching Tyler's eye from beside me before we twirl on the seats.

I'm out of breath, but far from exhausted. I suppose the stimulating gummy could still be strumming through my veins or the sloe gin must have loosened me up. But I'm happy, at ease, and confident.

The final line hits, and while the vests kneel at the corners of the stage, I mimic the corsets as we straddle our chairs one more time.

We're approaching the last chant, and we chair dancers all

bring our hands to our chests. Some anticipatory cheers sound from the audience.

Oh no.

I keep smiling, and we pause, teasingly, while Gertie draws out the last line.

No, this is what women in Chadwick Hall novels do.

It makes us objects for the male gaze. It's derogatory.

Then again, maybe I'm just afraid. It's not like I'll be topless.

Show your fierce beauty to the world.

We all smile teasingly, and the cheers grow louder.

The corsets come off in one sweep.

Except for mine.

I chickened out.

AFTER A FIVE-MINUTE BREAK, AND A FEW PROP EXchanges, we're ready for "Circus."

This time, Tyler's the soloist, and he looks unbelievably awesome in a red corset costume with a flashy silver sequined skirt. I wonder, fleetingly, if he thinks of Freddy as he performs. I can't imagine he doesn't.

I take my place beside him, determined to have fun on this one. No more nerves as I stand by Tyler in the dark.

"Having fun?" he whispers.

"Fucking time of my life."

"Then this one's yours."

"What? Wait!"

He hands me the mic.

"No . . . no . . . no . . ."

But he's already snapping the removable silver skirt around my waist.

"You've got this, Lizzie."

Do I?

I break my rule and look out into the sizable crowd lingering around high, round wooden tables. Little quirky vases of bright carnations accent the tabletops and bar. The place is packed. I see an artsy, warm crowd wearing drag—colorful gowns, fun tuxedos, and sparkly tiaras. I see wigs and, even in the dim lights, dramatically dark brows honoring Dita Von Teese and Jean Harlow. In this moment, I'm a rogue Victorian-in-mourning, and I feel wonderful.

The music starts.

I've got this, and I love this crowd. I stretch my free hand out to them as I grip the mic and belt out the first part of the song.

Now the corsets part away from me as August and the other vests weave between us. But I strut forward. This is *my* show.

The corsets behind me straddle and swing on the chairs, twirling giant red ribbons. As the beat picks up, I pull off the removable skirt and—oh why the hell not?—I toss it into the crowd amid roaring cheers. I wink as a drag queen in a pink gown catches it.

August and another vested dancer lift me up into the air as I sing loudly, with a confidence I've long forgotten.

They bring me down and twirl away while I swing my foot up onto my chair. While the corseted dancers flank me, twirling the giant red ribbons, Tyler tosses me a large silver one from somewhere. My voice quavers, surprised, until I remember I'm in charge here.

Claps and cheers sound as I flick and twirl the ribbon in front of me, gripping the mic still in the other hand. I spin with the ribbon a few more times, before handing it off to August as he twirls by. Then I spin on my chair, syncing a nice leg kick with Tyler. Are my moves perfect? No. I'm far from a Rockette. But I'm having the time of my life, and the crowd knows it.

And then, when I'm almost down to the last stanza, I hear Philip's voice in my head.

When are we going to take those dancing lessons, Lizzie?

I'm dancing again now, Philip. I'm dancing now!

I belt out the last part of the song with everything I have.

Two more lines.

I've torn off the skirt. Can I take more off?

Oh gosh . . .

It's now or never. My row waits for their cue. This isn't about the male gaze. I might love this crowd, but I'm not doing this for them. I'm doing this for me. I put everything into the last line.

And I rip the corset off as the crowd erupts in cheers and whistles.

"YOU WERE BRILLIANT!" TYLER GUSHES AS HE HANDS August and me to-go cartons of the bar's lamb scouse and walks us out to our waiting Uber. Both he and Gertie were beyond pleased and wanted me to stay longer to hang out with the cast. Unfortunately, it's almost one o'clock in the morning. I texted Ms. Fernsby and Henry to let them know I'm safe and fine, and I would be late. I told Ms. Fernsby not to wait up for me. But I'm losing steam now. The excitement of dancing, the adrenaline rush from the touch of stage fright, and likely the gummy have worn off.

"Tonight was wonderful, a beautiful dream," I say to Tyler as he kisses me on the cheek goodbye. He's wearing a long jacket over his costume in the cool night air. I've changed back into my own clothes, but the spell isn't broken. Although exhausted, I'm deliriously happy.

"*Ab-so-lutely!*" Tyler says as we hug. We've already exchanged numbers and plan to stay in touch. After August and

I load into the car, Tyler pulls one of the ostrich fans out from inside his jacket. "Here, take this. As a souvenir."

"Are you sure?" I ask.

"Yes," he says, smiling. "But you need to promise me you'll use it again."

"I promise," I say, taking the fan and squeezing his hand one more time before the car window goes up. I catch a glimpse of the wrist tattoo again. He blows us a kiss and turns to walk back into Fin de Siècle as the Uber drives away.

Both of us starving, August and I dig into the cartons of steaming scouse; warm bites of lamb, carrots, and gravy flood my mouth.

"You're welcome," August says cheekily after a big bite of stew.

Like me, he's back into his normal clothes, but hasn't washed off the eyeliner yet.

"Thank you. I needed that more than you know."

As we pull up to the row house, we stuff the empty cartons and plastic spoons into the trash bag. I move to get out of the car, and he lightly touches my arm. "Late-morning coffee in Westminster tomorrow morning—eleven o'clock-ish?"

I smile. "You bet."

18

After a very good night's sleep, I wake up feeling refreshed. If it weren't for the used makeup remover wipes all over the bathroom countertop, my sore muscles, and the ostrich fan on my nightstand, I would have thought I dreamed last night. But I didn't, and I remember every remarkable detail from my time at Fin de Siècle. Tyler, the dancers, the audience. I tapped into a part of myself I've left dormant for twenty years, and now I know why Philip gently nudged me over and over to dance again.

After taking a long Epson salt bath for my muscles, I walk downstairs, pour a cup of coffee and sort through my mail at the kitchen island. Heathcliff sits beside me eating one of Ms. Fernsby's perfectly rolled chocolate crepes. Ms. Fernsby had been asleep when I got back, but she told me she'd leave her phone on in case I needed her. This morning, she had a gardening club meeting, so it's just me and Heathcliff and the crepes.

I sign the film rights and then the book contract and put them back in the mail. (I'm still loving my no-email policy.)

Then I pour another mug of coffee and take a bite of crepe. Ms. Fernsby's crepes are not only meticulously shaped, like something on the cover of a *Great British Baking Show* cookbook, but the subtle flavors of cognac, coffee, and chocolate blend deliciously in the whipped filling.

"I miss Uncle Ian and Grandpa," Heathcliff says, chocolate staining his upper lip and the front of his pajamas. "When can we see them?"

I picture Dad, alone in his den eating Twinkies and struggling miserably through the Match app.

"This fall. Maybe Thanksgiving?"

"Sure," he says, licking his fork one more time and then running to the parlor to watch cartoons.

Suddenly, I'm longing to be with Dad, to support him now as he's supported me. I'd test bake a thousand lasagnas with him just to try to get one as perfect as Mom's.

I make a mental note to check in with him later this afternoon.

I open a letter from my department chair, Patrick, admiring the vintage stationery page, a raised Edgar Allan Poe silhouette at the top. I smile into my coffee mug and take another bite of crepe, wondering how Patrick handled Brad McGregor in my Jane Austen seminar.

Dear Lizzie,

I hope you are well. I know you're not checking email and Willoughby's perpetual dumpster fire is the last thing you want to hear about. But this is just too good . . .

Someone put xeroxed erotic love letters between Evie Caldwell and Bill

Rhodes in everyone's mailboxes. They were sleeping together sometime in the mid-eighties and addressed each other as Cupid and Psyche. The affair ended badly, and because both have the maturity of eight-year-olds, they've hated each other to this day. All hell's expected to break loose at the first fall faculty meeting. Bring popcorn.

And sorry... you MIGHT hear from Sandra. She thought we should tell you about Rhodes's interview with the paper. I told her not to bother you with it, but she might have sent it anyway. Don't worry—he's just jealous. Admin knows they'd be crazy to get rid of you.

In other news, Brad McGregor is still a gaping asshole.

All the best,
Patrick

He could have texted me, but these letters are much more satisfying. No jarring message dings, no stimulating screens. I can merely mull over business and friendship gossip from this sunlit kitchen without distraction

Smiling, I make my way to the last of my letters, finding one from Sandra. Ah. This must be the interview. I'm wildly curious about what Bill Rhodes has to say about me. I pour another cup of coffee and open it.

She includes a brief note wishing me well and telling me she hopes I'm enjoying myself. Then: *Patrick disagrees, but I thought* you should know what this wretched man is up to. Don't worry. We all have your back in the English department.

A neatly cut article from the local paper shows Bill Rhodes sitting in his office at Willoughby College. A large, framed print of Voltaire looms on the wall behind him, emphasizing his short stature. His dark-framed readers stand out on his round face, and he scowls, arms crossed across his chest. Overall, he looks like a crankier, academic version of Wallace Shawn in *The Princess Bride*. But instead of the charming Sicilian robes, he sports trousers and an ill-fitting sweater vest. I remember all the reasons I dislike the man.

Is Local Professor and Bestselling Author Receiving Preferential Treatment?

Twentysomething journalist and former Miss South Carolina Mackaylee Hillsdale conducted the interview. Over my coffee, I roll my eyes. Ambitious, she's clearly working at the local paper as she claws her way to one of the national news shows. She loves trying to crack open local scandals. Dysfunction at Willoughby would be right up her alley.

Mackaylee: Dr. Bill Rhodes, distinguished professor of philosophy at Willoughby College, is here to talk about what seems to be an increasingly concerning issue for students and faculty—the untouchable position of bestselling author and English professor Dr. Elizabeth Wells. Dr. Rhodes, would you like to tell us, in a nutshell, what's going on?

Bill Rhodes: Well, it's quite simple. Dr. Wells has displayed increasingly bizarre behavior on campus and hasn't been doing her job.

Mackaylee: She recently lost her husband, right?

Bill Rhodes: Yes, yes, of course we all felt sorry for her when she lost Peter.

Mackaylee: Do you mean *Philip* Wells?

Bill Rhodes: Sure, whatever. But she started coming to campus dressed like a nun—full black, black leggings, black blouses, black skirts. Rumor has it she even carries her husband's ashes around with her. She's been skipping meetings, only communicating through paper letters rather than email, and she went on an unhinged tirade at a student during class. The student was traumatized by the event. Yet she was never held accountable and instead was given paid leave. It's my understanding that she's romping about in England somewhere on Willoughby's dime.

Mackaylee: And yet, tuition has gone up 10 percent this past year. Is that correct?

Bill Rhodes: Absolutely. The bottom line, Mackaylee, is that just because Dr. Wells is a bestselling author—of *juvenile* literature, might I add, and not actual scholarship—the administration sees her as immune from any meaningful responsibilities or discipline. It's favoritism, and parents who pay substantial money for their children to attend Willoughby deserve better from their faculty.

Mackaylee: Wow. So you're saying that just because she writes lucrative work unconnected to her position, she's not expected to have the same responsibilities as other hardworking Willoughby faculty?

Bill Rhodes: I am saying that, Mackaylee. And if it were up to me, I would hold professors like Dr. Wells, who write their popular trash and hide behind *New York Times* bestseller lists without doing their jobs, accountable. This is an insult to all other responsible faculty working here. Finally, I would like to add that my latest book, *Metaphysical Intellectualism in Neoclassical England*, is on shelves now.

Mackaylee includes an addendum noting that she reached out to the administration but received no response. However, when she contacted Willoughby College's English department chair, he replied promptly:

Patrick Anderson: I will say that as Dr. Wells's department chair, I support her to the hilt. Apart from her wildly successful publishing career, Dr. Wells is an excellent teacher, Brontë scholar, and researcher. Willoughby College is lucky to have her. Dr. Rhodes is merely speaking from jealousy as sales for his book have been abysmal and the latest academic review deemed it "a real snoozer with facile and outdated scholarship."

I smile at Patrick's loyalty. He was always better than me at the pithy playground retorts in academia. The entire interview would be comical if it weren't for the Mirabel situation. Obviously, this article could add to her case that I'm mentally unfit.

I check in with Henry and ask him if he's seen it.

He texts back in seconds: Hey! I was just getting ready to text you. I can't put WH down. But OH MAN—why does everyone swoon over Heathcliff? He can act like a real dickwad on some of these pages. The guy HANGS HIS WIFE'S DOG!!!!

Me: Yeah, we all try to forget that he does that. No one ever said he wasn't a bastard—just broody and hot. And his and Catherine's hearts are one, etc., etc. 😊 But the INTERVIEW—should I be concerned if Mirabel's lawyer sees it?

Henry: Hell no. They wouldn't have a leg to stand on. I'm still digging, but I'll touch base soon about the case. There's some crazy stuff in that family!

I'm wildly curious about what he's finding, but I'm meeting up with August in an hour. I finish my coffee, quietly admitting to myself that I'm trusting and liking Henry more by the day.

WHILE WALKING BESIDE AUGUST, I REMEMBER HOW much I love summer strolls through Westminster. I've been here several times over the years for research and fun, and it always takes me by surprise, like a window breeze or a whiff of roses.

Under the midmorning sun, the waves of the Thames roll softly. Big Ben chimes over the background noise of cars and buses. I take a sip of my milky iced coffee with stevia and one pump of vanilla. August has a similar concoction. Philip always drank his with a splash of soy milk. We rehash the highlights of last evening, both agreeing that although we started out a little like Johnny and Baby in their infamous awkward first performance, everything went uphill from there. I open up to August a bit more, reminiscing about Philip, and how he always wanted the two of us to take dance lessons.

"I envy your love," August says.

"You've never been in love?" I ask.

"Well, that's a million-dollar question."

"Sorry if it's too personal. But have you?"

He takes a sip of coffee and stops walking momentarily to stare at an interesting, red-painted houseboat. I've hit a nerve, and I suspect he's stalling.

"I suppose so. But I haven't found it yet. I don't worry. Didn't Oscar Wilde say something about not trying to spoil love by making it last forever?"

"Probably."

"There you have it. It's a good creed."

"But tell me about someone who was really special to you. That one woman you can't forget."

"You don't stop, do you?"

"Never."

"Alright, well then. There was one, Cressida. I was . . . thirty . . . I think? We met at a writing conference, and everything happened quickly. I could have seen myself marrying her, but then she made a bad choice that rather broke my heart."

"She cheated."

"Yes."

I'm waiting for him to tell me how it made him feel or if she tried to win him back. But he's quiet, suddenly interested in the pavement.

"Before Philip, I had a boyfriend who cheated on me. It's the worst. He really broke my heart."

"But you were able to love again."

"Yes, I suppose I was."

"You should be bloody proud of that, Elizabeth."

We're quiet for a while as we stroll and finish our coffees, and I mull over his *love again* statement. Does that mean he *hasn't* been able to love again after such betrayal? Maybe the cad persona is a means to protect himself.

"So . . ." August says slowly, staring down at the pavement again as we walk and then up at me. His blue eyes are startling in the sunlight. "I had an event yesterday afternoon for *Blood Oath* and have an ungodly amount of oysters and champagne at my flat. How about heading over for an early lunch? Champagne at noon?"

He raises an eyebrow. It's just lunch—a lunch of oysters and champagne with a dashing bachelor, unchaperoned at his flat. I see him standing beside me in the dark last evening, bare, toned arms under the lights. I remember how he lifted me up into the air during my solo. Oh . . . of course Queen Victoria wouldn't do it, but . . . I glance down at my long, black sundress . . .

"That sounds lovely!"

August's Bedford Gardens flat looks exactly how I would have imagined A.D. Hemmings to live.

A luxury apartment with modernist furniture and odd, pricey-looking sculptures displayed in nooks in walls, and everything is a testimony to his books' success. He gives me a quick tour. Framed book covers hang over a pristine mahogany desk in the study. There's a guest bedroom and his bedroom, both tastefully decorated. I blush when I peek at his king-size bed, inappropriately imagining how much excitement happens there.

He continues the tour. Glass coffee tables, comfortable sofas, and a large, theatre-size screen make up the main living room. August clearly has a decorator and housekeeper as there's not a speck of dust anywhere. Even the throws are symmetrically folded at the corners of the couches.

As he rattles about in the kitchen, pulling out platters of oysters and popping a champagne bottle, I walk over to a glass case filled with first editions in a dozen translations of *Blood*

Oath. With this place and these accomplishments, he must feel proud. He comes across as cavalier. But I wonder suddenly if he's happy.

We sit down, and I realize I'm famished. There's something rather fun and sexy about slurping oysters. The sand on the tongue, the controlled messiness. All my caution fades as we talk about everything from our books to classes. I find myself describing my pleasant Midwest childhood, the wavy cornfields, our 1915 farmhouse with glass doorknobs, cozy, cushioned reading nooks, and floor-to-ceiling bookshelves. He tells me about his socialite mother, who brunched once with Truman Capote in the mid-'70s. August remains close to her to this day, always giving her early drafts of his books and skiing in Switzerland with her on holidays. After two and a half glasses of champagne (shockingly, before 1:00 in the afternoon!) and a shameful number of oysters, somehow I find myself on the living room couch making out with A.D. Hemmings.

"I've wanted to do this from the moment I met you," he says against my mouth. It's a cliché remark, straight from the Alec d'Urberville playbook, and yet—

At first, I try not to think too much about what I'm doing, how I'm breaking a million, zillion widow's rules. The champagne and August's expert kissing help. But as we're tangled on the couch, intrusive thoughts surface, sort of like Mom's occasional dinging texts when Philip and I were trying to be intimate.

The "séance" is still fresh in my head.

What if spirit-Philip can see me?

What if spirit-Mom can see me making out with a British man I barely know after a lunch of champagne and too many oysters? She'd be asking poignant questions about venereal disease and that sort of thing.

August's hand slides down the side of my rib cage, his thumb grazing my breast. I melt. My *god*, I forgot how much fun it is to be touched by someone for the first time.

My senses fire up and then—the *scent*. August smells amazing, like salty oysters and expensive cologne. But inside I recoil, my chest tightening. He doesn't smell like Philip. My body can't catch up to what my brain is consenting to. Philip smelled like Old Spice soap, and my senses reject this new man.

Damn biology.

His mouth moves down my neck, and the jet necklace twists, tightening uncomfortably.

"Owww..."

"Oh, sorry." He pulls back a little.

"No, it's okay." I quickly unclasp the necklace, and it falls to the floor. Lust is a devil. I'm like my friend Heather, removing the purity ring in romantically heated moments.

Now I know why I couldn't have kissed Henry. This first-kiss fire can be too intense. Spirit-Philip, Spirit-Mother, jet necklace, new scents—a barreling train can't stop me. I roll sideways, unbuttoning August's shirt.

Something hard uncomfortably presses against my hip. Well, that's natural. As I'm almost finished unbuttoning, August rolls more on top of me.

"*Owww!*" I scream, pain searing into my hip.

We bolt up alarmed.

I pull the bird urn from my sundress pocket, and tears burn my eyes.

Philip's ashes injured me while I was fooling around with another man. If that isn't a screaming sign, I don't know what is.

"I'm... I'm sorry. I have to go," I mutter, sitting up, smoothing my hair. I retrieve the jet necklace, fastening it around my neck. I grab my purse.

"Elizabeth."

"I'm sorry . . ."

WHEN I GET BACK TO THE ROW HOUSE, MS. FERNSBY and Heathcliff are cutting out cookie shapes in the kitchen.

"Lizzie?" She looks up, alarmed.

"I'm fine," I mumble through tears and run upstairs.

I fall onto the bed.

This went further than that moment with Henry.

Who was I back there with August Dansworth?

It's only been a little over two months since Philip passed, and I almost-kissed his best friend and now I drunk-made-out with A.D. Hemmings.

And yet . . .

I swallow, acknowledging a hard truth.

Those moments felt so wonderful. As with the dancing last night, I was tenaciously connecting to a part of myself again.

I'm confused.

Sad.

Ashamed as I shed hot tears.

I know what my mother would say if she were here. *Shame is a useless emotion.*

She always said shame, jealousy, envy, anger did nothing to make us better human beings.

I scan my mind, trying to remember what she said about lust, and I'm drawing a blank.

I don't look at my phone because I don't want to see if August tried to contact me.

"Lizzie, dear, are you alright?" Ms. Fernsby asks through the bedroom door.

"I think I just need some sleep."

"Well . . . let me know if you need anything. Heathie will be fine."

Holding the bird urn in my hands, I think about the dreams where I'm chasing Philip. He keeps eluding me—in my mind, at the séance—and my longing feels like physical pain.

@BluestockingBadass: Starting @ADHemmings *Blood Ties*. Noticing the interchangeable sex and car scene adjectives. *Sleek. Supple.* The Bentley's burgundy paint *shines* with the same intensity of Penny's auburn hair. And Wales's rolling hills *rise and fall* as gracefully as Emilia's breasts. Oh please . . .

19

When I wake up, my eyes throb, bone-dry, and a fishy aftertaste from the oysters lingers on my tongue. I need to brush my teeth. How long did I sleep? It's dark outside. Street light breaks in through the curtain; Heathcliff must be in bed, as the house is quiet. I rub my eyes and stare down at my wrinkled long black sundress.

I'm terrified to look at my phone on the nightstand.

On one hand, I'm worried there will be nothing from August—he might have thought I'm a widow-freak, and I'll never hear from him again. On the other hand, I'm afraid he actually did message me, and what the hell do I say? It was one awkward exit.

Several messages are on my screen. The first couple are from Mirabel, wanting to talk. She can wait. It also looks like she tried to call once at 4:00 p.m. London time. Dad tried to call me soon after.

I scroll down. Oh gosh. August did message me right after I left.

August: Buggers, Elizabeth. I didn't mean to upset you. You are lovely, and, well . . . there was the champagne and the oysters. And we had such a roaring good time last night. I'm deeply sorry if I hurt you. Please give me a call and let me know how you're doing.

There's one more message from him, from two hours later.

August: Do you bloody hate me?

I wipe my eyes, eyeliner smudges on my hand. I can't leave him hanging.

No, August. Thank you for a very nice lunch. I'm sorry about the way I left. I was getting confused. Let's meet up tomorrow.☺ My day's free.

He responds immediately. I'm so glad. I've been worried about you all day. How about the Triton fountain, Russell Park, at ten o'clock ☺?

Perfect! I'll see you then!

Whew. So that fire's put out for now.
I go ahead and call Dad back. It's only five o'clock his time. As soon as he answers, I hear rattling in the kitchen. A timer.
"Dad, are you still baking lasagnas?"
"I'm very close to getting it right."
Lucy stretches on the bed, her body warm against my side.

A lump rises in my throat. Dad's serial-baking lasagnas. I freaked out and ran from August's apartment this afternoon. Is this what grief does to us? Does it just make us obsessive and crazy?

"Maybe you should get out a bit more. Ian says you're giving Match.com a go. Any luck?"

"No. Ian set me up with Beverly—you know, the divorced painter who lives down our street."

"Beverly Lamott? She's pretty!"

"She can't cook."

"She's a brilliant painter."

"I don't care about that."

Silence.

"Well, I think about you a lot, Dad. I just know how lonely this can be."

"It's very lonely." Then the fire alarm squeals, piercing my ear even through the phone.

"Sorry, Lizzie. But I have to go. This is the third time I've set it off."

I tell him I love him and hang up, worried.

I stare into the rumpled bedcovers wondering if losing our soulmates weirdly doomed Dad and me. We had such unique love for our partners and now we're broken and lost.

No. We have to come out on the other side.

We *have* to.

I walk downstairs, where Ms. Fernsby sits at the kitchen island browsing through a magazine. She sips tea, gray hair wrapped up in curlers.

"Gosh . . . what time is it?"

"Ah, not that late, luv. Only 9:00."

I groan, insisting that she stay seated as I make a cold roast beef sandwich and pour a glass of milk.

As I sit down across from her, she glances up, "Do you want to talk about it?"

I shake my head. "Not really. No, wait. I guess, in a way, I do."

"Then go right ahead." She takes another sip of her tea.

"Can love ruin us?"

She cocks her head.

"I mean, if we find love, like I had with Philip, and then we lose it, does that make us broken?"

"Don't let yourself believe such nonsense, Lizzie," Ms. Fernsby says. She's peering through her readers at a paparazzi photo of Bella Patel at a farmers' market with her new beau. (She and Everett broke up again.) She's wearing big sunglasses, a T-shirt and jeans, and yet is still standout gorgeous as she scrutinizes a pint of blueberries.

"Trust me, Lizzie." Ms. Fernsby holds the magazine out for me. "You *wrote* such a wonderful love story. You made this beautiful girl a star. If anyone can find their way back, it's you."

From *Blood Ties*:

It was Penny's need that drove him to the tryst with his optometrist.

One minute, Dr. Griffiths was peering into his eyes with the ophthalmoscope, and then suddenly she was peering into his soul. And then they were having sex in the examination chair, her short, choppy blond hair bobbing, her sleek legs wrapped around him. It was all sweat, and perfume, and office vinyl leather.

As he drives home, where pretty, dependable Penny will have dinner ready on the table, her long, sleek red locks as shiny as his last Bentley model, he wonders if he even has to tell her about the office romp.

Surely, she can't think what they have is forever.
But she does.
And that's what worries him.

From *The Heathcliff Saga*:

Cathy never understands how her desires transform in the cave. She loves Heathcliff. But Linwood—the way he defies mortal rules, taking the Fae power for himself—stirs her blood.

Inside Penistone Crags, the outside world melts far away from this world of trickling water and moss. Here, delicate ferns spider out from cracks and crevices, and a sprawling bed of wood sorrel and rose robe spreads at their feet. Linwood spins the Fae energy into glowing orbs high above them, casting light and shadows all around.

Cathy trembles with need in this place, for the beauty Linwood creates. She should leave. Nelly warned her about coming here. But now, in his arms, she can't move.

"Cathy . . ." he murmurs, his breath warm on her cheek.

"You're a devil for summoning this magic."

"Perhaps. But you'll stay here nonetheless," he whispers into her ear. "Remember, you yourself told me if you die, heaven will cast you out and the angels will fling you right back here."

Her chest heaves, heart beating furiously inside her corset.

He kisses her cheek, lips trailing down her throat, and then she melts, knowing in her heart that she's part devil too. It's why she yearns for both these men.

20

The next morning, I find August lounging languidly on a bench in front of the Triton fountain. He's wearing aviator sunglasses, which add a sexy accent to his scholarly tweed jacket, and holding two iced coffees. He smiles lopsidedly as he hands me mine, and I'm pleased that it's perfectly flavored—milky, dash of stevia, one pump vanilla.

"Well, this is awkward," I mutter, plopping down onto the bench. I had articulated a better conversation in front of the mirror earlier, but the words elude me now. Better to state the obvious.

"It sure as hell is." He smiles and there's the darn dimple. "But the way I see it, there's nowhere to go but up now, right? If you want to, at least?"

"Yeah, I think so." I take a long sip of coffee. The two hours of sleep last night is getting to me. Children around Heathcliff's age run around the fountain as their mothers and nannies stare at their phones.

"I'm not here much longer, August."

"This is the second time you've brought that up, and yet again, I'm not sure why that matters. Let's carpe diem, shall we? I'd like to spend that remaining time with you."

"More writer bonding?"

He leans a little closer. God. His cologne. "You fascinate me more than as a writer, Elizabeth. I'm intrigued by your eccentricities, your cute morbid nature, your splendid spontaneous dancing, and your light Southern accent."

"I'm not Southern."

"But you have this little lilt every time you say *light*. You must have picked it up from your Philip. You've absorbed the *Steel Magnolias* vibes."

My phone dings. *Mirabel*. I ignore it.

It dings again. I'm not sure why her texts sound more grating than anyone else's. I shut off the sound.

"Who in the world is trying to text you so persistently, Elizabeth?"

Maybe he's jealous. For some reason, this delights me. "Just a bad *Steel Magnolias* vibe. Can we talk about something else?"

"Righto. How about the pervy statue?"

I turn my attention to the twisting naked sea god and bare-breasted bronze mermaids.

"Let's pretend it's one of those inkblot tests. What do you see when you look at it?" he asks.

"I see an artist somewhere years ago chiseling away at their physical and mental health to create it."

"Of course you do, Negative Nelly."

"What do you see?"

"Rose Haworth. Secondary school, year twelve. She was my first date to permit more than snogging."

I glance sideways at him. "You're acting like a cad again."

"Free spirit, you mean."

In spite of his rakish facade, I really am grateful to him for introducing me to the Fin de Siècle. August has been good for me. "I liked kissing you yesterday." I keep my eyes on the statue, hot blush creeping up my neck. "It's just hard for me."

"I understand."

"Next time, I won't weird out and run away."

"Promise?"

"Promise."

He leans forward, kissing me in front of the children, nannies, and naked sea god. It's a chaste kiss, warm, soft, our mouths tasting slightly like coffee. It's very nice, proper even by Victorian standards.

"Can I make us dinner reservations tomorrow evening, 7:00?" he asks against my mouth.

"Uh-huh."

STILL SWOONING FROM MY MORNING WITH AUGUST, I get back to the row house early afternoon. After a light lunch of cranberry chicken salad, Ms. Fernsby asks if she and Mabel can take Heathcliff to the Old Operating Theatre Museum. I readily agree with them that he would enjoy the ghoulish exhibits and a fake amputation demonstration. Perhaps it will make him less afraid of shots.

After they leave, just as I'm deciding how to spend the rest of my afternoon, someone knocks on the door.

"Bella?"

Bella Patel stands at the doorstep. But she's wearing a short blond bob wig under a running hat and round dark sunglasses. The casual workout leggings and top only accentuate her sleek, toned physique.

She puts a finger over her lips and steps in.

The minute I shut the door, she collapses against it with a long exhale. "Whew! I think I got rid of him!"

"Who? Are you prepping for the next spy movie? You're the latest Bond girl, right?"

"I wish! No. I've just had this fucking aggressive paparazzi guy *trailing* me all morning! Apparently, I'm *so interesting* since Everett broke up with me, and I'm with someone else. It's all been pretty messy and complicated."

"It wouldn't be fun otherwise."

She chuckles. "And I hope you don't mind me stopping by like this. I've wanted to hang out, and it was kind of spur-of-the-moment. I was going to text you, but you had your phone off, so—I hope you don't mind—I called Sarah to see where you were staying in London."

"Oh, no worries." I must have forgotten to turn the sound back on after Mirabel's texts.

"I need some girl time. I've been struggling being around the guys for all these events—and then we have a publicity shoot up north soon. Everything feels so off. I mean, I had *no idea* Harry's gay. Did you?"

"Not at all."

"Well, apparently everyone knew but us. It explained so much! I wanted to support him, but my therapist says I still mourned the relationship I thought we had. Anyway, I rebounded and flew right back into Everett's arms. But Everett eventually said it was just too weird acting as my lover on film and then dating me in real life—which I guess is fair. So now, the three of us pretend like everything's fine, but you can't just shut off your heart, right?"

"Right!" I affirm with false cheer, thinking of my own heart's ups, downs, stumbles, and fuckups these past weeks. Bella doesn't know about Philip yet. She'd care, but I don't feel like looping her into my grief right now.

"I'm on my way to my workout. Would you like to join me?"

I hesitate. I jog and ride my bike. But given her body, I'm

sure Bella's idea of a workout is far different than my own. Then again, I've missed her and really want to get caught up.

"Sure! Let me go get changed."

"WORKOUT" WAS A MISNOMER FOR BELLA'S PRIVATE SPIN instructor's torture session. Colin was like a British version of Paul Ryan, buff and handsome in a dry, anemic way, but coldhearted and fierce, willing to exhaust clients to death before slicing maternity care and school lunch budgets by late afternoon. Every time I thought it was over, and we would finally slow down, he'd yell, "Standing climb, *now*! Come on, no bloody slacking!" In the end, every single muscle in my body screamed in agony. I just wanted to collapse in a hot bath of Epson salts and eat a pint of ice cream. Irritatingly, the workout seemed to make Bella glow. The excess perspiration only brought out her beautiful dark eyes. She didn't even stink. I guess some people are just born goddesses.

Afterward, we head to the luxury gym's spa, where cool mists of lemongrass-scented sprays shoot out from the shower walls at our limbs. Then an assistant wraps us in ever-so-soft bamboo-viscose robes, and a masseuse gives us heavenly shoulder massages. Clearly, this isn't a typical gym, and I try not to gawk when Tom Hardy in a towel steps out of the sauna room.

Soon, still in our robes, we lounge in heated, plushy chairs as we're served kale smoothies that taste like what I imagine Mirabel's azalea garden trimmings would. Bella takes a long sip, settles back, and asks about Philip.

I avoid eye contact, stirring my thick smoothie with the boba straw. "He passed away a couple months ago."

She puts her hand over her mouth, setting the smoothie on a table. "That's awful. Why didn't you tell me earlier? I was going on and on about my own shit, and you . . . you've been dealing with this."

I shrug.

"Oh, my god—how are you carrying on?"

I glance over, and her eyes are wet with tears.

"It's kind of why I'm here. I just had to get away from it all."

She's quiet for a minute. "God, I loved him. When he visited the set, I didn't get a chance to talk to him as much as the guys did. I think they went out to drinks."

"They did." I swallow the lump in my throat. I remember Philip beaming when he got back to the hotel room that evening. I'd been sitting up reading in bed. He collapsed beside me, unfastening the top buttons of his shirt as he adjusted his glasses and looked up at me. *Whoa. If you ever told me one day I'd be on a film set and then doing shots with Everett Dane and Harry Waters, I'd call you crazy. This was an unbelievable day, Lizzie, and you made it happen. You are AMAZING.* And then he'd leaned in, cupped my cheek, and kissed me.

"I lost my mom last year too. It's all been a lot."

"I can't even imagine," she says, sniffing and wiping her eyes.

We finish the smoothies in silence. As gross as the blended kale tastes, it distracts me.

"We should each get a tattoo," she says suddenly, handing her empty glass to a nearby assistant.

"Huh?"

"I always get a tattoo when I'm going through a transition or a change. See!"

She points down to her calf, where she has the most beautiful ivy wrap. "I got this just after filming the movie. Everett and Harry have matching ones on their biceps. They just cover it up with makeup on the set. You've been through so much—I'm here for you. Let's do something permanent to remember our time together."

"I don't know . . ." I'm pretty sure Victorian convicts and sailors sported tattoos, not respectable widows.

"Come on! There's only one artist I trust in London. He's fabulous!"

"I don't know. I've never had a tattoo, and I'm pushing forty..."

"We can get *Wuthering Heights* themed tattoos..."

I hesitate. Tattoos definitely aren't in my proper widow's rule book. But then again, a Brontë-inspired one—that's a different story.

This is a hard call.

SOON, I FIND MYSELF SPRAWLED ON A COMFORTABLE heated massage table while Vincent, Bella's London tattoo artist, inks two delicate heather flowers and an elegant script on my lower back. He just finished Bella's identical flowers. She chose simply the words *Wuthering Heights* for her lettering. I knew the quote I wanted from the minute I walked in the studio door: *Whatever our souls are made out of, his and mine are the same.*

As I lay prostrate, chin resting on my hands and the vibrating sensations of the needle channeling my thoughts, a myriad of memories washes over me, as sharp as photographs. Philip stopping our canoe in the middle of Lake Marion to ask me to marry him. He'd seemed strangely shy and nervous, his hand shaking a little as he pulled the ring box from his jacket pocket. Philip standing behind a five-year-old Heathcliff, guiding his arms as he taught him how to fly-fish in an upstate creek. Philip in the bathroom with me after I miscarried our much-wanted pregnancy. He'd sat on the tub edge beside me, holding me as we both cried. Soon we found out we were expecting Heathcliff. I remember how nervous we were, clinging to each other that entire first trimester with cautious hope.

I'm not sure what stuff souls are made of, ethereal or more solid. I tried to connect to Philip the other night in Darcie's eccentric parlor. Wherever he is, he still feels so much a part of my fabric that it's too strange not having him living and breathing at my side. Grief is so fucking disorienting.

The needle stops as Vincent begins gently cleaning the area. I wipe my eyes, embarrassed that I'd been crying. As I stand to look at the tattoo in a tall mirror, my surrounding skin still pink around the design, I feel like I'm going to cry again. The heather blooms are beautiful, the lavender hues subtle and the small lines even. The script is perfect.

"It's gorgeous," Bella says from beside me.

"Yes."

"Just what you needed," she whispers, hugging me and lightly kissing my cheek.

LATER THAT EVENING, I'M SITTING COLORING ON THE floor with Heathcliff.

Bella and I parted when we left the tattoo parlor. She'd been wearing the wig and sunglasses again as she'd hurried down the street. She's here for a few more weeks for events; she'd heard there's a possibility they might do the film announcement's publicity shoot in Haworth if the weather behaves, but she's not sure. She said she'll keep me updated.

I smile as I try to keep my red colored pencil in the lines of Superman's cape, still disbelieving that Bella Patel and I now share matching tattoos.

Suddenly my phone rings, and Henry pops up on FaceTime.

"Hullo, Henry!" Heathcliff shouts, scribbling hard over Poison Ivy with a green crayon.

"Hello, buddy!"

"Guess what!" Heathcliff yells loudly.

"What?"

"I went to this cool museum where they had *real torture devices*."

"Well, nineteenth-century medical devices," I say, winking at Henry.

"Cool!" he exclaims, and then I notice he's outside somewhere. It's still afternoon in the Carolinas.

Heathcliff chatters for a bit more about the gorier parts of the museum. Then he gets back to coloring.

"Hey, Lizzie! This might be kind of a weird question . . ."

I hear the crunch of bushes, see ivy rising up behind him over painted gray bricks. I catch a glimpse of a familiar flowerpot.

I take the phone into the dining room.

"Are you *at my house*?"

"Yep, I'm breaking and entering."

"Ha, ha. No really, what are you doing there? My neighbor, Edith, watches everything, and she'll call the police."

"Philip told me he found a packet of old family letters in an envelope. I was hoping to wait until you got home, but I think I need them now. They'd be in the safe, right?"

"That's where he kept everything important. Philip did have a manila envelope in there, but I always thought it just had extra hard copies of the will."

"I need to check it out."

"Now?"

"Unfortunately, yes, so tell me what window you want me to bust."

"*What?*"

He's behind my azalea bushes at the back of my house, tapping at my windows.

"I really am breaking and entering. Damn *it!*" He jumps and yells, stumbling back from the bushes. "Do you know you have a garter snake back here?"

"Snakes live in bushes, Henry."

"Oh . . . hey! You must be Miss Edith! No, it's okay, I've got Lizzie on the line." He flips the phone around. "See?"

In the grainy FaceTime image, I see Miss Edith standing at the picket fence between our yards, arms crossed over her floral housedress as she glares.

"It's okay, Miss Edith. Henry's a friend!" I say loudly after Henry puts me on speaker. She nods, glaring at him one last time before walking back into her home.

"Strange male friend breaking into my house while I'm out of the country—you're making a spectacle out of me, ruining my reputation and all that."

He laughs, out of breath as he peels a stubborn patch of ivy back from the window. "Now you sound like you really are in one of those novels you love. Wait, does Miss Edith have a key?"

"Ha. I love her, but I wouldn't in a million years give her a key to my house. She'd read my diary, drink all my Chardonnay, and go through my drawers."

"I guess I'm going to have to get in the old-fashioned way. You know, I've always wanted to do this. Which window?"

"I suppose that one," I say, pointing to the pane closest to him. "Heathcliff already cracked it with a baseball this spring."

"Yes, ma'am. Here we go! And you'll take the call from your security system when it goes off, right?"

"Right."

He puts in earplugs, wraps a towel around his hand, and punches through the pane. The alarms starts screeching. He hoists himself through the window. As I wait for the security system to call me, I can't stop laughing. This is like a crazy reality television show. The security company calls; I give them the password, and the alarm goes quiet.

"Whew. That would wake the dead! I have to say, though, this was one of the most exciting afternoons I've had in a while. So where's that safe?"

"Bolted in my bedroom closet."

I direct Henry to my room.

He comments on the dangerous number of LEGOs all over the floors. "No need for a security system with these all over. Jeez . . . It's like *Home Alone* in here." He sets the phone down and disappears for a minute. When he comes back, I give him the safe code. Once he's in, there's a rustling of paper and then I hear, "Jackpot!"

"You found them?"

"Yep. A whole bundle. Philip told me he came across these when moving something down from Mirabel's attic a couple months ago. It's where I bet he found the photo. I think it was the letters that kicked off his interest in the trust and Mirabel's relationship with the Duboses."

"So the letters are between them?"

"That's what it seems like. I've got some reading to do tonight."

I hear more paper rustling as he walks back to the broken window. "I'll be in touch. And don't worry, Lizzie. I've already paid someone to come out to fix this as soon as I'm done."

"I appreciate that."

"Anytime." He pulls ivy back to cover the broken pane.

His phone dings suddenly as a text arrives. He goes very quiet.

"Henry?"

His expression crumples a little. He tries to hide it, scratching the corner of his eye. But his eyes water when he brings his hand back.

"Hey—are you okay?" I ask gently.

"Allergies."

"Liar."

"Just got a text from my attorney. The divorce is final."

"Oh—I'm . . . sorry."

He shrugs. "It is what it is. It had to happen. It's just—it's been ten years, and it's not how I wanted things to turn out."

"If you need to talk, I'll be here."

"I know you will be, Lizzie."

I give him a minute. It's difficult to know what to say. I've been aware there were problems for years, but still my chest tightens in pain for him.

"I guess I'd better go. I'm going to try to make yoga class tonight, and then I've got these letters to sort through and a batshit romance book to finish." He's trying to be cheerful, but I hear the heaviness in his voice.

"Just take care of yourself, Henry. Please."

"I will."

After we hang up, I stare at my phone. His is not the same grief as mine, but this will be hard. There's no easy way through loss of any kind. I'd give anything for him to have a Ms. Fernsby at his side now, with a listening ear and steaming cups of tea.

@BluestockingBadass: A tryst with a hot optometrist in an office chair? @ADHemmings even you can do better. #womenreadersaresmarterthanthis

Six Years Earlier

New Year's Eve

WE INVITED HENRY AND GINGER OVER FOR NEW YEAR'S Eve on a whim.

Although neither of us is a party animal, Philip and I always spent previous years at his law firm's downtown gala. There, Philip mingled with local judges while I sipped champagne and tugged awkwardly at my satin opera gloves, grateful this was the one and only time of year I'd be expected to wear them. Fortunately, this year, two-month-old Heathcliff gave us an excuse to bow out. Our holiday has been a long, sleepless stretch of pajamas, Netflix, breastmilk, poopy diapers, and takeout. (It's amazing how comfortable we've become with baby poop.) But it's been sweet nonetheless—bonding with this squalling tiny creature the universe thrust into our arms to love and keep alive.

Now, as I pump breastmilk in the den while Philip puts together a charcuterie board in the kitchen, I feel nothing but gratitude for our little family and this low-key evening with friends. Henry and Ginger snuggle Heathcliff in the living room, and I relish a few minutes alone.

Maybe it's the postpartum hormones, but I tear up staring at our hybrid Christmas tree of everything Midwest and Southern. A little train runs around the tree base, circling a ceramic snowy village, the scene Dickensian and vintage except for the little cousin Eddie figurine in his bathrobe. (Philip's touch.) University of South Carolina football ornaments and an artsy blown-glass set from Mirabel dangle from the branches. A large shiny "Baby's First Christmas" bulb from Patrick hangs near the tree's star. Every decoration gestures to the life Philip and I've built together these past eight years.

Although Heathcliff must be hungry, I can't help but stop in the kitchen, where Philip arranges the smoked meat and aged cheeses. I hug him from behind, nuzzling my cheek against his warm back. He turns around with a half smile. "What's that for?"

"I just love you. I really, really do."

He gives me a lingering kiss as he opens the olive jar.

I sigh happily, tightening the breast milk bottle cap, and walk to the living room.

I never see Henry as much as Philip does, and I haven't had more than passing conversations with Ginger. She's nice enough, but I'm not sure we'll ever be close friends. She's an active member of the Junior Service League and loves everything monogrammed. Even her beer koozies.

"It's all your fault," she hisses angrily.

I pause uncomfortably in the doorway. They're standing near the fireplace, in front of the draped garlands. A sleeping Heathcliff snuggles against Ginger's chest.

"I've said I'm sorry a million times," Henry says.

"I'd still have my Zoie if you hadn't been fiddle-faddling around with your tackle box."

"Sweetheart, she was barking at a goddamn alligator. I tried to save her."

"I don't think I'll ever get over this."

"You seem to not be getting over a lot lately—how I wash the dishes, how I fold the towels, how yoga's just not my thing, the way I cook mac and cheese."

I blush, hiding back in the doorway shadows. I should go back to the kitchen and warn Philip that they might need a few minutes.

Then I hear sniffing. Oh gosh, she's crying.

I ache for them. Philip and I are far from perfect, but as a couple, we're in sync. Only my parents and a handful of my friends have our type of marriage. I've thought about Henry and Ginger on and off since their wedding reception. I've hoped they could eventually find their way to one another.

"Ginger..." His voice is gentle, husky. Sad.

"Are we ever going to get it together, Henry?"

"Sure—it's a new year..."

"But is this going to be the year we finally feel good enough about *us* to bring one of these sweet bundles into the world?"

"Sure..."

"Oh, come on!"

He sighs. "I don't know."

Heathcliff starts grunting, nosing Ginger's chest, rooting around for a breast.

"Just in time!" I say, entering with false cheerfulness. I gently take Heathcliff from Ginger, warm bottle in hand. Flustered, she turns away to dab her eyes, and I pretend not to notice. Henry sighs, thrusts his hands into his pockets and turns toward the window, his expression miserable and defeated.

21

Soon after dinner, August calls to let me know he made reservations for tomorrow evening at a swanky restaurant in Sloane Square. I look it up quickly on my phone. Geesh. The champagne is thirty-five pounds a glass. Inspector Hall is lucrative.

After tucking Heathcliff in bed for the night, I walk downstairs for a cup of tea. I'd like to enjoy tomorrow, and I'm determined to get a good night's sleep. I take my time steeping the tea, savoring the chamomile steam.

"Do you think sleep will be any better tonight?" I ask as Ms. Fernsby walks through the room.

She smiles a little mischievously. "I hope you don't mind, but I picked you up something that I thought could help you with the anxiety."

"That's so kind of you."

"I'm just one woman helping out another. Come on. It's upstairs."

I follow her up. It's probably a new essential oil diffuser.

Several widow blogs recommend essential oils for insomnia. Maybe Ms. Fernsby bought me some lavender or eucalyptus scents. I've heard they're particularly good for restfulness.

I follow her into her neat and cozy bedroom. I admire the floral wallpaper and busy rose-patterned bedspread, perfectly mimicking the roses she plants and prunes outside. A bulky antique chest sits at the bottom of the bed, and I wonder how many centuries it's been in the Routledge family.

A paperback novel lies half-open on the nightstand. It's one of Ms. Fernsby's many bodice-rippers. A woman with a gown slipping off her shoulders makes out with a half-dressed man—*Emma and her Scottish duke*.

Ms. Fernsby opens the top drawer in an old maple dresser and pulls out an unwrapped package.

"Oh . . ." My face burns.

"I know. I hope this doesn't embarrass you, but my own Magic Wand has given me so much comfort over the years and helped me drift off on many a sleepless night."

I take the package, smiling but tongue-tied. It's a classic. Long electric cord, silicon knob. A glorious grandmother's vibrator.

Quite literally.

Nostalgically, I remember around the age of ten snooping in my grandma's room. It was a slow summer for Ian and me at her Martinsville farmhouse. Sunlight spilled across the blue quilt of her spindly antique Jennie Lind bed. Her curiously large hurricane lamp rested near the bedside. I don't remember why I was in there. I think I was just bored and thought it might be fun to poke around her drawers. I found the Magic Wand in the nightstand. The box said it was a body massager. That looked like fun to me, so I plugged it into the wall, a little surprised at how loud it was. Giggling, I rubbed it on my lower back like I had a backache.

"Lizzie? What are you doing?" my mom barked sternly from the doorway, a basket of folded laundry in her arms.

"I'm playing with Grandma's body massager. This is *so fun!*"

"Yes, well, *this* massager isn't for little girls." She plopped the basket down, unplugged the "massager," and took it from me. She folded it neatly back in the box, telling me over and over again how rude it is to rummage through people's drawers.

It wasn't until I was a teenager when I learned what the "massager" actually was.

"You're not offended, are you, luv?" Ms. Fernsby asks, blushing a little.

"Oh no, not at all! It's just been a long time since I've seen one of these."

"Oh . . ." She looks a little sad. And, happily married or not, that was a rather sad thing of me to say.

But I keep talking, sounding more pitiful by the second. "I mean, who needs a vibrator when you have my husband, right?"

Again, really dumb. Every woman needs a vibrator, and I haven't indulged in years. Honestly, I'm not even sure where mine is. Probably stuffed in the back of one of my drawers with a spent battery.

"I do hope it helps," Ms. Fernsby says kindly.

I thank her and leave with the package, my face searing hot.

When I get back to the bedroom, I stare at the wand, wondering what to do. Why am I so embarrassed by another woman giving me this? I've always considered myself liberated. And yet, why haven't I used my own vibrator in years?

Back in graduate school, I remember a Gender Studies class where we discussed vibrators as essential to women's sexual pleasure and how the Victorians, oddly enough, *invented* the vibrator. Philip and I had a fantastic sex life. Yet why did I forget how fun these are? It's strange how amid this ritualized grief, I'm feeling more connections to my pre-Philip self. I touch the jet necklace around my neck. Long before the 1960s wand, Victorian women loved their vibrators.

Using Ms. Fernsby's gift might be my most authentic Victorian move yet.

I WAKE UP THE NEXT MORNING, SUNLIGHT SPILLING through the drapes. My brain feels strangely clear, like a dissipating fog.

I glance at my phone—I've slept *seven* straight hours.

This is the longest I've slept since Philip died. Before the advent of sleeping pills, vibrators must have made a world of difference health-wise for young wives advised to "lie back and think of England." (Although, as I always tell my students, there is *zero* evidence Queen Victoria actually ever gave this advice to any woman. As indicated by the scandalous loose-haired, bare-shouldered self-portrait she gifted Prince Albert, they had quite the steamy relationship.)

A text from Henry pops up. Almost to the finish line and will be in touch soon!

Wonderful! Can't wait to hear! I text back.

I stare at Henry's smiling emoji, heartbeat quickening. Whatever will come to light is what Philip was trying to tell me that night. I want to know, but I'm anxious. There are some big secrets at bay. I've had one awful shock this year, and admittedly, I'm also afraid of the truth.

I get out of bed, pull on my robe, and brush my teeth.

But I'm me and not Mirabel.

I'm my steely nurse-mother's daughter, and I'm not about

to keep the Wellses' Southern family skeletons crammed in the attic. Philip was going to tell me the truth that night, and I need to know it all—at least for our son.

After a leisurely breakfast with Ms. Fernsby, Heathcliff and I go to the Sherlock Holmes Museum. With a promise to Heathcliff to find some nondairy ice cream if he is good during the tour, we make our way through the museum's quirky rooms. Heathcliff likes the interesting toilet with the blue patterns. Dad always gave books as gifts for every holiday and birthday, and I still remember my thirteenth birthday, when he presented me with a shiny new *Sherlock Holmes* anthology. I stayed up all night reading *The Hound of the Baskervilles*.

As we leave, Heathcliff happily wearing a gift shop Sherlock Holmes hat, I think of Dad sitting alone in his study, rejecting sweet, artistic Beverly Lamott because she can't cook.

"I know what Daddy would say about everything," Heathcliff says, ridiculously expensive coconut ice cream dripping down his bottom lip.

I push the hat up to see his face better.

"What would he say now?"

"That Batman is cool, and you shouldn't be sad all the time."

"Do I look sad all the time?"

"Yes," he says matter-of-factly.

"Part of me will always be sad about Daddy. But you don't need to worry about me."

He sighs long and hard, exhausted by this truth. "Yeah, I know."

After taking Heathcliff back to the town house, I can't stop thinking about what he said. Although his comment is strange, I know exactly what he meant by knowing what his dad would say about everything. Philip was so involved as a dad and partner, the conversations keep going and going in my head. Heartbreakingly, I know what he would say in every moment.

Admittedly, sometimes I don't *want* to know what he would say. I know he would say I shouldn't be sad all the time. I know he would tell me Brad McGregor is a twerp, and I shouldn't let him get to me. I know he would say he can't believe I put him in a dumb bird urn and an old-lady necklace.

Feeling a new drive to move forward, I buy a cocktail dress. It's black of course. But it's the sexiest black outfit I've bought in my widowhood.

August made reservations for seven. I take my time, plucking neglected strays from my eyebrows and slipping my favorite pair of dangly earrings through my lobes. I pick up my widow jewelry, hesitating before I clasp the jet necklace around my neck. I'm not ready to give this up yet.

As I finish getting ready, he calls at about 6:30.

August groans into the phone. "Hi, Elizabeth, I really hate to do this, but my publisher called and I'm in a bit of a bind. Because the Inspector Hall Netflix series debuts next month, they want to get the third book, *Blood Offspring*, out ahead of deadline. It's pretty urgent, and I think I can finish if I pull an all-nighter tonight. Would it be bloody awful if we bumped our reservations to tomorrow night?"

"Not at all," I say. Although my stomach sinks in disappointment.

"You're wonderful, Elizabeth. Tomorrow night, then. I'm sure you'll look ravishing in something widowy-black. Enjoy your evening. For me, it's loads of coffee."

"I understand. Good luck."

"I'll be in touch tomorrow. Take care."

I sigh, staring into the mirror at my hair, half-secured in a French knot. Strangely, the jet necklace looks like an appropriate accent piece at my neckline. My gold earrings dangle elegantly. The cocktail dress fits perfectly, tailored at the waist and showing off my bare arms. It felt good to *want* to look good again.

Obviously, this is disappointing, but I can at least do something nice for him.

Slipping the dress off, I pull on my black leggings and tennis shoes.

HE'S ONLY A FEW BLOCKS AWAY FROM THE TOWN HOUSE, so I grab the coffee from our favorite shop. We've had enough coffee together, and I know exactly how he likes it—extra shot of espresso, milk, two sugar cubes.

I buzz up.

"Elizabeth!" he says through the intercom, sounding slightly surprised. He was probably deep into a Chadwick Hall chase scene.

"Hey, August, I brought you something to help out. A little pick-me-up from one writer to another! Don't worry. I won't keep you."

He lets me in.

For some reason, I expected more evidence of writerly chaos—cups of tea in random places, takeout cartons on the kitchen countertops. Stray beer bottles. I thought he'd be sporting sweatpants and sexy tousled hair.

Instead, he's well-groomed and put together in pressed slacks and a dress shirt. A bottle of champagne and two flickering candles rest on the table.

"Ahhh . . . you're a darling." He takes the coffee from me.

"Is this the mood you set while writing?" I'm trying to sound lighthearted and not possessive. But I really want to ask if someone else is here.

He glances nervously in the direction of a clock on the wall.

"Yes—um . . . peculiar quirk of mine. When I'm deep into writing, I dress like I'm going into the office, and I sip champagne. It makes me feel bloody successful." He smiles, the dimple deepening.

I smile back—as if it makes sense.

The doorbell sounds, ringing right by my head.

"Hullo, Professor!" A young twiggy blond woman appears on the security screen. She's wearing a cocktail dress like mine. But she's fifteen pounds skinnier and has clearly had breast work done.

"Uhhh . . ." The dimple disappears as his face reddens.

"A student?" I mutter, my voice barely audible.

His mouth hangs open. For once, he has nothing clever to say.

"Right."

"Elizabeth . . . wait . . ." He reaches for me.

"Just leave me alone," I say, wrenching away from him.

I leave quickly, passing the pretty girl outside without a word.

I walk up the streets, evening settling around me. I walk through busy Covent Garden, the young professional crowd off work, clustering around the pubs with pints. I walk slowly, my arms crossed across my chest—lonely in the happy throng, tears in my eyes. I remember this ache of betrayal, and it hurts now like a phantom limb. I remember how it felt as I walked the narrow, uneven streets of Haworth after catching Wes with Samantha on the antique icebox. I remember wondering how I'd get through the last few days of that excursion, how I'd sit near Wes on the plane. I wondered how I could keep my dignity around him and not break down in tears when I couldn't wait to get home and cry in my practical mother's arms.

I meander the streets, not ready to go home. As I pass Victoria Square's private garden, I pause at the statue of a young Victoria. This might be my favorite monument to her. It's years before she delivered eight children and then lost Albert. Her back to me, I can't see her expression in the lamplit darkness. As I wrap my fingers around the cool wrought iron fence, I stare at her form, the folds of her bronze skirt, the swooping braids in her hair, and I feel something slip in me. *Wes was a stupid weasel, and you should never cry more than five minutes over such a person.*

I'm not only grieving Philip. I'm grieving *Mom*. Although Dad took me out for ice cream and listened as I cried, Mom was the structure behind everything, baking and cleaning and making sure we all took our vitamins and went to bed by nine. She kept Dad, Ian and me going like clockwork. We're unmoored without her.

I'm terrified of the grief. There are many reasons I've adhered to these rituals. But I realize now, I'm clinging to Mom's order because whenever the world felt like it was falling apart, she was there holding us all together. And then when my world fell apart, she wasn't there. When Philip died, I needed her more than ever, and everything crumbled for me. There was no remarkable Nora to keep me wound up and running. I needed tangibles and rituals and black clothes and jewelry to keep me rooted. I needed structure because Mom wasn't there.

22

Previous Summer

The evening I fly back from Mom's funeral, I feel exhausted. Heavy. Philip, Heathcliff, and I pick up Greek takeout, but I leave mine mostly untouched. Once Heathcliff is in bed, I take a hot bath and suddenly notice streaks of dust along our tiny square cream and tan ceramic bathroom tiles. After putting on my robe and wrapping my hair in a towel, I know what has to be done.

I pull an unused toothbrush out from under the sink and fill a bucket with hot water and cleaner. The grime will have to be taken care of with a toothbrush. Only then can I mop the entire floor. Then it will all be clean.

Just as I'm scrubbing the edges around the tub, Philip comes to the door.

"What are you doing, Lizzie?" he asks gently.

"What does it look like I'm doing? I'm scrubbing the floor here because it's gross."

"Since when have you been concerned about housecleaning?" he asks, the corner of his mouth twitching.

"Since *now*!"

Then he understands.

I drop the toothbrush and start sobbing, my face in my hands.

Philip sits on the floor beside me as I lean into him.

He holds me for a very long time.

Present

WHEN I GET BACK TO THE ROW HOUSE, I'M RELIEVED that Heathcliff and Ms. Fernsby are out.

Alone, I sink down on the parlor couch ugly-crying. I've lost Mom. I've lost Philip. Philip's loss hurts more because I've lost Mom. And I've been phenomenally stupid these past few weeks.

I'm furious at myself. What had I expected? I hadn't known him for more than a hot minute, and he just *screamed* dashing cad from the instant I laid eyes on him in the British Museum. But he kept saying not to think too far ahead—carpe diem and all that crap, and I went along with it. Underneath, I think I knew this was the kind of thing he'd do.

And yet . . . stupid eternal optimist that I am—I hoped he'd fill a fraction of the gaping hole Philip left. I lost my soulmate, and I held out hope that I might mean something to August Dansworth.

No. That's not completely accurate.

I'm even more confused.

I was less afraid to kiss August than Henry because underneath, I knew it would never last. August was a paper moon, safe and illusionary, because I feared the possibility of real love.

Finding love again feels like a betrayal of Philip.

I'm not finding my way through a labyrinth. I'm lost in a dark, tangled maze.

What would Mom tell me to do?

Mom and Ms. Fernsby would tell me to get a hot cup of tea.

In the kitchen, I pick out the prettiest antique teacup covered in a pink rose pattern with a curved handle. I reach for the tea bags before laying eyes on the brandy.

Once I'm upstairs, I get into my pajamas, crawl into bed, and call Ian. I'm still ugly-crying but the teacup of brandy warms me.

@BluestockingBadass: Two-thirds through *Blood Ties* and Inspector Hall has slept with poor Penny, a bar server, a flight attendant, and an optometrist. Who will he bed next? @ADHemmings (aka Sex God) seems to know a lot about inconstant man-sluts . . .

@ADHemmings: @BlustockingBadass How many women's studies degrees did you earn to grow so bitter? Enjoy your chaste evenings with your vibrator and cats.

@BluestockingBadass: @ADHemmings Whoa. Apparently I hit a nerve. Just curious: Do you even know where a clitoris is located?

@ADHemmings: @BluestockingBadass Sod off.

Ian listens as I cry, sniffling and using up half a box of tissues.

I moan about what a fool I've been, and how I can't believe I'm crying over one man while still grieving Philip. ("What's wrong with me?")

After getting over his initial shock that I've been cavorting with A.D. Hemmings ("Jeez... Lizzie. I can't wait for the Netflix series to come out! I had no idea..."), Ian tells me there's nothing wrong with me, and Dansworth can go fuck himself. Ian promises to write some bad online reviews and troll him relentlessly. Ian says a million funny things to make me laugh and feel marginally better.

"Hey, how's Dad doing?" I ask, blowing my nose.

Ian sighs. "The same. He's given up on the lasagnas. But he's still down."

"So no more dates?"

"Not that I'm aware of. He's just kind of lost."

"I know, Ian. I know."

Before we hang up, Ian tells me he loves me and that my next book will sink Hemmings on the *New York Times* list. I hang up, grateful as always for my brother.

Soon Ms. Fernsby returns from the market with Heathcliff.

I splash cold water on my puffy face to look a little less terrible before going down. She notices, kindly telling me if I want to talk with her I can. But she doesn't prod. I help her put away groceries, trying to shelve my grief and worries. It's difficult. I don't think I've ever felt so confused in my life. After tucking Heathcliff into bed, I refill the teacup and settle into one of my bedroom chairs with *Wuthering Heights*. Lucy peeks at me through one eye from the other chair, and I toast her. After a day like this, there's nothing to do except read and sip brandy.

Soon my phone rings as Henry tries to FaceTime me. He's at his home-office desk.

"Lizzie?" He takes off his reading glasses, peers at me through the screen. "Are you drunk or . . . upset?"

"Both. Do I look that bad?"

"You couldn't look bad in a potato sack, but you just look *sad*. Do you want to talk about it?"

"Thanks. But not really."

He's quiet, rubs his beard.

"Well, I had some news. But if there's a better time, it can wait . . ."

"No, now should be fine." I set my book and half-empty teacup aside. My heartbeat picks up. I hope we finally have answers.

Henry puts his reading glasses back on and clicks through a screen on his desk. I see the stack of letters he took from the safe the other day.

"Lizzie, did Philip ever take you to the Summerville Grits Festival?"

"Once, when Heathcliff was a toddler. It was quite the tribute to grits."

"But a big ole deal if you're from that area. Do you remember there was the parade, shrimp and grits at every stand, and even a grits dunk tank?"

"Unfortunately, yes."

"Let's go back together to that festival in the summer of 1982. It was a sweltering one even by South Carolina's standards. But everyone and their mama turned up, and the lemonade stands made a killing. It was a golden era for Frank and Lila Mae Dubose and your in-laws. Mirabel and Lila Mae's gardening shop was thriving. Frank was mayor. And Ted had just been promoted to bank manager. The couples rode together in the mayor's float at the front of the parade. Mirabel and Lila Mae tossed store coupons and candy into the crowd. Have a look..."

He shares his screen, flashing a photo from the parade. Mirabel wore a short, tight denim skirt and puffy white blouse. Both women sport '80s bouffant hair and thick, deliciously colorful eye shadow. They smile widely and nearby Frank beams proudly, wearing a blue pin-striped seersucker suit and red bow tie. He waves at the crowd, handsome sunburned face smiling under his panama hat. Ted stands meekly at the back of the float, looking like he wants to be anywhere but there.

Henry flips the screen back to him. "After the parade, Frank had a little party at his downtown Summerville house. As I said, it was *hot*. Guests sucked champagne pops and stuck their feet in kiddie pools in the backyard. It was sometime on that hot afternoon that Mirabel and Frank, drunk on Lila Mae's specialty champagne pops and whatever other cocktails came out, slipped off alone in the house."

"Oh..." I mutter, completely sober now.

"Whether Ted or Lila Mae noticed their missing spouses that afternoon is unclear. But in the days to come, Miss Lila Mae knew something had happened. Tensions brewed at the gardening shop, culminating in the Piggly Wiggly fight. Mirabel found herself pregnant by the end of the summer, and it was clear to the couples that what happened that afternoon wasn't about to go away. The shop closed. Afraid of scandal, Frank stepped down as mayor."

"And Ted?"

Henry smiles and shrugs. "He kept working at the bank."

My mouth goes dry, and I swallow. "Are you telling me what I think you're telling me?"

"I sure am. I hope you don't mind. I didn't want to scare you with my suspicions, but when I went to the house, I didn't just go for the letters. I took some hair from one of Heathcliff's combs. My investigator sent me the results today. Lizzie, Frank Dubose was Philip's father."

"Mirabel slept with the mayor, and he fathered Philip? *This* is the secret she's been going nuts about?"

Henry nods. "I don't think the affair lasted long, and even though the couples parted ways, Frank wanted to do the right thing. He set up a trust fund for Philip, and over the years, as his real estate grew, he contributed regularly. It's fairly sizable at this point, and when I finally got my hands on the paperwork, I saw it's true—none of the money is Ted's. It's all from Frank Dubose."

I blink away tears. "This was what Philip wanted to tell me that night. He put it all together and confronted her."

"It is," Henry says gently. Then he taps the bundle at his desk. "The letters, the photos. They opened up suspicions he'd had for years. That's how I got the whole story—flirtatious notes between Mirabel and Frank. Furious letters from Lila

Mae to Mirabel. It was quite the soap opera, and I can't help but wonder why Mirabel hung on to them for all these years, up in that attic for Philip to find."

"I'd like to know that too. And I get that hooking up with the mayor is something she's probably not proud of, but why is she so anxious about it now? It was almost forty years ago. Philip wouldn't have judged her for what she did. But he would have wanted her to tell him the truth. He must have been so hurt. I wonder what happened that night. Like did she try to lie?"

Henry shakes his head. "I think Mirabel's the only one who can fill in those blanks. Look, the trust paperwork is sound. I know you're not really in a place where you need money, but the trust should cover Heathcliff's college. Frank handled the legal part right. The issue now is closure for you—and I think for all involved."

I bite my lip. It's not going to be easy to get Mirabel to talk.

"I'm curious, Henry. Did Frank ever see Philip?"

Henry rubs his beard. "I'm working on that end. So far, the Duboses have been as closed-off as Mirabel. But in my line of work, I've learned people can act pretty shitty while underneath all that almost everyone has a beating heart. You can't tell me he put that money faithfully into that trust for his son and grandson and didn't think of them at all. I just can't believe that."

I pick up my teacup and take another sip.

"That's not tea in there, is it?" Henry asks, grinning.

"No."

"If you don't mind me asking again, you looked in pretty bad shape when you accepted my call. Is everything ok?"

"Not really."

"Do you want me to fly out there? If you need me to be with you, I will."

At his earnest expression, I realize he would. I realize he'd do anything for me.

When did that start?

"Lizzie?"

"You don't need to do that, Henry. But thank you."

"I'd do it, Lizzie."

"I know you would."

BLOCKED TEXT FROM AUGUST DANSWORTH:
Hello, Elizabeth. I'm sorry about last night. I was ghastly. Call me!

24

The next day, I wake to discover that I really can't do anything other than scroll through TikTok videos of cute pugs, eat cereal, and watch Batman cartoons with Heathcliff. I can't stop thinking about Dansworth and the stew of Southern drama waiting for me when I get back to South Carolina. Why couldn't she come clean with her own adult son? I can only imagine how Philip felt that night he called me to tell me everything. I see her manic in her garden hat with her pistol; I see her leaning out the bathroom window smoking those cigarettes. Amid my annoyance, I feel sorry for her. She must have been eaten up by guilt all these years. She needs to tell the truth and let it all go.

Then there's August . . .

With great effort, I try not to dwell on the pain I still feel from last night. I can't believe I got myself into this situation. I wanted to believe his rakishness was a facade, that the charming smoke and mirrors covered good character. I was naive. Even more shocking: What is happening between me and Philip's best friend? Shame seeps through my gut. My feelings are promiscuous and weird. Henry and Philip went fishing together. Had beers together. He's the *last* man I should be attracted to in the wake of my husband's death—even further down the list from British playboys who ply college students and silly, grief-stricken widows with champagne.

I came to England to reassemble myself after losing Philip. I intentionally created rules to help me navigate my loss. Mourning rituals provided convenient paths for me to follow, comforting boundaries for my pain. But I couldn't create rules for my heart. Black dresses, jet necklaces, little bird urns aren't talismans to ward off grief and love. There are some things that I can't control no matter how improper I believe them to be.

Who am I?

Although I'm on the journey I set out to take, I'm still as fucking lost as I was when I broke down in my seminar class.

"You're using the wrong colors," Heathcliff says indignantly. Oops. He's right. I'm coloring Poison Ivy blue in the coloring book.

"She's supposed to be *GREEN*," he says scornfully, like I'm the world's most ignorant slut. It's like he knows I'm a poor excuse for a Victorian widow—a true wid-*hoe* if there ever was one.

"Now, you be nice to your mum," Ms. Fernsby says reproachfully as she walks through the room with a large bundle of fresh thyme.

She knows something upsetting happened last evening when I went to meet August, but she's been giving me space today. She's been mostly running errands and busying herself with the patio garden.

Heathcliff scowls at both of us before going back to his coloring book.

In the late afternoon, I'm helping Ms. Fernsby with dinner.

While she cuts up onions for her chicken gnocchi soup, I knead sourdough bread dough on the kitchen island. Jazz music plays pleasantly from the Alexa on the kitchen counter as we chat. Mabel will be stopping by for dinner, and I'm looking forward to it. Always bright and cheery, she'll be good company to distract me from my angst.

My phone rings suddenly, and I see it's Henry. Wiping my floury fingers on a towel, I excuse myself and step outside to the small back patio.

"Hey," I say, slumping into a wrought iron chair cushioned by a jade garden pillow. Ms. Fernsby's roses bloom nearby in the late-afternoon sun.

"Hey . . ."

I wait out a long, awkward pause as he clears his throat. I thought this might be more Mirabel drama, but my stomach sinks a little. That's not why he called.

"I couldn't sleep last night," he says.

"I'm . . . sorry."

"Listen, um . . ." He sighs and then chuckles. "There's just no smooth way to say this."

I'm quiet.

"I don't regret almost kissing you. I think about it every day. I can't *stop* thinking about it. I miss you, Lizzie."

I hold my breath, watching a tiny hummingbird dip into one of the feeders poking out from the roses. Of course, I sensed *this* in his voice last night. But why does he have to tell me now? I'm in the worst place to hear a love confession, particularly from Henry.

"Lizzie?"

"Why are you telling me this?"

"Because I have to. I mean . . . I know the timing is weird . . ."

"Weird? More like *terrible*. Where can this go? You were his best friend, for god's sake. Philip just died, and the ink on your divorce papers isn't even dry."

"Look, I know, Lizzie. But there's never a good time. You can do with this whatever you want, but I need you to know how I feel."

"You're hot-off-the-press divorced. You don't know what you're saying. I'm just filling a void for you, Henry. That's all this is."

"You really think that's all you are to me? Something to fill a void?"

"Yes."

"It's not like that. And it's not like we just met. We've known each other for years."

"Which makes it all the weirder." Tears well up, filming my vision. "Please. Let's just not talk about this anymore."

I hang up before he can say anything, and wipe my eyes. I'm angry at him for calling out what's been between us these past few weeks. My feelings for Henry *have* grown. My fondness for him from all these years *has* bloomed into something different. But any way I look at it, it feels wrong.

Everything feels wrong with Philip gone, and I'm in pieces. I take several deep breaths, determined not to cry, and go back inside to knead bread.

By 9:00 in the evening, I'm reading *Wuthering Heights* on the parlor couch. I'm at the scene of Cathy's death. Women had such vague causes of death in Victorian literature. There's Cathy—hysteria and heartbreak; Lily Bart and Emma Bovary—debt and drugs; the Lady of Shalott—isolation and art. I fall asleep wondering how I'll die.

In this dream, I'm in Yorkshire hiking through Brontë country. It's cool and windy, and I'm surrounded by the rocky terrain, rippling purple heather, pink foxglove, and sticky thistles.

Philip treks on ahead, sun glinting on his green Patagonia windbreaker. I yell for him to wait up, but he keeps going. I stop to catch my breath, pissed and exhausted. Then I remember the rules of these Philip dreams. He's always just out of my reach, and it's nothing but yearning. Always.

No.

This time I'll catch up with him.

There's nowhere for him to hide here—no crowds, no bushy azalea gardens. I run, yelling his name, keeping my eyes glued on him. But in the way dreams work, space and time don't make sense. Although I'm sprinting and he's hiking, he remains ahead of me. Out of reach.

I stop on the trail, teary and exhausted. When I look up, I see we're approaching Top Withens, the crumbling farmhouse that likely inspired the Earnshaw home in *Wuthering Heights*. Now it's all stone walls and open space.

"Philip! Wait for me this time!" I yell with Cathy Earnshaw passion.

He pauses at an open door. He turns slightly in my direction, but I only see his silhouette. He can hear me. He knows I'm here. But then he walks inside the ruins.

I run up the hill and into the ruins. "Philip?" I call, looking around me. But it's all broken rocks and grass and sunlight. He's nowhere here. And it's eerily, unnaturally silent. No nesting bird warbles, no wind roars. I stand frozen there, confused and trying to pinpoint a spreading emotion. *Fear.* Not fear that I'm in danger, like someone is going to attack me. It's much worse because I don't think I can fight back against this. I really am alone, and it's terrifying.

I wake up. In the dark parlor, my phone says it's 1:30 a.m. I sit up, rub my eyes, rumpling a large eiderdown quilt Ms. Fernsby must have laid across me as I slept. *Wuthering Heights* lies open on the floor. Everyone's asleep. Heathcliff. Ms. Fernsby. Lucy sleeps in her cozy hearth bed.

I might be awake, but the fear from the dream continues. I feel the weight of my separation from Philip. I'm living a life I didn't want to live. If Philip could see me now, he'd be ashamed of me—having a nervous breakdown in class, whisking Heathcliff away to this fairy-tale little row house in London. Attending séances, wearing and carrying pieces of *him*.

Who am I?

In spite of the early hour, stray cars still pass on the street. I see the glare of headlights through the curtain slits, hear the soft braking of a car and men's voices.

Someone knocks at the door.

Wiping away tears, I get up. I'm in such a grief fog that only as I'm unlatching the door do I think it's odd for someone to be knocking at this time of night. And I'm in London, so—Jack the Ripper?

"Dad!"

He's standing there in his tweed jacket and trousers, barely rumpled in spite of the international flight. His gray beard is trimmed, tortoiseshell glasses perched neatly on his nose. It's been a while since I've seen him face-to-face, but he still smells oh-so-wonderful, like pipe smoke and dusty books.

He shuffles uncomfortably.

"Ian called yesterday. He said you were having a hard time. Maybe we could go out for ice cream later and talk about it?"

I burst into tears and collapse into him, the tweed rough against my cheek.

AT 5:30 A.M., HEATHCLIFF WAKES, EXCITED TO SEE HIS grandpa curled up on the little futon in his room. I make strong coffee and scramble eggs with fresh spinach and Tabasco sauce the way Dad likes them. As I sip my coffee, I enjoy watching Dad with Heathcliff.

Dad studies a little LEGO house Heathcliff made, looking it over through his glasses as if it's a scholarly essay to be edited. As Heathcliff chatters, Dad nods, interested but not quite able to follow a six-year-old's stream-of-consciousness thoughts, where the Joker, kittens, and chocolate donuts somehow make it into the same sentence. He's treating Heathcliff the way he treated me and Ian as children, with love and care, but also with slight bewilderment, as if we were hobbits or some other little strange creatures that magically ended up in his world.

Heathcliff doesn't seem to notice, and I have to keep reminding him to eat his scrambled eggs and strawberries as he chatters away.

A little after seven o'clock, Ms. Fernsby walks downstairs in a daisy-print housedress, hair pulled back in a neat gray knot at the back of her head. Without looking around, she tells me good morning and goes on about the lemon sponge cake she needs to make for her gardening club event this afternoon.

"I *should* have started last evening, you see—the lemon glaze should set overnight—but then I poured my nip of brandy and started *The Governess Falls for the Duke* and, well, I couldn't put it down— *Oh* . . ."

She stops mid-sentence, suddenly seeing my shy father at the kitchen island with Heathcliff.

"Oh . . ." she says again more quietly, patting her hair.

Dad nods but doesn't say anything. Obviously, he isn't an extrovert, and I'll need to introduce them. But I'm trying not to smile into my coffee. I'm more delighted than I want to let on by Ms. Fernsby's response.

I make the introductions.

"Well, Gaylord, it's nice to meet you," Ms. Fernsby says, regaining some of her composure.

Dad shifts in his seat. "You as well, Annabel."
This is too cute.
Ms. Fernsby tightens her apron strings and springs into action, doing what she does best, making everyone feel comfortable. "I have some iced scones in here—they'll go well with that coffee..."

As she pulls the tray out of the fridge, I start to tell her that he never eats sugar. But he catches my eye and shakes his head.

"Yes, I'd love one. Thank you."

I gulp my coffee, watching Dad eat a scone as he adds to Heathcliff's LEGO house. Ian said he ate a Twinkie recently, but I don't think I actually believed it until now. Ms. Fernsby bustles around me, pulling out the ingredients for her cake. She keeps casting side glances at Dad, her cheeks blushing rosier by the minute.

25

By afternoon, Dad and I eat at a little ice cream shop in Covent Garden. We sit on the outside patio chairs under a shady trellis. I'm eating a giant cup of white chocolate and raspberry gelato, and he's licking chocolate ice cream from a waffle cone. It's the least professor-y thing I've ever seen him do. Also, I thought he might call it a day with the sugar after having the iced scone this morning, but he seems to really enjoy the cone.

I tell him about August *and* about my feelings for Henry. I tell him about August's lies last evening and how upset I was. I also tell him about Mirabel and the big Southern stew I have to sort out when I get back. I tell him I miss Philip so much it hurts. I tell him I miss Mom so much it hurts.

I tell him that I have no idea what to do about any of it.

Dad doesn't say anything as he eats his ice cream. He just sits here with me. I remember this is why I always feel comfortable falling apart with him in my neediest moments.

"I can't believe I was so stupid with August Dansworth.

I'm so ashamed, Dad. I really am. Philip would be disappointed in me."

"And why would you say that, Lizzie?"

"I'm supposed to be in *mourning* and instead I'm having all these inappropriate feelings. I came here to sort myself out and now I'm more confused."

I'm stupidly teary. This is the falling-apart moment. I put down my spoon, dab my eyes with my napkin. I'm blubbering with Dad over ice cream just like I did in fourth grade and in graduate school.

"Who told you that you were supposed to be in mourning?"

"Well . . . me—I guess. And you know, one of the great things about Mom was that she always kept order and rules going even when things went badly for us. A period of mourning and maintaining mourning rituals seemed like a good idea. It helps keep me together."

He glances down at my jet necklace over my black sundress.

"It's Victorian-style mourning, Dad," I mutter.

"Naturally," he says dryly, as if he expected nothing less of me.

He takes the last bite of cone and wipes his mouth. I can't believe he ate the whole thing.

"You aren't *supposed* to do anything except take care of yourself and Heathcliff. Keep it simple. I thought for decades I wasn't supposed to eat sugar. I ate a Twinkie last month, and nothing happened."

I remember that scary moment when August asked me what would happen if I stopped my rules and rituals. I think about giving them up now without as much fear.

"Nora was our backbone. But your mother didn't always follow the rules." He looks off at the rippling ivy on the trellis beams. "We danced again before she died."

"What?" I murmur, my voice barely audible.

He keeps his eyes on the ivy.

"We danced. She had strict orders not to get out of bed unassisted. She was too weak. But one of those last evenings when I walked into the bedroom with her medicine, she was up, queuing the salsa music on the nightstand stereo. She looked so frail under her robe. But somehow, she'd summoned the strength to slip on her old satin dancing shoes. I urged her back to bed, but she said, 'Be quiet, Gaylord. I want to dance with you one last time.' So we danced. She put on one of our favorites, Héctor Lavoe's 'Periódico de Ayer.' She was so weak. I had to support her. But she remembered every move perfectly. My darling didn't miss a beat."

"Oh, Dad . . ."

We're quiet. I can't quite finish my gelato, so I push it aside. We watch a woman tether a large French poodle to the ice cream store patio's iron gate as she walks inside to order. I watch a young blonde nanny share an ice cream cone with a toddler.

He turns to me. "My point is that you really shouldn't follow all the rules all the time. You'll end up missing out on something important.

"As for Mirabel," Dad continues. "You'll know what to do when you get home. She's always been like she is. The longer she keeps the lid on her secret, the more monstrous it feels to her. Do you remember the Pandora's box myth we read when you were young?"

"Yes."

He shrugs. "Philip, and now Henry and you, sprung open a box lid that needed to come off. Philip wanted the truth out, no matter how troublesome. Now you have to resolve it all, and part of that is helping Mirabel come to peace with it. I know that's a weight, Lizzie, but you can do it."

Although I knew with childlike longing that I needed ice cream with Dad, I realize why. For all his aloofness, he always believed in me. This helped me believe in myself.

"As for Dansworth, well . . . I think we both know what your mother would say about him." Dad's mouth twitches. "Henry Lawton's a harder one. But let your heart do the sorting rather than the rules about what you think you're supposed to do."

I cringe remembering how I snapped at Henry last night. The hard truth is I'm overwhelmed and afraid.

I take a deep breath. "And in the meantime, in my last days here—what am I supposed to do? I'm still not sorted out, Dad."

He crosses his arms on the patio table and pushes his glasses up on his nose.

"Take another trip."

I KNOW WHERE I NEED TO GO.

That evening, I make a flurry of calls and text Henry to tell him I'll be away again. I book train tickets and an Airbnb. Dad offers to take care of Heathcliff for the next two days. I know between him and Ms. Fernsby, he'll be in good hands. I tell them I'm only going to accept texts and calls from them. I've already blocked August, but I'm (temporarily) going to block everyone else—even Henry. For now. I need to be alone with my own thoughts.

Dad, meanwhile, seems to be in no hurry to leave London. He remains vague when I ask him how long he's here. Ms. Fernsby looks prettier by the day, wearing all her nicest housedresses, and I've never seen her blush so often. Dad continues to play with Heathcliff, taking him on walks and reading to him. Heathcliff doesn't seem to notice Dad's shyness. If anything, he seems to enjoy having a constant companion listen nonstop to his favorite Batman story plots. Dad doesn't get tired like I do with Heathcliff's energy and chatter. Also, I don't think I'm imagining that Dad seems to be quietly making himself available to Ms. Fernsby—sitting often at the kitchen island between meals with a cup of tea, reading in the parlor. He eats everything she puts in front of him no matter how sweet, and each time she beams.

I pack quickly—jeans, my warmest pair of black leggings, new hiking boots. Even though it's summer, I buy a black windbreaker and fleece vest. I know I'll need them where I'm going. I still take my widowhood trinkets, the jet and fingerprint necklace, Philip's urn.

Henry texts me: I know I'm the last person you want to talk to now. But you need to know you might hear from Mirabel. She's threatening to sue us. Don't worry about it.

Me: Ok

Henry: You're not going to tell me where you're going to?

Me: No

As if on cue, Mirabel texts me.

I'm suing the goddamn pants off you and your lawyer, Elizabeth.

I inhale. Exhale.
Then I block her.

AFTER BUYING MY TRAIN TICKETS THE NEXT MORNING, I wander around crowded Platform 9¾. I scan the glossy hardback books and Hogwarts scarves and pins. I purchase far too many Bertie Bott's jelly beans. (Heathcliff will be delighted.) Philip and I read the series out loud during our first year of marriage. We'd lie on the couch, taking turns reading each chapter. Even now, I can feel the warm weight of his feet tangled up in mine under our colorful granny-square afghan.

By the time I board, a strange peace settles over me. I have knots to unravel, and there's one place I need to be. But amid it all I feel hopeful and even happy. For a few minutes, I see clearly the journey before me and the ongoing one that stretches beyond this trip. I see that I can miss Philip always and allow myself to still feel happy.

BLOCKED TEXT FROM AUGUST DANSWORTH:
Elizabeth, first let me apologize again for my ghastly behavior. To be honest, I've never been out with a widow, and you're a rather rare bird. Not to be crass, but you'd still be married to the chap if he hadn't died. To know there's someone (even eternally) out there that you love madly, deeply, more than anyone else—well, it's a lot for a guy like me to take. Anyway, please do return my call.

After my train reaches Keighley, I take a bus to Haworth and arrive toward evening. As I walk through the quaint town, I pause at a high point where I can look out over the surrounding countryside. A bronze glow settles over the lakes and rolling hills. Long green swaths of farmland and rustling thick summer foliage cover the land. Creeks ramble through clusters of forest, and a hawk circles the skies above. I remember seeing Emily

Brontë's watercolor of her rescued hawk, Nero, displayed in the Brontë Parsonage on my last visit. With her brush, she painted the bird's speckled breast, the cream-and-chestnut plumage, the curved beak in startling detail. The sisters had years to explore the nooks and crannies of this beautiful landscape, and I envy how they plucked its secrets.

I think of my other two times here. I remember that first ill-fated trip after my grad school friends and I found cheap plane tickets and a dodgy, drafty eighteenth-century cottage on the edge of town where we could all stay for almost nothing. Of our group, I was the one most taken by this place. While the others pub-crawled through Haworth, I spent my days wandering through the Brontë Parsonage, absorbing each room's details and reading every exhibit description in the museum collection. I could stare all day at the sisters' carefully embroidered dresses, visualizing them as living, breathing women. Charlotte, particularly, was tiny, less than five feet.

I've always thought it was somehow significant that my first real heartbreak happened in Haworth. Although the well-behaved daughter of an Anglican priest, Charlotte Brontë struggled to keep her heart in check. For me, one of her most interesting biographical gems was her unrequited passion for her married teacher Constantin Héger. She wrote to him, and when he didn't respond, she wrote yet again—this time about waiting in vain for his letters: *Day and night I find neither rest nor peace—if I sleep I have tormenting dreams.* We know now Héger threw the letters away until his wife pasted them back together, preserving Charlotte's mad infatuation for the world to see. It comforts me to know that even a Brontë sister could lose herself in lust and heartache, slipping from the straight-and-narrow path.

My second journey here, when I was with Philip and expecting Heathcliff, had been better than the first. I was no longer chasing after an insouciant ass. I was happily married, and life felt wonderful. It had been a few months before Christmas, the last time my doctor would allow me to fly when pregnant; the streetlamps were wrapped with garlands and red ribbons. Candles and sprayed frost decorated the dripping glass panes of shop windows. We took things pretty slow that holiday and would sit for long periods in the Black Bull, the infamous pub where Branwell Brontë drank away his afternoons. Philip and I would talk about the impending birth of our son: *You do know my vagina will never look the same . . . I love your dad, but we can't use Gaylord, even as a middle name . . .* Sometimes we'd just quietly read. I'd nurse my apple cider as Philip sipped stout beer.

I always loved it when lawyer-Philip entered my literary world, and after two pints one afternoon, Philip said we should name our son after one of the sisters' characters. He pulled out the copy of *Wuthering Heights* he'd bought from the Brontë museum gift shop that afternoon. "Batshit crazy" is what he called it. After several healthy debates where Philip vetoed St. John, Fairfax and Crimsworth, we decided on Heathcliff. Although I loved the name, I wondered if it was all right to name our baby after such a broody rat-bastard. Philip just laughed and said, *He'll have edge.*

On this journey now, I'm here alone.

No man-slut boyfriend.

No Philip.

It's only me.

I walk the steep cobbled streets to my Airbnb. The place is small and cute—a cozy bedroom, kitchenette and sitting area. The floors are uneven after the centuries, but it's perfect. There's a little ivy-lined balcony looking out over the village. The owner left a warm note and a bottle of brandy on the table. I pour a snifter, wrap myself in an afghan, and sit on the little rusted chair on the balcony. I take a deep breath and plan my next day.

IN THE MORNING, I MAKE MYSELF A BIG BREAKFAST. I always loved cooking and eating, and Ms. Fernsby certainly has revived my interest in big breakfasts. As I sizzle the bacon crispy and put the big sourdough slices in the toaster while frying three eggs, I think sadly of my unused stove at home. I remember how happy cooking those weekend breakfasts with Philip made me. I slather butter and blueberry preserves on my toast slice and pour an enormous mug of coffee. After breakfast, I put on my black leggings and oversize black windbreaker, strap on my duffel bag, lock the door, and walk down the narrow fire escape steps.

Little has changed in Haworth since my last two trips. A bittersweet déjà vu seeps through me as I walk by familiar pubs, tearooms, antiques stores, and bookshops. The quirky, uneven ivy-draped brick buildings rise around me, window boxes blooming with rainbow coleus leaves, thyme, lavender, and bright salvias. On my last visit, these same boxes displayed small fir branches, the painted wood draped in festive wreaths and garlands. Frost speckled the needles.

The Brontë Parsonage isn't crowded. This week, there's a festival in nearby Keighley, draining much of the tourist crowd. It's nice to find myself mostly alone in the rooms. I walk through the small kitchen, with white-painted cabinets, little tea towels hanging from a wooden rod affixed to the ceiling. I picture Emily, the most elusive of the sisters, kneading bread on these countertops while brainstorming windswept scenes for her novel. Although I've been through these rooms before, for the first time, I experience these women as a woman and not as a scholar. I stand for a long time in front of the table where the sisters wrote their books. Patterned wallpaper covers the walls above the painted white trim and wainscoting. George Richmond's drawing of Charlotte hangs above the fireplace mantel. I've always loved this image. She wears fashionable lace and ribbon about her throat, and her hair modestly conceals her ears. Yet I've always thought Charlotte's expression seems dark and edgy—a far cry from the proper demure Victorian woman.

When I continue to Charlotte's bedroom, I'm fascinated by her displayed dress, particularly the bell sleeves and faded violet material. Like her Jane Eyre, Charlotte was petite. One of Anne's necklaces drapes over the dress, and Anne's monogrammed ivory stockings hang nearby. I walk through Branwell's rooms, nightshirt on the bed, papers, feather pens, and inkwells displayed in an intentionally disheveled manner. Branwell. The family always thought he would be the celebrated artist. A portrait painter by training, his life spiraled out of control before the age of thirty. With his unwise love affairs and addictions, he was a tender headache to the sisters.

Light rain pelts the windows.

All of them died young here amid these windy moors and the gothic parsonage graveyard. Perhaps because of this, everyone thinks the sisters lived sad, gloomy lives. I touch the glass above a pair of spectacles on display. The family suffered. The siblings lost their mother to cancer and their older sisters to illness when they were young. Charlotte outlived all the siblings before dying at my age; she lost Branwell, Emily, and Anne within a year.

When I lost Mom to breast cancer, it was devastating. But you do expect, difficult as it may be, to lose your parent at some point. Other deaths, like Philip's, are more startling. I feel Charlotte's stinging loss at seeing her sisters and brother die in the prime of life. I see Charlotte wearing spectacles as she writes one of her more raw letters, admitting about her deceased sister: *I could hardly let Emily go—I wanted to hold her back then—and I want her back hourly now.*

In spite of losing their mother and sisters, the siblings wrote about magical worlds with battles, women rulers, and searing love affairs. Charlotte and Branwell created Angria, and Anne and Emily, Gondal. The siblings bickered and drew and painted and wrote. They showed compassion to their servants, caring for their beloved housekeeper, Tabby, after she broke her leg. Even after losing Branwell, Emily, and Anne, Charlotte still went on holidays in the Lake District. She held her own in the London literary scene, sparring with indomitable male writers such as William Thackeray. She attended art exhibitions and wrote letters drenched in sarcasm and wicked humor to fellow female writers like Elizabeth Gaskell. I walk back to the gown and imaginatively reach through the display glass to feel the texture of the dress's patterns. I feel another world where others grieved and yet lived on creatively and warmly and deeply. There could still be humor and delightful fabric patterns and friendships.

After purchasing a *Jane Eyre* umbrella in the museum shop, I meander through the graveyard paths. The lichen-covered gravestones are long, some standing upright, some leaning or toppled along the ground. But all are uneven, many sunken in the rows framed by winding dirt paths. I've heard there are between twenty and sixty thousand bodies in the grounds. With that many, the headstone can't be guaranteed to label the body underneath. I'm humbled, wrapping my mind around all these buried bodies. After death, each Brontë was carried through here to the St. Michael's Church crypt. A stone marks the graveyard gate through which they passed.

Rain falls lightly on the stones around me, and as I sit on a damp, rough stone bench, I think about all the nineteenth-century widows like me visiting their husbands' graves here.

They would have worn black, a jet necklace protecting a lock of his hair if they could afford it. Of course, these women would all be dead now, lost in the crowd of bones under my feet. In my imagination, I tip my hat to them all.

After visiting the monument in the church over the Brontë family crypt, I walk back through the village to the Black Bull. It's late afternoon, and I order a kidney pie, laden with gravy and rosemary and covered in a buttery potato crust. When I was expecting Heathcliff, I could eat an entire pie. I do so now without the pregnancy heartburn, fueling up for the long hike I have tomorrow.

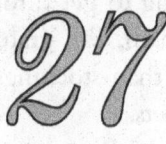

27

After breakfast, I stock my backpack with a sandwich, snacks, and water. I don black leggings, sturdy hiking boots, and a few layers, including a jacket for the moor winds. I still wear my fingerprint and jet necklaces. I carry the bird urn in my bag.

As I set out from Haworth for the trail, I think of the Brontë sisters themselves and how many times they walked these paths for peace, exercise, or to visit a neighbor. A woman's love of solitary walking could be controversial in the nineteenth century. Hetty Sorrel and Tess d'Urberville bumped into their seducers while strolling about alone. Lizzie Bennet's walking habits sparked Caroline Bingley's snark. Why did I never take up the scandalous practice of walking solo? Philip and I used to like to run outside or hike upstate during the peak of autumn. But I never actually explored extensively on my own.

I pass the Parsonage Museum, move through the graveyard and a kissing gate, and head for the trail to Top Withens. I feel a strong pull for solitude. Noise and parenting and texts, even good conversation, have made it impossible for me to hear my own heart's needs. If I'd been widowed in the nineteenth century, without sympathy texts from friends and Grubhub deliveries and online widow blogs, I know I would have done a lot of pie baking and walking to get through the day. As I stride briskly, mindful of the path, I'm grateful I can wear leggings and hiking boots rather than stockings and layers of petticoat and lung-crunching corsets.

Before long, I reach the Penistone Hill marker. The midmorning sun breaks through the clouds, and in spite of the wind, I'm sweating by the time I make it down the soft, grassy paths, then onto rougher ones to the Brontë waterfall. There are only a few people out here, and I sit on a rock to eat a protein bar and drink from my water thermos. I thought the trek would be peaceful, but something strums uncomfortably inside me. Part of me wants to turn back—I mean, Heathcliff might need me. I should have called Ms. Fernsby this morning. He could have taken a Batman leap off the second-floor window.

I inhale, then let out my breath slowly.

I'm resisting.

I watch the water spilling over the wide, steplike rocks; the rising sun hits the surface in gold glints. Charlotte wrote about walking around these falls with her Irish curate husband. We know she felt deeply. Her letters to Héger reveal her inner passionate nature. In her brief remaining life after losing her siblings, I wonder if she felt fear. That swallowing grief-fear that never goes away, but only ebbs and flows, unpredictable and unchecked.

Chloe told me once that fear should be one of the seven deadly sins. I'm scared to be alone with my grief in this place. I want to walk back to the village and sit in one of those cozy tearooms listening to conversations around me as I sip a steaming chamomile. Or I could go to the Black Bull pub, sip a glass of wine, and continue reading *Wuthering Heights*; I can call to check in on Heathcliff. In fact, I should check on him. All these options would qualify as self-care and good parenting.

But I know that's all giving in to my fear.

I keep going.

Soon I'm on a narrow path in the moors. I hiked this with Samantha (before the pantry incident), but never alone. Gorgeous pink foxglove blooms everywhere, near every craggy rock, fence, and stone enclosure wall. I've heard somewhere that this path was once a packhorse trail for taking supplies to these hard-to-reach homes. The landscape is beautiful but isolated, thick with mud and slippery rock edges, good for twisting ankles. The climb is arduous, nearly entirely uphill and steep, and I'm out of breath as I continue up the approximate mile between Brontë Falls and Top Withens. Because I was pregnant during my last trip here, I haven't hiked this trail in almost twenty years. It's a little more rugged than I remember. (Thank you, middle age.)

As crumbling Top Withens comes into view, I stop, fear strumming through my chest. I remember following Philip here in my dream. I feel fresh that pain of separation, where he's just beyond my fingertips.

I buckle over, my hands heavy on my knees. I can't stand this—where one stupid, superstitious part of me thinks I can reach him. It's why I wanted something from that boozy séance. But it's all a delusion. At the end of every day for the rest of my life, I'll be alone, and I must—I *have* to accept that.

I straighten, breathe deeply, and step forward.

This is my labyrinth, and I'll keep walking.

I approach the house, reading The Brontë Society plaque bolted on the stone wall in 1964. Although no one knows for certain this was the farmhouse Emily had in mind for Wuthering Heights, Charlotte's lifelong friend Ellen Nussey surmised that it was. Many scholars agree on the possibility. But the connections are inconsistent and slippery. Top Withens certainly doesn't match all of Emily's Wuthering Heights architectural descriptions. For me, though, now, it works, and I choose to see this place as the scene of destabilizing heartbreak.

I wander around the towering stone wall to the crumbling west foundations. I step through one of the old stone windows and make my way into the roofless, grassy interior. There are the ruins of the old stone fireplaces, the space for the vaulted cellar. I imagine families living here over the centuries—fires roaring in the hearth; potatoes, parsnips, and turnips stored in the cellar. Now the harsh moor winds blow through the open spaces, and I search to find a sheltered spot. I sit on a stony piece jutting out from a wall and remain entirely still.

I close my eyes, inhaling, listening to nothing but the wind. I know how the sisters imagined remarkable things in these moors. Through the wind, Jane heard Mr. Rochester calling for her. Catherine, child of the moors, transferred her oneness with the landscape to her lover: "I *am* Heathcliff." And she dreamed if she died, she'd be cast out of heaven and tossed back to this place she so ardently longed for.

I sit still, and I breathe.

Lizzie, we need to talk.

We had needed to talk. He wanted to talk about Mirabel and her secret. She dreaded the world knowing she wasn't perfect. Philip wouldn't have minded her peccadillo. But I know he hurt knowing she never told him who his actual father was. He had wanted me to help him walk forward with this new information. I would have held his hand, and I would have helped him help his mother.

Suddenly, I sense Philip, not supernaturally, but as a part of me I still carry. We do need to talk. Silently, I tell him about the grief, how sometimes it feels like a cancer eating away at me inside. How Heathcliff and my coffee and Ms. Fernsby's scones and crepes are the only things getting me out of bed in the morning. How my colleagues bicker like they're never going to die, but they will, and their nemesis from another department will dance on their grave. I tell him the decades ahead seem bleak, that I want to love, but I feel like I'm betraying him. That I wear black clothes and pieces of his hair around my neck and carry his urn because Mom isn't here to help me forward. That I'm worried that if I don't do these things, my grief isn't real and our love will fade away. Or it will overwhelm me altogether.

I sit in the silence. The wind blows cold on my tears.

I know his reply.

Lizzie, we need to talk.

He's proud of me beyond words. Just getting out of bed at all is a victory. He tells me there's no cancer; it's festering grief and gradually, day by day, I'll feel more joy and the sting won't be so sharp. He doesn't want my decades to be bleak, and even though remarkable Nora isn't here anymore, I have her strength and can carry on with her steel and grit. He wants me to channel my pluck, to stay determined to move forward and not back. He wants me to ease away from the black clothes unless I genuinely like them as a glam Audrey Hepburn style. He lets me know he'll be just fine if I leave his ashes and hair in my jewelry box because it won't mean I love him any less. He tells me my colleagues are jackasses and to use their pettiness and his death to learn how to live a better life. He tells me all these things and ends with a sincere wish that I try to love again and it's okay if it's Henry. He tells me I can love anyone who makes me happy because if I'm happy then he's at peace.

And then there's just the wind.

I LINGER AT TOP WITHENS, EATING MY LUNCH, WONdering what it would be like to live here and sleep on the grassy floor. Beautiful at times. But I decide it would be impossible in the winters and downright frightening during stormy Yorkshire torrents. And of course, there are most definitely tormented ghosts wandering these moors.

After brushing crumbs off my leggings, I leave to get back on the trail. Because no one is around, I blow a kiss back at the ruins for what they offered me.

I'm taking a circular route, not backtracking as I did in grad school.

A light rain starts as I continue on, passing through a kissing gate. The trail grows muddy as I walk, my boots sticking in the thick sludge, now splattering my leggings. A long, hot bath will be in order when I get back to my rooms.

Then I look up to meet eyes with the largest ram I've ever seen. I've seen plenty of sheep during my hike, but they're content, well-behaved, fluffy, and just generally ignore me. But not this one.

Oh fuck.

And my god. It's big.

The size of a small motherfucking pony.

And the horns . . .

Ian went on a safari after undergrad. He said he was taking a drunken walk back to his tent when a hyena stepped in front of him on the path. Although he was within the camp boundaries, it got in through the sewers to check out the campfire scraps.

"Lizzie, in the PBS shows, they just look like large crazy dogs. But this one—it was the size of a pony. A fucking large pony with teeth."

"Oh god, what'd you do?"

"The wrong thing: I ran. I ran like hell, screaming. But I was the luckiest man in the world because a camp guard just happened to be nearby, fired his gun and chased the fucker off."

"Hey," I say sweetly as if I'm talking to a very large dog and letting it know that I don't pose a threat. "I'm not going to hurt you."

The ram lowers its head, the curved horns facing me. Obviously, my Brontë studies never helped me read a ram's behavior. But this looks pretty darn aggressive.

"Do you want me to get off your path?" I say, hands up in surrender. "Fine. I'm happy to get off your path. I don't mean any harm. I'm just a silly, middle-aged professor who wishes she wore petticoats."

It snorts nastily.

I step gingerly off the path toward a crooked, windswept juniper tree. Unlike in Ian's situation, there's no guard on duty nearby.

The ram kicks its hoof in the mud and runs toward me at full speed.

I scream at the top of my lungs and try to climb the juniper tree. I clamber up the twisted trunk, awful flashbacks to gym class when I tried to climb up the rope and ring the bell before the teacher's timer went off. My leggings snag, my backpack drops in the mud, and I brace for sharp horns in my derriere at any minute.

Hanging on for dear life, I scream. The wind blows hard in my ears. I can't hear anything, but I sure as hell hope someone hears me.

"HELP!!!"

Oh god.

My grip slips, and I slide downward, knotty bark scraping my fingers painfully.

And I fall, screaming all the way down.

But it's a soft landing in someone's arms.

"Dr. Wells?"

I'm staring up into Everett Dane's gorgeous blue eyes.

BLOCKED TEXT FROM AUGUST DANSWORTH:
Hello, Elizabeth. Please pick up. Again, I've been such a nasty bugger, and I'm sorry. You have every right to never want to speak to me again. But I really want to at least talk to you. Once. Pretty please?

Soon I'm nestled in a private booth at the back of a Stanbury pub with Everett, Bella, and Harry. No paparazzi. The three gave the hostess a generous tip to keep quiet about us being here. Still, Bella wears a glam baseball cap, the brim pulled low over her face. Her dressed-down style does little to mask her beauty, with long, black hair cascading in a ponytail down her back and her professionally applied winged liner highlighting her eyes. Both Harry and Everett sport sexy bed head and wrinkled sweatshirts. Even in the pub's low light, I see the makeup sheen on their cheeks. I'd completely forgotten about the publicity shoot. The actors had just wrapped it up and were taking a little stroll themselves when they heard my screams.

Bella and I compare our lower back tattoos. Both are healing nicely.

"We really are like sisters now," she says, smiling.

"Except you're the one with the better eyebrows."

She laughs. Then over pints, we joke about the awkward but serendipitous meeting. My relief outweighs my embarrassment. Thanks to these three, who scared off the ram, I walked away with an intact rear. And now it's time to celebrate our wonderful news. Maybe it's the British accents and long working hours, but despite our almost twenty-year age gap, they all seem more mature and far friendlier than my Willoughby colleagues.

After our meals arrive, Everett asks about Mr. Wells, and Bella suddenly looks mortified.

"I'm so sorry, Lizzie. I haven't told them yet."

Everett and Harry stare at her and then me.

"Philip . . . he passed away a little over two months ago—car accident."

"Oh fuck. That's awful," Harry says softly. "I had no idea."

I press my sore palm against the sticky table surface. "You couldn't have known. I never put anything about it on social media."

"He was so cool," Everett says, staring down into his bitter ale.

"When Bella had that all-day indoor scene to shoot in LA, you know, the bad one where the sheepdog shat all over the set kitchen, we did shots with Mr. Wells at The Varnish. He stopped after two to call home to check on Heathcliff. He was such a bloody good dad. And he couldn't stop talking about you." Everett shakes his head glumly.

"I've never seen another couple as happy as you two," Bella says.

"We were so young when we met. We didn't know anything."

"You know *everything* about love."

"I'm not sure about that . . ." I mutter, moving my fork around the congealing sauce of my black sheep kidney pie.

"No, you did know everything about love. Even the shitty parts," Bella says.

"I'm sorry, but I don't understand."

Everett takes a bite of fried haddock, chewing thoughtfully. "It's the book."

"Definitely," Harry agrees.

Everett continues, "Our agents made us read *Wuthering Heights* as soon as we signed. I thought it would be boring, but it really gets to all the craziness love brings on. Then your book cranked it up a notch."

Bella smirks at the guys. "We three have had some drama—some highs and some really fucking low times. Remember when I sobbed on your shoulder after our news appearance?"

I nod.

"That was one of my lowest points. That was when I learned you can really love someone even though you're so wrong for each other."

She meets eyes with Harry, and he smiles.

"And we've learned loads about ourselves through it all—it took poor Harry here most of a year to come out."

"And they supported the hell out of me," Harry says.

"Even when I threw the mimosa at you in that Rome café that morning you suddenly broke up with me."

Harry grins. "You were blindsided."

"And Everett and I were together pre-Harry and post-Harry."

"But post-Harry was just a rebound," Everett says, raising one eyebrow. Bella smiles as they playfully click their pints.

"And it's been *so fucking awkward* since, but we've been hashing through it all, and we've decided we can be friends. At least we're going to try. We're teasing our love for one another in a different direction. Right now, I'm very happy with my new guy."

"And cheers to him," Everett says, lifting his pint.

This should feel awkward, but I'm giggling.

"Can you tell us about the next book?" Bella asks.

"I haven't started. Any suggestions?"

"Ummm . . ." Bella looks thoughtful. "You could make the story even more about Cathy."

"You know I wanted to title the last one *The Catherine Saga*."

"Do it for this one! Push back if they give you problems," she says excitedly. "What do you think, guys?"

"Oh absolutely!" Harry says as Everett nods.

"No one wants to see my duff face on-screen all the time," Everett says through his Greek-god grin.

"Oh, shut up, you." Bella playfully slaps his arm.

"I'll do it," I say. I've signed the contract already. Given the first book's success, I certainly have more leverage this time around.

"And she gets another happy ending this time. That's non-negotiable," I say smiling as I finish off my pint.

We talk a bit more before karaoke music and dancing starts. The pub is significantly more crowded now than when we first arrived. I'm sure the festival drew people from Yorkshire and beyond. I hear local and Scottish accents in the midst. Pretty soon, as the music starts, we have to practically shout across the table to hear one another.

After the Spice Girls' "Wannabe," Madonna's "Like a Virgin," and Britney Spears's "Toxic," I'm tapping my boot under the table.

Bella wrinkles her nose and orders another pint. "Who *chose* this list?"

Harry groans. "If they're going to go '90s/early 2000s vintage, they can at least throw out some cerebral radical British hits via The Cranberries or Chumbawamba."

Everett mock sings a few lines from "Tubthumping."

Except for our table, everyone seems to be having a great time. Of course, almost everyone on the dance floor is over thirty. Ancient by my youthful movie star friends' standards.

"What's next? *Destiny's Child?*" Everett asks sarcastically as our shots arrive.

I'm suddenly tickled. At least at this moment, I'm cooler than these three.

I down my shot and stand up with a wicked grin. "Sure. Why the fuck not?"

And then, a few minutes later for the first time since 2001, I'm belting out "Survivor" from the small, sticky pub stage, while Bella, Everett, and Harry have joined the older millennial crowd, not caring if anyone recognizes them. They dance, lip-synching and cheering me on from the floor.

WE TAKE A SELFIE AS WE LEAVE THE PUB, AND BELLA hugs me tight before I get in my taxi. On the short ride back to Haworth, I watch stars poking through the night sky's fabric. It's so dark here. My tight cord loosened today. I've put myself through so much—guilt over my feelings for Henry, guilt for blinding myself to August's waywardness. But Bella, Everett, and Harry helped me see that the craggy rock path is fine, and we can come out on the other end wise and even happy.

Philip, a good soul, is safe wherever he is. It's me who's been adrift. I needed this journey to feel secure. I'll always grieve him, but I can lose this rippling fear that our love ended with his death.

THAT EVENING, I TAKE A LONG, HOT BATH, SOAKING MY sore feet and chaffed hands in Epson salt. I call Ms. Fernsby briefly to check in on Heathcliff and then shut my phone off. I settle back in the soapy water, dwelling on my gratitude for what I had with Philip and my good odds for a bright future.

BLOCKED TEXT FROM AUGUST DANSWORTH:
Hello, Elizabeth. Please pick up. I'm dying here. ☹

After cleaning and then locking up the Airbnb, I visit the Brontë Parsonage gift shop to buy some souvenirs. I buy a T-shirt for Heathcliff, "I *am* Heathcliff" (How meta, right?); a Victorian cookbook for Ms. Fernsby; and a pretty copy of *Jane Eyre* for Dad. (He needs to branch out in his reading.) And then I hurry off to catch the bus.

29

It's early evening as I walk up to the row house.

Light shines invitingly through the windows.

I unlock the door, and the warm, caramelized scent of blueberry pie wafts through the parlor. As I remove my mud-crusted boots, Ms. Fernsby's soft laughter rings out from the kitchen. Lucy steps gingerly around Heathcliff's LEGOs and several Nerf gun bullets. A new wooden block Windsor Castle sits half-assembled on the floor surrounded by a pile of wooden soldiers. I smile, thinking about how Heathcliff's been spoiled in my absence.

I might be flying home in three days, but I feel like I'm home now.

Ms. Fernsby rushes through the kitchen doorway, wiping flour on her apron.

"Oh . . . you're back, Lizzie. You look wonderful!" She kisses my cheek lightly.

She leads me into the kitchen, where Dad sits at the island

sipping a brandy snifter while Heathcliff plays on his tablet. Dad looks good. He looks *happy*. His expression changes when he sees me, and I almost cry, because he suddenly looks proud.

"Dad..."

"Hello, Lizzie." He tilts his nose up a bit, as if to see me better through his lenses. "You seem better." A touch of professor-like scrutiny, his voice soft: "Are you?"

"I am."

Ms. Fernsby dabs the corner of her eye before pulling the pie out of the oven. With her cheeks flushed, her energy seems even more vibrant than when I left. It's obvious she and Dad have been enjoying each other's company.

"You're back," Heathcliff says drolly without looking up from his screen, his Batman mask pushed up on his head so his thick blond hair sticks out behind. A brand-new high-powered Batman Nerf gun lies on the table in front of him.

I kiss his head, inhaling his sweaty little boy scent.

"Hey, Lizzie."

"Henry?"

He stands on the bottom step of the staircase just off the kitchen, smiling. I blink a few times to be sure he's really here. He seems out of place in this cozy, frilly London row house. And I don't know what to say. I was hoping to come up with something beautiful and articulate when I got home. I was banking on the plane ride to sort it all out.

He grins. "Seemed like you didn't have enough folks crashing the place, so I needed to fly in."

"You know there's always room for you, Henry," Ms. Fernsby says firmly as she inspects her pie, blueberry syrup and steam oozing out through the slits.

"It's been a good time. I've learned loads about American transcendentalists and Batman."

"I've enjoyed getting to know Philip's friend, Lizzie," Dad

says with formality. "I've learned about South Carolina legal history and the art of fly-fishing."

Heathcliff interrupts, chattering about something on his tablet and shoving the screen forcefully in Dad's face. I hear something about a cat and Mickey Mouse, but I can't focus. I can't take my eyes off Henry, and he looks like he wants to say something.

"Hey, ummm . . . can we chat for a minute, Lizzie?"

"Sure."

As soon as we're in the parlor, Ms. Fernsby soundlessly kicks the kitchen doorstop away to give us some privacy.

I sit on the sofa.

With the curtains shut, we're bathed in semidarkness. The cobblestone street is quiet outside; the little cuckoo clock ticks away rhythmically. With the exception of Henry's modern clothes, my scandalous bare ankles, and a dangerous amount of LEGO, Nerf bullets, and wooden toy soldiers strewn about, we could be in a Rossetti poem. I half expect to hear the clacking of carriage wheels on the stones outside.

"Are you mad?" he asks, sheepishly.

"No."

He exhales. "Whew. Good. You weren't very happy with me the other night when I bared my soul."

"I mean, I was mad—but it was more about me, and I had to figure myself out."

"Did you?"

"I think so. As much as I can. It's been quite a journey . . . in a lot of ways."

"What happened?" He nods at my bandaged palm as he sits down next to me.

"I had a run-in with Yorkshire's largest ram."

"Huh?"

"Long story."

We sit in silence for a few moments. Spoons and dessert plates clatter from the kitchen as Ms. Fernsby dishes out the pie. I hear Dad's measured voice and Heathcliff's insistent demands for soy ice cream. Neither Henry nor I is brave enough to say what we both want to say.

"That Ms. Fernsby," Henry says, chuckling. "She looks like she stepped out of one of those PBS shows you like to watch. I'm never sure whether she's going to bring me a 'biscuit' as they call them over here or accuse me of murdering the rector."

"She's kind of magical. I think she's charmed even Dad."

"I've noticed."

Silence again.

"So . . . someone needs to talk to Miss Mirabel," he says, still evading.

"Ugh."

"If you'd like, I can go."

"No. She's going to be a real pill, but I need to talk to her myself. Or at least I need to talk to her first."

More awkward silence.

Henry clears his throat. "You look good now. Really good. But I was kind of worried about you when we hung up the other night."

"So you flew all the way here to check on me?"

"I guess so, and for another reason . . ." He reddens, rubs his beard.

"What?"

"There was this new exhibit at the Tate Modern I wanted to see."

"Which one?"

"Ummm . . ." He squirms on the cushion beside me. "You know, that newly discovered Shakespeare play. Supposedly, it's even signed by him."

"What? That would be incredible! But it would also be all

over the news." I'm smirking and kind of enjoying this. "Besides, something like that wouldn't be on display at the Tate Modern."

He grins. "Okay, fine. I'm clearly the world's worst damn liar."

He takes a deep breath, exhales. "I came here to tell you I love you."

"You do?" I stutter, my heart pounding.

"I fought it hard. I mean, I'm just coming out of a divorce from a decade-long marriage. And it seemed weird—you were his wife. And I didn't want you or anyone else thinking I was taking advantage of you. Like I said, I wanted to kiss you that evening, and my feelings for you have just grown."

My bandaged hand rests on my knee, so close to him our fingertips almost touch.

"After we talked the other night, it kept gnawing at me: what I wanted—*you*—versus what I thought I was *supposed to want*—anyone but you. I wanted to drop it, to 'move on' and just be your attorney. I went upstate with Bonnie and did a lot of fishing in Philip's favorite spot. I finished *Wuthering Heights*, and dang—those people are nutjobs, tearing up coffin sides so they can decompose with each other, howling at the wind . . ."

"Hey—watch it!" I joke.

He chuckles. "I guess they inspired me to do something nutty like fly all the way here to show you that you're not filling a void. I miss Philip so much it hurts. I'm sad my marriage didn't work out. But I love you apart from all of that. In such a short time, you've challenged me in so many ways. You're just wonderful, Lizzie."

I stare at him stupidly in the semidarkness. I never expected Henry of all people to be so *romantic*.

He blushes. "Come on, say something, Lizzie. I'm *really* stepping out of a limb here . . ."

We jump at a loud knock on the front door.
Flustered, I get up to open it.
"August?"
He's standing in the doorway, disheveled hair, face blanched white in the parlor's dimness. He reeks of scotch. Red streaks ghoulishly from his mouth. Heathcliff would think he's the Joker.
"God, August—are you hurt?"
"What? Oh . . . no . . ." And then as he wipes it—ah, lipstick, not blood—irritation flares up in me from the other night.
"What are you doing here?"
"You never returned my texts."
"That's because I blocked you."
"Gosh, you look bloody ravishing, Elizabeth."
"Why. Are. You. *Here?*"
"I'm truly sorry about the other night . . ."
He glances at Henry. "Who's he?"
"Henry Lawton," Henry says, standing up politely and putting out his hand as he walks toward us.
August ignores the gesture. "Henry? Wait . . . he's the Southern chap you were on the phone with that night after the Jack the Ripper tour."
Henry glances at me quizzically, before it clicks. "Hemmings?"
August sizes Henry up, looking over his rolled-up shirtsleeves and khakis. "Nice accent. It's like you've stepped out of a bloody Tennessee Williams play."
"I think you should leave," I say.
"Can we have some privacy, Elizabeth?"
"No."
"Fine."
Henry shuffles his feet awkwardly beside me.

"Elizabeth, before you disappear forever, I want you to know I've been beastly. It was a lapse in judgment. Her name was Alice. It's over now. I'm just under so much pressure from my publisher, my agent, and then there's the Netflix series. I was telling my therapist today how stressful the success has been. I mean, *Brad Pitt* and I have become such good chaps, and I don't know what to do with all the money in my bank account."

"Do you know what you sound like?" I snap.

Evidently not, because he leans in close enough to kiss me. God, he *is* drunk.

"Whoa! Hey there!" Henry says, stepping forward as I shove August away.

"What are you *thinking*?" I yell.

Suddenly, the kitchen door bursts open.

"Don't worry, Mom! I *got* him. Die, Joker!" Brandishing the high-powered Nerf gun, Heathcliff promptly shoots A.D. Hemmings in the privates.

"*Owwwwwwwwww!!!!!*" August doubles over in pain.

"Heathcliff, what have I told you about shooting that in the house . . . ?" And then Ms. Fernsby freezes in the doorway, one hand clapped over her mouth.

"But he's the Joker, and he was going after Mom, so I shot him in the nuts!"

Henry and I stare at August, tears in his eyes, voice barely audible. "Buggers. I think I'm going to throw up."

"Mr. Dansworth?" Heathcliff narrows his eyes, confused.

Dansworth gives a pathetic little wave to Heathcliff while still doubled over, face twisted in pain.

Dad appears silently behind Ms. Fernsby, taking in the scene.

"Mr. Dansworth was just leaving," I say firmly.

"Come along, Heathie," Ms. Fernsby says, shooing him away. "It's past your bedtime."

"Am I in trouble?"

"No. But your mum can take care of herself."

She leaves, but Dad stands in the doorway with the hint of a smile.

August straightens himself and attempts to regain his composure as he glances back and forth between me and Henry.

"Is it because of *him*?"

"I wouldn't go on another date with you in a million years. But Henry here, he's amazing."

"So, Elizabeth, you're really going to fly back to America with this William bloody Faulkner gent, have lots of babies and eat—" he grimaces "—*grits* every morning?"

Henry smirks, clearly amused.

"We still have to decide about the grits and babies parts, but . . ." I look over at Henry. "Yes, I'm flying back with him."

"Very well, then, I guess that's my cue. Too bad. Elizabeth, you and I—we could have kept dancing; we could have been the literary golden couple, the new Zelda and Scott."

"I prefer happiness."

Henry politely holds the door open.

"Sod the fuck off," August mutters to him as he leaves.

I cross my arms, sighing as Henry bolts the front door.

He turns around with a grin. "Dancing?"

"We danced one night, and it was fun," I admit.

Henry cocks his head.

"Sorry you all had to see that," I say to Dad, still standing in the doorway.

"Was that A.D. Hemmings?" Dad asks. "You didn't tell me *he* was August Dansworth."

"I didn't think you'd know who Hemmings is."

"I've given Gaylord *Blood Oath* so he can read it before the telly series comes out," Ms. Fernsby says proudly, returning to his side.

"Ms. Fernsby, I'm sorry that was so unpleasant."

"Never you mind that. I knew he did something to hurt you. I don't care how handsome he is—he showed up here trying to win you back, and he's smeared up with some trollop's lipstick." She shakes her head, chuckling. "Lizzie, you should *check the tabloids* . . . this feminist is making quite a name for herself roasting him online. Her account is incognito with a clever name—*BluestockingBadass*—and *everyone* wants to know who she is! He ignored it for a while, but it got under his skin the other night and he went off at her, and he was quite sexist. I'm sure a good many women right now want to shoot a Nerf gun at his willy!"

Henry laughs softly from beside me.

"*Ms. Fernsby!!!*" Heathcliff yells from upstairs.

"Oh dear, I promised Heathie we'd have a nice bubble bath and read a story. He's anything but patient."

As Ms. Fernsby hurries upstairs, Dad pushes his glasses up on his nose. He catches my eye and clears his throat. "Good work, Lizzie," he says before letting the kitchen door swing shut to follow Ms. Fernsby.

Alone again, Henry and I stare at one another in the darkness. Moonlight streams in through the damask curtains, highlighting the knots in the polished walnut floorboards. We're standing very close.

"Was he a diversion?"

"I thought he was a fling for a bit. It all started really quickly, but he's a textbook playboy." Tentatively, and then more bravely, I touch Henry's arm. He's broader than Philip. Different. Henry's familiar, known, and yet new to me in *this* way. I need another couple of breaths to remind myself that I do know how to fall in love again, and this isn't betraying Philip.

This—all of it—is okay.

He puts his hand on my cheek, thumb caressing my jawline. And then I pull him into a kiss worthy of any Brontë sister's page. Following the Victorian rule book was a good crutch. But now I need to follow my gut. Nothing can erase my love for Philip, and nothing is wrong with me falling in love with his best friend. Dansworth was the distraction, the side plot that allowed me to explore romance again. That was less intimidating than what I have with Henry—something real and grounded.

The cuckoo clock ticks from the mantelpiece. Heathcliff runs on the floorboards upstairs as Ms. Fernsby draws his bathwater. Lucy scampers into the parlor with us, scattering LEGOs and Nerf bullets.

I push it all to the margins and kiss Henry.

@ADHemmings: *noir-filtered photo of a scotch* Learning that the creative life can be both glorious and lonely. #writerslife

@BluestockingBadass: @ADHemming Awww . . . the Sex God is lonely tonight. Probably wasn't a smart move to insult women everywhere.

@ADHemmings: @BluestockingBadass I told you to sod off, you pernicious woman.

@BluestockingBadass: @ADHemmings I will not be silenced, you pretentious baby.

WE STAY UP LATE INTO THE NIGHT EATING MS. FERNSBY'S blueberry pie. We talk a little about everything: Philip, nutty Mirabel, Ginger's dog, Zoie. He tells me about Zoie's ill-fated encounter with the alligator at Lake Marion, and I pretend I'm hearing the story for the first time. The conversation takes a turn as he tells me how unsuited he and Ginger were to one another.

"Why did you stay?"

He dips his spoon into melting soy ice cream. "We just couldn't ever get on the same page. We tried. Year after year. She was the braver one for leaving."

He rubs his temples wearily. "Once the movers left, I felt a little lost. When she walked out, I asked her what we were supposed to do. She said, *Now we can learn who we really are.*

"And that's what I've been doing these past months—fishing with Bonnie, reflecting on my friendship with Philip. I realize now I knew what it was all along. I should have had the courage ten years ago at my own goddamn reception to see I didn't have it with Ginger."

"And you're sure you know now?"

He laughs, glancing shyly sideways at me. "I've never been one to take risks, and now I'm the guy who'll shell out the money for a red-eye flight to London just to tell a woman I love her. Well, after I tell a really bad lie about going to the Tate Modern."

"A newly discovered Shakespeare play that somehow wasn't all over the news? *Whoa.*"

"Hey, it was the best a non-bookish guy like me could think of."

And then I kiss him again, lightly, happily, our mouths tasting like blueberries.

30

@BellaPatel *selfie with Lizzie, Everett, and Harry*:

Lucky meetup and then dinner with the lovely @LizzieWells. The woman GETS love—the grief, the joys, and all the in-betweens. Dr. Wells—you inspire me.

Henry, Heathcliff, and I relish our last days in London. We take Heathcliff to the Tower, where he wonders why Poison Ivy hasn't stolen the Crown Jewels yet. We stroll down unfamiliar streets to find the best tucked-away pubs, the charming ones with teal painted shutters and window boxes overflowing with ivy and water hyssops. One afternoon, we devour a plate of perfect Scotch eggs. Heathcliff eats two sides of fries, and Henry and I wash the savory sausage crusts down with ale. On our last day, we linger, taking everything slowly. I toss bread to the ducks of St. James Park while Henry shows Heathcliff how to fold the perfect origami paper boat. It sails, tiny and determined, under the hazy late-afternoon sunlight.

We watch Heathcliff kick around a ball with some other children. The joys and challenges and uncertainties of this new chapter play in my head.

"Where is Philip in all this? I mean now that we're together."

"That's a pretty big question, Lizzie. But, well, something in my gut tells me that our happiness honors him. We'll miss him always—nothing's going to change that. I'll always feel the twang in my chest when I'm fishing alone. But he'd want us to be happy and not pine away for him when it's not going to do either of us any good. And I'll keep his memory alive for Heathcliff. I'll tell him so many stories about his dad."

"Thank you, Henry. I'd like that."

I give him a little hug, before Heathcliff's ball rolls over to us. I bend over to pick it up and toss it back to him. My shirt rides up a little in the back.

"Did you get a *tattoo*?" Henry asks.

"I did." I pull my shirt up a bit to let him see it.

"Can I?" he asks.

"Sure."

He gently touches the ink, his fingers calloused against my lower back. "'Whatever our souls are made of, his and mine are the same . . .'" he reads. His thumb lingers a little over the skin, slightly raised and still healing.

"I like it, Lizzie. I really do."

I slip my shirt back in place and take his hand.

THAT EVENING, I SIT ON THE LITTLE BACK PATIO SIPping tea while Ms. Fernsby tends her flowers. I watch her carefully clip the brown stems off her hybrid tea roses, revealing damp green interiors. The air is cool and pleasant; patches of waning sunlight fall on the worn lichen-spotted patio stones.

I tell her about August.

"I assumed it was something along those lines. Insufferable man. And then to come here thinking he could win you back after that. It's my opinion that men like that underneath it all really want women like you. They're just too selfish to give it a go."

Angrily, she sprays herbal repellent on the stems.

"You're much better off with Henry. I can always tell when these things will work out. Lord and Lady Routledge argued to high heaven behind closed doors. And I knew, underneath, even after Mabel's birth that Lord Routledge would never love me. Now, you and Henry—that's another story. I have more than a good feeling that you both will be very happy together."

Through the window, I watch Dad at the kitchen island work on a crossword puzzle. I remember him lonely and lost, making all those lasagnas in our kitchen.

"I see some happiness for you as well, Ms. Fernsby."

She blushes. "Gaylord told me last night he's in no hurry to leave. And I'm glad for that."

IN THE MORNING, I MAKE SURE I'VE PACKED EVERY-thing, peeking under my bedroom chairs, inside the wardrobe. Lucy rolls lazily out of my way as I pull back the bedcovers looking for loose socks. I leave the vibrator in the nightstand drawer. I've heard horror stories from girlfriends about forgetting to take the batteries out and then the darn thing goes off at the airport security checkpoint. I'm still Victorian widow enough to feel mortified at the idea of *that* happening.

Dad knocks softly on the open bedroom door.

"Can I do anything to help?"

"No, I think I have everything."

He leans against the doorframe.

"Did you find what you sought at Haworth?"

"I did."

In my mind's eye, I see Philip at windy Top Withens. He's peaceful. Watching.

I blink away the tears, take a deep breath.

"Dad, it was like walking a labyrinth. I didn't have a destination. But the path changed me and brought me peace."

"I believe you, Lizzie."

As I straighten up the bed, fluffing the pillows, I catch his eye. "Ms. Fernsby says you're not in any hurry to leave."

Dad reddens. He was crazy about Mom. But I've never seen him in the flush of a new romance. It's sweet.

"It doesn't make sense to fly home right now. It's only me there."

"You can stay here as long as you want, Dad."

"We're getting along well."

"It's okay, Dad. It doesn't mean you love Mom any less. You'll always love her."

His lip quivers. In my almost-forty years, I've never seen him cry. He takes off his glasses, dabs the corners of his eyes.

"Thank you, Lizzie."

HENRY, HEATHCLIFF, AND I LEAVE BY MIDMORNING TO make it to Heathrow. It's all hugs and goodbye kisses in the parlor. Ms. Fernsby vigorously embraces me and Henry. I hug Dad before he gives Henry a professional goodbye handshake. Heathcliff tries to hug Lucy, and she hisses, swipes at him with sharp, curved claws. As I whisk Heathcliff out the door, Ms. Fernsby thrusts an enormous bag of dairy-free toffee into his hands, and we're off.

From the last page of *Blood Ties*:

"Your *eye* doctor?" Penny asks through tears.

"I had to tell you," Hall says, packing. "I don't want to

lie to you. At least not anymore. From the start, you knew what I'm like."

A stinging slap. Ouch. He supposed he deserved that.

Her gaze is furious. "Ah . . . so now that you've delivered your Copycat Strangler to Scotland Yard, you've caught your mouse and now you're done with Tintern and with me! We're *over*?"

"I told you, Penny. We've had a good run, and yes, it's over." He zips up the suitcase. "I'm sorry. I can't change who I am."

"No, you can't. But mind me, you've destined yourself to a hard road. I don't know when, but someone sometime will break your bloody heart, and when that happens, it will break *you*."

From *The Heathcliff Saga*:

As she pins the freshly washed bed linens to the clothesline, Nelly glares at Cathy walking home from the moors. She sees how the lass's cheeks are reddened from the wind and Linton's charms.

"You've been out to the cave again, haven't ye?"

Cathy turns her nose up impudently. "And so what if I have?"

Nelly shakes her head, and her sunburned crow's-feet deepen. "You can't be fiddling around with the Fae's powers without paying a price."

"What are you talking about?" Cathy feigns anger, but there's fear in her eyes. "You'd better answer me, Nelly."

"You love both those boys—Linton and Heathcliff. But the ancient powers here won't let Linton keep meddlin' for nothing. Sometime, somehow, they'll come calling for one of you three. And I know, either one of those headstrong boys will sacrifice themselves for you. Even I'll admit, the love between you three is rarer and deeper than what the Fae can conjure. They'll be threatened. Jealous. You can bet on that and mind me they'll come a-calling."

Cathy shakes her head, lip quivering slightly. "You're wrong, Nelly. We have it all under control. Heathcliff and I just need to keep Linton from taking all the magic for himself."

"But it doesn't work that way. You can't control it, and a sacrifice will be required. It might not be for years to come—but it's coming nonetheless."

31

......

Six Years Earlier

I wipe away the breast milk splashed across my laptop keys as I get back to work. At two months old, Heathcliff seems to be settling into a three-to-four-hour feeding schedule. It's 7:00 p.m. now, so perhaps I can cram in three good writing hours before his next session, when I'll likely crash from exhaustion. My at-home desk has never looked so messy. In addition to my laptop, course binders, and committee folders, now I have a breast pump, stained burp cloths, and nipple ointment for my very sore breasts.

"How's it coming?" Philip asks as he walks into the den with a hot mug of tea. I hear the repetitive music of Heathcliff's swing from the nursery.

"Thanks," I say as he gently sets the cup in front of me. Steam and the warm, tart scent hit my nose. Elderberry. One of my favorite flavors when I'm trying to focus.

"Good." I push my blue-light glasses up on my nose. "It's coming along. I'm twenty thousand words in, and it's basically

Wuthering Heights with magic. There's an enchanted cave and lots of teen angst. Just tell me this isn't a complete waste of time."

"You want to do it, right?"

"It's why I'm sitting here keeping my fanny at my desk instead of sleeping."

"Well, there you go. I've never seen you work on committee meeting notes in your spare time just because you *like* doing it. I've never seen you review a journal article because you *like* doing it. I haven't seen you this motivated about a project in a very long time. I support you and want to do whatever I can to help you along."

This is another moment where I feel how much he loves me and how very lucky I am.

"You really mean that?"

"I do." He leans down, kissing my temple lightly. "Now write."

Present

FIVE DAYS LATER, HENRY AND I ARE ON OUR WAY TO THE Azalea Dream.

I tried kindly to reach out to Mirabel to meet. But she refused, responding only with three more lawsuit text threats in slightly different wording. After much debate and some surprising twists in the case, Henry and I developed a plan to talk to Mirabel today because we know she'll be home. She's hosting a Methodist Women's League fundraiser in her front yard. I feel guilty crashing her party, but this is important. I'd prefer not to think of my presence as an ambush, but rather a loving intervention.

Except in my dreams, I haven't been to the property since

Philip's death. Bittersweet memories surface, like sand stirred up at the bottom of a pond. As we ease off of I-95 South and deeper into the Low Country, we pass through black water swamps bordered by tupelos and weeping willows, algae and lily pads blanketing the surfaces. I still see toddler Heathcliff bouncing gently from the carrier on Philip's back during our weekend hikes. As a child, Philip roamed these woods and canoed through the lakes and swamps. He knew the location of the rarest bald cypresses, every tucked-away mossy chapel ruin. I can never be here without feeling Philip close by.

"We have the plan down?" Henry asks as he pulls into the driveway.

"Yes. I handle Mirabel while you take care of your side of things."

"Sounds good. You've got the sharper end of the stick, though."

We drive up Mirabel's long driveway shadowed by towering pines and lined by sturdy azalea bushes. The house and lawn come into view.

It looks like the event just started. Two large white tents stand in the middle of the lawn sheltering long, linen-draped tables with platters of shrimp on ice, creamy grits, and collard greens. A slew of well-dressed servers stroll about with trays of champagne flutes.

"Fuck. This isn't going to be pleasant."

"Ahhh . . . you've got this," Henry says.

He's right. But still—it's *Mirabel*. She pointed an arrow at me in my dream.

He lets me out of the car, tells me he'll return soon, and heads back down the driveway.

I take a deep breath, straightening my peach eyelet sundress and gold chain necklace. My bare legs feel strange and airy after wearing black tights and leggings all summer. My necklaces and the bird urn are safely tucked away in my jewelry box at home, and I'm (gradually) feeling fine about not having them with me all the time.

The Azalea Dream is never as beautiful as it is at this time of late summer, when the surrounding property is warm and dreamlike; a pink sunset edges the tops of the pines. Mirabel stands at the corner of the lawn, champagne flute in hand. Summerville's finest-dressed Methodist women surround her. Mirabel wears red. And when Mirabel Wells wears red, she looks like a Fury. She's like Jessica Lange ready for a scene. It's a clingy dress, and she's draped a pearl-colored shawl around her arms. Her red lipstick matches the dress.

She sees me approaching, and her back stiffens, eyes narrow.

A server places a champagne flute in my hand. Although I probably need a drink to calm my nerves, my stomach roils, and I just set it on a nearby table without having so much as a sip.

"What the *hell* are *you* doing here?" Mirabel hisses.

"Mirabel," I say gently. "This isn't an attack. But I'm not letting this go."

"There's *nothing* to let go."

"You know that's not true."

Mirabel's nostrils flare.

"No one's judging you. Nobody ever would—even and *especially* Philip. It was *years* ago. But you have to tell me what happened, and I need to know about that night when Philip came here."

Tears shine in her wide blue eyes.

"Please," I beg in a whisper. "It will help all of us if you do."

"You look *gorgeous*, Mirabel," Deanna Willa, wife of Orangeburg Methodist's rector, says as she passes us. "Why, you'd think you were a girl of thirty from your figure."

"Thank you." Mirabel beams, dabbing the corner of her eye as she smiles. "It's Jesus, high protein, and exercise."

"I'd love to know more about it . . . I just bought these protein shakes from Julia Barnwell, and they're not working . . ."

"Unfortunately, Miss Deanna, I have a can't-wait business meeting with my daughter-in-law. I'll be back out soon, and we'll talk about some quality shakes and diet prayers. As you know, Jesus takes care of everything. Now, please enjoy the grits bar."

Mirabel leads me up the front steps, past Ted and his friends. They all lounge in the nice white porch chairs with tumblers of Ted's favorite bourbon. Ted's telling everyone about what he ordered, course by course, from a new Savannah restaurant the week before. Deanna Willa's husband has already fallen asleep, tumbler tipping precariously in his right hand. Ted pauses when he sees us, blinks, and then continues describing the restaurant's lemon meringue pie.

I follow Mirabel through the front hall, along the waxed wood floors, past the oriental vases, the portraits lining the wall beside me.

She takes me into the parlor, methodically shutting the glass French doors.

The parlor is Mirabel's favorite room for retreat. A large dark-hued oil painting depicting a crystal bowl of floating rose petals hangs over the mantelpiece while two antique painted china spaniels flank the little fireplace hearth; heavy, bird-patterned drapes frame the windows from floor to ceiling. A mahogany glass door bookcase displays rare editions of novels collected by the Wells family over the years, and a mid-century rolling bar cart sits invitingly in the corner. Everything in the Azalea Dream showcases Ted's old money and Mirabel's enjoyment of it, and this beautiful room sits tucked away at the back of the grand house like a secret. I wonder how many times Mirabel sat in here contemplating her own.

I sink into the sofa while Mirabel perches herself on the

ottoman, legs crossed, arms folded across her chest. Her bracelets jangle as she tugs the shawl up around her shoulders.

"Alright. Here we are, Lizzie. Now, what do you want?"

"The truth. That's all, Mirabel."

She says nothing. She just kicks her crossed right leg vigorously, taupe heel moving up and down, up and down.

"Philip wanted the truth too."

Mirabel's lips tighten, then grimace. Her face crumbles, and I ache for the pain she keeps bottled up inside.

"I never planned on telling him. Why in the world would he need to know?"

She stares out the window at her groundhog-free rows of azalea bushes. I don't say anything, but just let her question hang in the air. For all her flaws, Mirabel is whip-smart. She recognizes underneath her embarrassment that Philip wanted and needed to know the truth for his own well-being. She owed him that.

She makes an angry sound in her throat like she's going to protest one more time.

Then she sighs, sadly, wearily.

"Since you're dead set on exposing my shame, I suppose I'll start from the beginning. I never really loved Ted. His family had old money, and my daddy worked at the Summerville post office. We managed. But every time we'd run errands in Charleston, and I'd see those Ashley Hall debutantes walk around in their pretty dresses, I'd go green with envy. I knew if I wanted wealth, I'd have to marry it. I wanted the Wells name and money, so I threw myself in Ted's path. Over the years, we've gotten along fine, but there wasn't a spark of chemistry between us."

On silent, my phone lights up with a text from Henry.

"As you probably know by now, in the early '80s, the mayor's wife, Lila Mae, and I became quick friends. We shared a passion for gardening and started that little downtown shop. It did well for a while. But then I started to get to know Frank. I felt things I'd never felt before, and he did too. Ted never looked at me like Frank did. We behaved ourselves for a good while. But then there was that Grits Festival parade."

She pauses, her gaze still out the window, like she's forgotten all about me. She's back in that summer of 1982. My phone lights up again, this time with a photo from the babysitter back home of Heathcliff at the playground. But I don't dare touch it. I can't risk anything keeping Mirabel from saying what she's about to say. I know if I don't keep her talking or if we get interrupted, I'll never hear the story.

"It was a hot afternoon, so goddamn hot we had to spread towels out on our leather car seats to protect our legs; the little garden lizards swarmed into all our houses to escape the heat, hiding in our houseplants and curtain folds. After the festival, important Summerville folk hung out in the Duboses' yard. Mayor Frank was known back then for his fine wraparound porch and elegant garden parties. There were backyard kiddie pools and champagne pops. Then Frank brought out an antique tray of his signature gin fizzes. While Lila Mae took the guests through her gardens, intent on showing off her newly imported Lady Banks's roses, Frank brought me inside. Between the heat and the drinks, I think we both knew what was going to happen."

She plucks a piece of lint off her dress.

"Don't *judge* me, Lizzie."

"I'm not . . ."

"I never had what you and Philip had. I was *starved* that afternoon. I made my choice of what I wanted out of marriage, but it felt good to let myself go. Just that once. Lila Mae suspected something happened right away. Women know these things. Tensions brewed between us at the garden shop, and then everything came to a head a month later when she called me a *cheap whore* at the grocery store. Mr. *Lawton*, intent on embarrassing me to no end, dredged up that awful mug shot. It pains me to this day to know it still exists.

"Soon after the arrest, I threw up, and my doctor confirmed what I'd already suspected. I'm not sure why I told Frank. He was the first person I called in a panic. I confessed to Ted too, but he didn't care." Mirabel wrinkles her nose. "If anything, he seemed relieved that another man gave me what he couldn't—not that he *tried* that often. Ted and I sat down with Lila Mae and Frank to discuss the matter. The closing of the garden shop, the arrest—we were embarrassing ourselves. It was best to part ways. But not before Frank set up that trust, determined to do something for the child."

Outside, a blue jay perches on the garden sundial, flapping its wings once before swooping off.

Mirabel's gaze follows the bird. Her right leg has stopped rocking. She sighs. She's fought hard to keep her secret under tight wraps. Maybe she's seeing that the world won't collapse if she lets it out. Her gardens will still bloom. She'll still host the Methodist Women's League fundraisers. She'll still be able to keep Ted's house nice for him.

"And Philip?"

"I don't want to talk about this."

"Please . . ."

She eyes me angrily, tightening her lips.

"One afternoon, when he stopped by for lunch on his way back from court in Charleston, I asked him to help me and Ted move my cherrywood chifforobe down from the attic. While up there, he found a box of old photos and letters between me and Lila Mae, and me and Frank. You're probably wondering why I kept them all. I suppose I was perversely nostalgic for the one time in my adult life when a handsome man desired me. Philip didn't say anything about finding them, but he took them home to read. Always the lawyer, he wanted to try to understand all the facts before confronting me. Two weeks later, he came over that night to talk about it. At first I lied, and this made him angry. He said he had the letters. We had a row and I accused him of trying to shame me." She wipes a tear away. "We'd never argued like that. He kept saying, 'I just want the truth, Mama, and I want to hear it from you.' I told him he had it and yelled at him to get the hell out of my house. Then . . ."

She breaks down in tears.

Moved, I remember what Henry said about how underneath everything, most people have a beating heart.

I move to the ottoman to sit beside her. I hesitate, then gently place my hand between her heaving shoulder blades. In fifteen years, I don't think I've ever touched her, not even for a holiday hug. It's unfortunate now that I think about it. She leans into me as she sobs, broken and vulnerable.

"Oh, Lizzie . . . help me . . . If I had just told him everything like I told you just now, he wouldn't have left so mad."

"It's okay, Mirabel. It's all okay," I whisper into her hair. "Nobody cares about a comedy of errors that happened forty years ago. The accident that night wasn't your fault. Just forget that. It was raining. It was dark. You know how many deer dart across that highway at night. A million things could have happened to make Philip's car slide off the road. It *wasn't your fault*."

She sits up, wiping her eyes with her fingers.

"Do you hear me?" I repeat, making her look at me. "It. Wasn't. Your. Fault."

She nods.

"And every time it crosses your mind, I'll tell you this again and again and again because it's the truth."

She puts her hand on my cheek. "You'll do that?"

"I will."

She nods. The shawl has slipped off her shoulders, and her

mascara has streaked. She straightens, smooths her hair, and opens a little drawer from a side table. She pulls out a handkerchief, a hand mirror, and tube of lipstick. She cleans up as I try not to think about how many times she's fallen apart and reassembled herself in this parlor over the years.

She purses her lips in the little mirror and fluffs her hair, her old steely expression returning. "Thank you, Lizzie. I never thought I'd look to you for help."

"Thanks?"

I stare at my phone. Henry's on standby. My heartbeat picks up and my palms sweat. Will there ever be a good time to do what we're about to do?

"These goddamn heels are killing me, and I think I need a proper drink before going out to my fundraiser again. I make a killer bourbon with pressed basil. How about one?"

"Sure." I watch my phone nervously, debating the timing for our plan.

She pulls off her heels, cracking her peach painted toes against the oriental rug before walking over to the bar cart.

Soon I'm sipping the best mixed drink I've ever had.

She takes a long swallow. "That's real good. You know, I made one of these for Philip when he graduated from the College of Charleston. We sat on the front porch sipping them. He told me no one made them like I did."

"He told me that too. In fact, he said we shouldn't even try to make one because ours couldn't top yours. We never even kept basil in our cocktail supplies."

She smiles. "He was a good son."

Between the drink and a good memory, she seems more relaxed. But I'm not. Beads of sweat pop out on my forehead. There's never going to be a perfect time.

Best to pull the Band-Aid off.

I text Henry: **Come on in.**

Soon Henry and Frank Dubose show up at the French doors.

Mirabel gasps, her drink's cubes rattling. Henry opens the door, letting Frank walk in first.

"It's been a minute, Mirabel."

My chest constricts at his voice. He sounds like Philip. He *looks* like Philip, and I see how my husband would have aged if we'd had the chance to grow old together. Endearing sunspots from years in the Carolina sun stand out around his warm blue eyes; Frank's sandy blond hair is fading in color but still thick. Although he's close to seventy, he's still a handsome man.

"Lizzie," he says, nodding politely, as if we've met before.

"Will someone tell me what the hell is going on?" Mirabel snaps.

"Now, please listen, Ms. Wells. This isn't an ambush. Frank here has some things to say," Henry says gently, as he and Frank sit on the couch.

Mirabel sets her tumbler down on a porcelain coaster a tad hard, splashing some bourbon on the coffee table.

"Look, Mirabel, I know we had an arrangement years ago to all go our separate ways. But I've sure as hell never felt good about it. I've had a lot of sleepless nights, and I've thought of my son every day. You've done a good job with him. Law school, a good career, a successful wife. I just couldn't be prouder."

Mirabel's lips tighten. "What's your point, Frank?"

"My point is that it's time to let sleeping dogs lie."

"And *Lila Mae*?"

He chuckles. "Oh, she was raging mad. She made me sleep on the couch for a full three months. But if it makes you feel any better, at the time we were in a bit of a rough patch ourselves. I'd just found out she'd been carrying on with Senator McCullom."

Henry's eyes widen as he meets mine. I shrug at him discreetly.

"The short fella who looks like Elmer Fudd?" Mirabel asks.

"The one and only."

"She could have done better than him." Mirabel picks up her drink and takes a long sip.

"She sure could have. And imagine how *I* felt—cuckolded by a man like him." Frank laughs. "My point is, over the years, my wife and I have had our good and bad times, but especially recently, we've both softened. She cried with me when we heard about Philip's death. And, Lizzie, I came to that funeral, watching from farther back in the graveyard. I felt just sick losing a son I never knew. When Henry started contacting us, we didn't know what to do. Lila Mae and I clammed up. It took us a minute to open a door we've kept shut for years. We were cowards. Then we realized it's just plain silliness to keep it up."

"What do you want?" Mirabel asks.

"Lila Mae and I want to let it all go. And—" he looks at me "—Lizzie, we'd like to meet our grandson."

32

@ADHemmings *noir-filtered selfie of August Dansworth in a suit with new eyeglasses*:

Almost finished with *Blood Offspring*. Cleaned up for a rare night out. Thoughts on the new specs? #lonelywriterlife

@BluestockingBadass: @ADHemmings Watch out, ladies, the Sex God emerges from his #writersmancave

The next evening, I'm over at Henry's house stirring up coleslaw in the kitchen.

Through the window over the sink, I watch Henry putting chicken thighs on the grill while Lila Mae Dubose talks to him, glass of Chardonnay in hand. Frank throws a ball back and forth with Heathcliff. The game, though, has become more of a race between Heathcliff and Bonnie over who can get to the ball first. Heathcliff's having a blast.

I should probably consider getting him a dog.

He'd love it.

Patrick calls.

"Hey!" I balance the cell phone between my cheek and shoulder as I take a bite of the coleslaw, determining it needs more sauce.

Patrick and I make small talk about my trip. I don't tell him I went to Haworth. I don't tell him I snogged A.D. Hemmings. Maybe I will at some point. It just feels too personal now.

"So . . . you know the first faculty meeting is coming up next week . . ."

"Yep."

"Well, I hate to bother you about this, but Bill Rhodes is on my case. He says he still needs the *Fiscal Advisory Report* data for the last academic year. He says his twenty-five reminder letters are still lying unopened in front of your office. I told him your husband just died, and he can kiss my ass."

"Thanks for the heads-up. I'm resuming email again next week at 9:00 a.m. on the morning I return to campus. Everyone will have the report by 9:30 a.m."

Patrick chuckles. "He wanted it by five o'clock tonight, but he can wait."

"He'll have to."

"Are you better?"

"In a million ways. You don't have to worry about anymore class meltdowns."

"I'm glad you're better. You know Elaine and I have been thinking about you a lot. We still can't believe Philip's gone."

"Me neither." I stop myself, take a breath.

Henry comes in, setting the platter of barbecue chicken on the kitchen counter. *It's Patrick* . . . I mouth, rinsing slaw sauce off my fingers. Henry pours me a large glass of wine, smiles meaningfully and takes the bowl of chilled fruit back outside to the patio table by the crackers and vegan cheese plate. Apparently, Frank, too, is lactose intolerant.

"I'll let you go," Patrick says. "But before you step back into the arena, you need to know that Bill and Evie's ongoing war is at a take-no-prisoners level. More xeroxed letters keep ending up in our mailboxes. We still have no idea who's doing it, but I'll bet anything it's the new junior faculty hire in Mathematics, Betsy Byers. Dr. Caldwell gave her such an awful time at her pre-tenure review! Anyway, details of the Caldwell-Rhodes affair continue to leak, and all I can say is *ewww*."

"Well, it explains why they hate each other."

"It's not really something we need to worry too much about. But between the humiliation and humanities budget cuts, tensions could be high next week. And there's good old-fashioned jealousy. I emailed everyone the news that you've signed another movie deal. Whatever happens, just remember, I'll have your back."

"I know you will, Patrick."

After we hang up, I put the large serving spoon in the coleslaw bowl. Henry helps Heathcliff wash his hands before dinner. I look out the kitchen sink window at the back deck patio table, citronella candles glowing in the center. Bonnie sniffs around Henry's rows of box gardens. Frank and Lila Mae sit at the patio table, her hand in his. I take a moment and then let out a long breath of gratitude.

After loss, there can still be an evening like this.

AFTER LILA MAE AND FRANK SAY GOODBYE, HEADING back to Charleston, we put on a movie for Heathcliff and return to the screened porch. I settle back on one of the painted white wicker cushioned sofas; Henry sits beside me. Bonnie lies in a deep sleep at our feet, wiped after chasing Heathcliff all evening. The sky sprawls pink beyond the backyard's pine trees.

Autumn coolness is already starting in the Midwest, but summer's warmth continues, stubborn and thick, here in the South. I've lived here for almost twenty years, and I always welcome this late-summer heat like a warm blanket.

"Are you ready to go back to all the work drama?" Henry asks.

"I suppose I'm as ready as I'll ever be. You probably think I'm crazy for staying at Willoughby."

"Maybe a little. Why not just write?"

I think of Kayla, all the bright students in and out of my office every day. I think of Patrick and how we've become such good friends over the years. I think of how happy I am when I teach literature. It all outweighs the Brad McGregors and Bill Rhodes and budget cuts.

"I just really love teaching."

Evening cicadas hum beyond the screens. Bonnie stretches with a giant yawn.

I lean into him, his shoulder warm against my cheek.

"Henry, why do you think people act the way they do? My colleagues? Mirabel keeping a secret all those years?"

He sighs, stretches his arm out behind me, and strokes my hair.

"I don't need to tell you, Lizzie, that people just aren't rational. My clients dig themselves into the biggest shitholes out of greed, fear, and shame. And it's the most put-together ones who live in upscale properties with pretentious names like *The Azalea Dream* who are the darn nuttiest. But that's just my two cents."

"You may be onto something. I think I've learned a thing or two about that in my field as well. As you've pointed out, no one acts sane in the books I teach."

He grins. "Speaking of books, are you going to watch *Blood Oath* when it comes out?"

I groan. "Please don't tell me you're into the series."

"I've already preordered *Blood Offspring*—you know, where supposedly he falls for a widow and finds out he has the kid from his brief time with Penny."

"Ha. Wait. No, really. Have you?"

"I sure have. This Hemmings guy came to your house drunk, ready to beg for you back. The guy'll base a character off you."

"Funny. He did say he'll have a widow character in his next book and Inspector Hall would be snogging her by the third chapter."

"Well, there you go."

I laugh. "I'm a bit worried about what that would look like—peculiar youngish widow who carries her husband's ashes in a bird urn. He'll probably make me a serial killer."

33

....

That weekend, Chloe's wife, Abby, has a regional pottery conference in Greenville, and Chloe invites me to go hiking with her in nearby Jones Gap State Park. Henry keeps Heathcliff for the day, promising him a fun, jam-packed schedule, including IHOP pancakes and the zoo. With the day to myself, I take my time driving north. I sip a large iced coffee as I meander along winding back highways, admiring the hillier terrain and the mountains rising in the distance.

Philip and I used to love this area.

With Asher strapped to her chest in a baby carrier, Chloe and I follow a rocky trail past several waterfalls. Sunlight breaks through the treetops, falling in rainbow streaks across the rushing Saluda River. We're on the cusp of autumn, only weeks away from when the surrounding hemlocks, sweet gums, and maples burst out in warm foliage. When that time comes, hopefully I'll be back up here with Henry and Heathcliff. We'll pick apples and buy heirloom pumpkins and cider from roadside stands.

As we hike, I tell Chloe every detail about London: about taking the gummy before the Jack the Ripper tour and attending a séance where Philip was a no-show. I tell her about what happened with August, how it hurt and confused me, and how I took the side trip to Haworth to sort it all out. It all spills out—not just what happened, but the layers of fear driving my journey.

"I tried to walk the labyrinth, to follow the path without agenda. I thought it would be more pleasant, like walking around in your garden labyrinth on the church grounds. But it was dark and awful at times. More like a maze."

She looks sideways at me as she helps me over a log, her expression full of sympathy.

"I was terrified I'd forget I loved Philip."

"I should have warned you that the path isn't always peaceful."

After about another mile, Asher starts crying, so we stop for a snack break on a shady rocky ledge. While I unpeel my banana, Chloe takes Asher out of the carrier to feed him a bottle.

"I hope you've realized you'll never stop loving Philip."

"I have. It's just been hard to sort through all the feelings—loving someone else, feeling happiness, but also missing Philip every single fucking day."

Asher sucks the bottle greedily. Chloe watches him, a breeze blowing a spiraling dark curl across her forehead.

"You know, Lizzie, I have to share with you my favorite word in the world. It's a Portuguese one with no solid English translation. *Saudade*. The word refers to a deep longing for something gone or for someone you love who's passed away. You ache for them and for the joy they brought you. It's bittersweet, bundling the sadness and happiness of love together."

Chloe reaches across Asher's head and gently pokes my sternum. "You'll feel the ache for Philip right there always. It's not depression or ruin. It's just the part of you that knots and swells because it's only filled by him. And that's okay to keep feeling it. You're still going to feel love and happiness, but you'll have to be alright with the little ache too. Just be at peace with that."

I'm wiping tears away.

As she brings Asher up to her shoulder, gently patting his back to make him burp, she smiles at me warmly. "I love you, Lizzie. So many people do."

After she straps Asher back in, and we start to head back from the trail, she smiles sideways at me, mischievous.

"On a lighter note, I have a little confession for you."

"Go for it."

"It wasn't very priestly of me, but I just couldn't help myself. I got so mad at Chadwick Hall's womanizing, I started my own feminist troll account against Hemmings—BluestockingBadass."

"BluestockingBadass was *you*?"

"Guilty." She smiles sheepishly. "I had such a love-hate relationship with the books—I mean, I couldn't put them down, but I also just *hate* the misogyny. The silly account made me feel like a more responsible reader. I've deactivated it, because, well—it wasn't nice. Jesus wouldn't have done it. But I don't feel so bad about it now that I know how he treated you. So there it is. I might be a priest, but I'm still human. Oh, Lizzie, do you think I'm awful?"

I smile. "I think you're awesome."

TWO DAYS LATER, MIRABEL AND I MEET IN SUMMERville for lunch at her favorite downtown tearoom.

It's not the typical place I would go for a meal. In addition to tea and tiny triangle cucumber sandwiches on antique plates, lunch comes with doll-size sides of potato salad flavored with hard parsley sprigs and cracked pepper. It's overpriced, and unsatisfying, but Mirabel says it's the best luncheon spot on this side of the Ashley River. I'll probably stop at a drive-through on my way home.

As Mirabel pokes at her salad with her little silver fork, one of her cap sleeves slips away to reveal a nicotine patch. She looks up at me sharply.

"Lizzie, I've been smoking cigarettes on the sly for years."

"I had no idea."

"Nobody did. It's a bad habit, but mighty helpful when my skin crawls. I'm sure as hell tired, though, of asking Dr. Jenkins to keep whitening my teeth year after year. And as much as I don't like it, I'm a woman of a certain age. It's time for me to quit."

I take a sip of hot, weak green tea.

We make small talk, about how Heathcliff's doing now that school has started again, her four new azalea bushes, and her manicurist quitting suddenly. It's hard to bury the tensions and threats of these past months. Conversation doesn't exactly come easily, but we're trying.

"I suppose Frank and Lila Mae are back in the picture now," she says rather abruptly.

"They are. They're really enjoying Heathcliff."

"Well, they should. He's a sweet boy." She dabs the corner of her eye before lightly touching the patch. "Jesus. I could use a goddamn cigarette."

I reach across the table, laying my hand across hers.

She sniffs, blinking away tears. "This is a hard thing I'm about to say, so listen up, Lizzie, because I'm going to say it once. I hated you for a good while. Like, really hated you. But thank you for doing what you did. In the end, it was the right thing to do."

34

I'd just picked up my burger on the way back from lunch with Mirabel, enjoying the satisfying flavor of meat and mayonnaise, when Sarah calls.

"Your director bailed."

"What?"

"Yes, he pulled out. There's a more lucrative sci-fi film he wants. You'll still get to keep the first part of the option money, but this isn't good."

"What do we do?" I ask, setting my burger down in my lap and taking a long sip of Diet Coke.

"I'm going to make some calls. Our agency knows another director who *might* be open to the project. Just give me some time. But keep your phone on. I might need you to make a quick trip to New York."

TWO DAYS LATER, I'M SITTING IN SARAH'S AGENCY OFfice getting ready to meet virtually with *The Catherine Saga* director and present my fleshed-out book proposal for approval. I've only been to New York City one other time, and I'm always amazed at how sleek Sarah's world is. The long conference table takes up most of the room with floor-to-ceiling windows. She has a snappily dressed assistant named Rory who brings her shiny pens and foamy cappuccinos. I'm sure he doesn't blare Fox News segments from his desk.

Sarah sits beside me as she reads my latest ten-page proposal. She taps her pen and bites her lower lip thoughtfully. Mostly she nods and smiles at various moments. It's only when she gets to the end that she pauses, tightens her mouth, and gives a long "Hmmm . . ."

"Well?"

She pats her elegant French knot at the back of her head and then taps the last sheet. "For the most part, I love it. You've spun quite the classic teen love triangle in the vein of *Twilight* or *Vampire Diaries*. It's sexy, intoxicating, and depending on the decade or circumstance in the saga, she's with Heathcliff or Linton. The passion and tensions and twists are really brilliant. I love the general plot of battles and dark magic. But . . ." She drums the page again. "It's this ending that bothers me. Remember, it was supposed to be *happy*."

"But it is."

She raises a microbladed eyebrow.

"I mean, it's happy-ish. Certainly not a downer. I wanted to write an authentic happy ending."

"In terms of hills to die on, how strongly do you feel about this ending?"

"Ten out of ten."

"Well, Sophie's calling in a minute, and if she's not on board, you and I are going to talk. You know I always respect your artistic wishes, Lizzie, but there's a lot of money riding on this."

"I understand."

Soon we have the director, Sophie Kendrick, pop up on the large conference screen. I was thrilled to hear she might be taking over the project. I'd been hoping for a female director on this one. Kendrick is sitting in her large, sunny Los Angeles office. After introductions, Sarah dives into our pitch. Sophie listens carefully, but her expression is difficult to read, particularly through the monitor glare on her large glasses.

"The ending is interesting," she says after a brief pause.

Sarah holds her breath next to me.

"Describe it again please . . ."

Sarah reads it again.

"Certainly not the potboiler we expected."

"We're open to amending . . ." Sarah starts.

"No. I won't hear of it." Sophie leans back in her chair and removes her glasses thoughtfully. "I've been wanting to edge my work more into the nuanced and bittersweet. This ending is wise and unexpected. Beautiful at all levels."

"Then we're keeping it!" Sarah exclaims happily, tapping my knee under the table.

"Absolutely we're keeping it. Count me in! And good work, Lizzie. I'm looking forward to working on this project with you."

JUST BEFORE I BOARD MY PLANE BACK TO SOUTH CAROLina, my phone dings.

Tyler: Hi, beautiful friend! Missing you already. I'll be back in the States next year, and I've booked some gigs. I'm in Charleston in April. Would love to catch up and I'd love it even more if you joined me onstage. *GIF of a pleading kitten with big eyes*

Me: Fuck yes! I wouldn't miss an onstage opportunity with you for the world!

I scroll down, finding that I missed an earlier text from Henry. It's a phone pic of the ostrich fan.

Henry: Hey, Lizzie, so I was putting away the suitcases and this fell out of a zipper. I'm kind of scratching my head . . .

Me: Getting ready to board, but what can I say, I'm a burlesque dancer on the side.

Henry: LOL Love you, and have a safe flight

I smile into my phone. Too bad I don't have any pics from Fin de Siècle. Maybe Henry can come out to Charleston next Spring. I'm not afraid of that side of me anymore. He should see it, and he can meet Tyler.

35

The next week, I return to campus.

I pull up to the line of faculty spaces, honking as I cut off Brad McGregor's red BMW a second before he takes my space. I smile and he scowls before hitting the accelerator and heading down the row to look for another reserved space. Patrick told me he didn't pass the seminar, and Dean McGregor is not happy.

Gathering my satchel and jacket, I lock my car and intuitively reach for the jet necklace around my throat. I still do this fairly often since getting back from England. But now I'm wearing another necklace. Today, it's a string of pearls Philip gave me on our thirteenth anniversary. We'd been in Indiana supporting Mom after her breast cancer diagnosis. I'd been sick with worry and had forgotten our anniversary date. But that night, just before we went to sleep in my childhood bedroom under my hideous 1980s-era pink canopy, Philip clasped it around my neck. I'd burst into tears, touched that, amid everything going on, he'd remembered.

"You're back!" Sandra exclaims as she takes her bifocals off and turns down the volume on her MAGA podcast. From the computer, I see she's finalizing the course schedules. I thank my lucky stars that Patrick assured me Brad won't end up in any of my fall classes.

Her gaze skims down my emerald-green blouse, capris, and cranberry flats. "You look wonderful. You're wearing colors again!"

"I am, Sandra."

She tells me she's been putting my campus letters outside my office door and then I turn the corner.

Oh dear.

A laundry basket of envelopes sits outside my office. I count Bill Rhodes's twenty five letters reminding me about the *Fiscal Advisory Report*. There are fifteen from Evie Caldwell demanding I change item nine in the report or her department will censor the English department. (*Censor?* Jeez. I don't even remember what that means in university policies.) I stop reading at the tenth student letter complaining about Patrick taking over my class. I unlock my office door and put all the letters into the shredder.

Then I sit at my desk. Strangely, in spite of the laundry basket, it feels good to be back. I grouse about my job, but I love teaching. I remember again how lucky I am to get paid to talk to students about my favorite books.

I stare at the degrees hanging above my desk and my disorderly stacks of committee notes to be filed. I pick up the framed picture of Philip and me on our wedding day. Taking a deep breath, I refocus, determined to teach, write and learn. I will not lose any more chunks of my soul to campus politics and administrative squabbles. Or to emotional vampires like Bill Rhodes.

After pouring a mug of coffee, I log into my Willoughby College campus account. I announce my return to email and send out my report. Then I open the faculty meeting's agenda.

Drat . . . I'm up first.

I tap my fingers lightly on my cup.

I have one more letter to write.

PATRICK AND I WALK INTO THE PACKED FACULTY MEETing. Throughout the lecture hall, conversations buzz about anticipated budget cuts and the latest leaked Rhodes-Caldwell letters. In this batch, Rhodes fantasized about her coming into his office wearing nothing but a toga and feeding him grapes. Gross. Soon, though, we retreat to our department teams and draw swords.

The administration sits at the front ready to hear faculty reports. Dean McGregor stiffens when he sees me; he leans over to whisper in the provost's ear as she glances in my direction and nods coolly. President Hummel sits beside them in her power suit and splashy Jimmy Choos. With news of the second book and upcoming film, she offered me a course reduction and generous raise over the phone yesterday. Of course, I took it. The money will be nice, and I'll have more time to work on the book. Still, I'm fully braced for more jealous colleagues to want my blood.

Betsy Byers projects the meeting agenda on the screen and records notes from the corner. Although she seems shy behind her curly hair and glasses, I second Patrick's guess that she's the leaker. It's always the quiet ones . . .

Soon President Hummel stands and calls for the meeting to begin. All eyes are on me as I open my letter.

"In this moment, I'd like to share something more meaningful than the *Fiscal Advisory Report*. All of us, myself included, have a history of arguing about low-stakes issues. Arguing is now the fabric of our campus existence. I've spent time far away this summer, and with my journey came perspective. You all know what happened to my husband, Philip. What happened to him could happen to any of us. Life is a beautiful and fragile gift. These turf wars and power struggles to wrest the most money for our own departments—it's all meaningless in the end and not how we want to be remembered. In one of my favorite Victorian novels, *Jane Eyre*, Jane's childhood friend Helen tells her, 'Life appears to me too short to be nursing animosity or registering wrongs.' I'm convinced that we can all do our jobs well, and that we can all be excellent scholars, teachers, mentors, *and* generous human beings. That's all I have for now."

Betsy types away in the minutes, pushing her glasses up on her nose.

I'm not sure what I expected, but definitely not this silence. The provost and president glance sideways at each other. My colleagues say *nothing*. Maybe this is a good sign. Did I just tip the scales for Willoughby College to be a kinder place?

"So where's your report?" Bill Rhodes grunts.

"I emailed it to everyone this morning," I say, logging out of my laptop and locating my car keys.

"It's in your inbox, *Bill*," Evie Caldwell snipes. "And it looks like your department already spent your allowance. So you'll have to cut back on the cocktails at your post-structuralism conference in Venice. We *all* saw the receipts last year."

Chuckles erupt throughout the hall.

Bill turns as red as a beefsteak tomato and begins one of his exhausted attacks on her infamous Post-it note stunt. He calls her an academic has-been trying desperately to be relevant. President Hummell interrupts, calling for order. Recently tenured Sylvia from the history department interrupts President

Hummell to demand salary transparency and address the rumor about my raise for a "popular period-drama *Twilight* series that's certainly not serious scholarship." While others speak up in agreement, Patrick chivalrously defends my artistic work, arguing that it's as "well-esteemed" as my scholarship.

Normally this would stress me out. But the voices around me drone away into wind. I see Philip ahead of me at sunny Top Withens. I feel that bittersweet ache in my chest.

I blink, bringing myself back to the present.

As I pull out my keys and snap the buckle on my satchel, my colleagues turn on the provost, criticizing line-item A in my report. Anthony from Speech Pathology stands and demands administration transparency while bemoaning the end of faculty governance.

Nobody notices as I leave, and I feel the satisfying whoosh of the lecture hall door swinging shut behind me.

I wasted my breath. Sure, I'll stay in this job for now. I'm tenured, so my position is highly protected. It's Friday, and I'd like to take Heathcliff to the park. Henry and Bonnie are coming over this evening. Patrick and Elaine are showing up tomorrow to watch the premier of *Blood Oath* when it drops on Netflix. Tomorrow is Dad's birthday, and I want to FaceTime with him. Late-afternoon light from the glass entrance doors spreads across the floors and empty classrooms. Students don't move back until this weekend. This campus, my colleagues, these halls—this isn't my *real* life, the one that matters in the end.

The lecture hall door behind me opens and closes.

"Lizzie," Patrick says, lightly hurrying down the corridor to me.

I turn around. He's smiling, his blue-light glasses still on. "Are you okay with a hug?"

"Yes."

And he gives me one of our infamous awkward-professor

hugs. "Thank you," he says quietly. "I appreciate what you said—even if no one else does."

"Thank you. And we're looking forward to tomorrow evening."

"We wouldn't miss it," Patrick says. He glances around sheepishly. "Don't tell anyone, but I binge read *Blood Ties* last weekend. Hemmings is no Edgar Allan Poe, but his books sure kept my interest. I saw him interviewed on the *Today* show this morning. He's got it all—looks, money, that suave accent. I'd love to have a beer with the fellow."

"Uh—yeah, me too," I mutter before he runs back to the meeting.

Bella Patel: Hey Dr. Wells! I hope you're well. I so enjoyed hanging out with you, and I still can't BELIEVE we have matching tattoos! If you've started writing yet, I wanted to make sure that you're going to write the next book as *The Catherine Saga*

Me: You bet!

36

I FaceTime Dad on his birthday. He's still in London, with no plans to come home yet. Although he doesn't text, he emails often to let me know how he's doing. He and Ms. Fernsby have been sightseeing—Stonehenge, Stratford-upon-Avon, Canterbury Cathedral. Ms. Fernsby texts me a photo of Dad in the London Eye. Although Dad rarely smiles, he looks happy, eyes twinkling behind his glasses. He's carrying a large bag of gift shop souvenirs earmarked for Heathcliff.

It's evening there, and Dad and Ms. Fernsby sit in the dining room behind a large frosted pink layer cake. This is the first time I've ever seen him eat cake on his birthday.

"Hullo!" Ms. Fernsby says cheerily from beside him. She looks pretty with pink lipstick on and her graying hair pulled back in a green cloth headband. "We've just come home from my favorite Thai restaurant. You and Henry will have to go out with us when you're here next time. (Although I think it might be a bit too spicy for Heathie.) We went out with dear Darcie, remember her?"

"Interesting woman," Dad interjects. "Extraordinarily fond of cats and wallpaper."

"Gaylord, can I tell Lizzie about the other night?" she asks Dad quickly.

When he nods, Ms. Fernsby leans forward excitedly. "Lizzie, we tried *it* again at Darcie's—we had the brandy, the candlelight, the hissing cats. She tried to summon your sweet mother—but *nothing happened*. At least for Gaylord. And it was most peculiar because Lord Routledge tried to make another appearance! I think he's jealous of me with Gaylord! Maybe he thought I would loyally clean his house for the rest of my days. Stupid man. Anyway, Darcie theorizes that in the happy relationships, the loved one doesn't need to go back."

"That sounds about right," I say, meeting Dad's eyes. "I miss Philip every day, but we had a . . . security . . . that didn't require anything else."

"Oh, Lizzie," Ms. Fernsby says, "That's so lovely."

Her phone dings. "It's almost time, Gaylord! Can you go make some tea and cut me a slice? I'll be in in a minute."

Dad says goodbye to me, takes the cake platter, and kisses Ms. Fernsby's forehead. He's come a long way from expressing his affection through smelling Mom's hair.

"I hope you don't mind, Lizzie, but we're going to watch *Blood Oath* tonight. I know Dansworth was an awful rat to you, but, well . . . Brad Pitt is playing Chadwick Hall and I really must watch it . . ."

"It's fine, Ms. Fernsby. Really it is. Dansworth wrote a good series. In fact, I have my own *Blood Oath* watch party coming up."

"Oh good! And I did want to tell you something about him the other night. I went down the online rabbit hole on A.D. Hemmings, and it turns out the man can't keep his pants on! Have you heard of Cressida Bishop?"

"No . . . Wait . . . yes, he mentioned a Cressida."

"She's an author in her own right, more literary fiction than the boilerplate pulp he puts out. Anyway, she talked about their relationship in an interview—they were a hot literary couple for a while, on some magazine covers posing with antique typewriters. They were engaged and had bought and moved into a Kensington town house. But then he had an affair with one of his writing students. Can you believe it? Cressida said she wishes him well, but she just couldn't trust him anymore."

"He told me *she cheated on him*. And yes, now I can believe he would cheat with a student. Jeez. What a creep!"

"Absolutely! And what a lot of nerve! He and Cressida are both public figures, so it's not like you wouldn't be able to find out about this."

"Right? Poor man. Doesn't he know he's going to find himself lonely and old one day?"

"He will soon enough . . ."

"Annabel, it's coming on," Dad says from the doorway.

I tell them both goodbye and close my laptop.

From the screened porch, I watch Heathcliff play in the backyard with a friend. They're both in full Batman costumes, chasing each other with plastic light sabers. Superhero hybrid play, I guess. Late-afternoon cicadas hum from the trees all around, and I take a long sip from my glass of iced lime water. I have syllabi to polish and *I don't want to know how many* number of emails waiting for me now that I'm plugged in again.

But it can all wait.
I know like I did in Haworth that I'm going to be okay.
And Dad is happy.

Three Years Earlier

THE WEDDING OF PHILIP'S LAW SCHOOL FRIENDS MEG and Will falls on one of those beautiful, butter-melting Carolina summer evenings. It's outdoors, in Meg's family's backyard, not far from the Azalea Dream. The ceremony over, the reception is in full swing, with a jazz band playing from the back deck of the large house. Long rows of white linen–covered tables decorated with ivy garlands and flickering candles in glass globe centerpieces line the yard. Servers bring steaming platters of Low Country boil to each table and refill champagne glasses generously.

Philip and I give our warmest wishes to the couple before visiting with some of his other law school friends at our table during dinner. But Philip and I enjoy each other's company best, and eventually find ourselves meandering to the celebration's boundaries, closer to the quiet edge of the Ashley River. Twilight settles around us as we walk along the banks. As much as I hate the South's stupid conservative politics and asshat politicians, I never tire of the landscape. Cicadas buzz around us, drowning out the noise from the party, and Spanish moss drapes curtain-like from the surrounding oaks.

I feel particularly cleaned-up tonight having splurged on a vintage, shell-colored cocktail dress with a scalloped skirt and chandelier earrings. Philip looks dapper in the suit he usually reserves for court. It's a glorious childless evening as Mirabel has Heathcliff for the weekend and we're staying at a Charleston

Airbnb. We both feel a rare lightness, like two teenagers allowed to stay out past curfew.

We've had a few glasses of champagne and everything has that nice fuzzy glow; we're both bolder, brave enough to talk about our deeper fears and longings.

As we talk about the ceremony, I bring up that part of wedding vows that always makes my heart skip a little with dread, that fly in the ointment. "'Till death do us part.' Does that bother you like it does me?"

"What? Death?"

"No, that one of us is probably going to die first."

We watch the fiddler crabs scurry along the pluff mud banks. Philip exhales loudly, then picks up a thin rock and throws it across the water so that it skips three times.

"I do. But that happens to everyone, Lizzie."

"But what about when it happens to *us*?"

"Lizzie," he says softly.

"No, you know what I mean. You and I, we don't have normal couple boundaries." And I'm buzzed enough in this beautiful Low Country twilight to keep going. "We're the rare ones like Heathcliff and Cathy where we don't know where one of us ends and the other begins. People in nineteenth-century novels die all the time of fucking heartbreak. What will we do when one of us dies before the other?"

He steps closer to me, puts his hands on my shoulders. The setting sun catches on his short, neatly trimmed blond beard. The wind blows at my ridiculously long earrings, and they tickle my neck.

"We keep living."

"How?"

"With happiness and purpose."

I lean forward, my face in the crease of his neck. He smells vaguely of dinner's heavy cardamom spice, the citronella-scented torches back at the reception. I drink in his smell and put my arms around him.

Present

AFTER SATURDAY DINNER IN MY BACKYARD WITH HENRY, Patrick and Elaine, we start popping popcorn and refilling wineglasses before heading to the den to watch the *Blood Oath* Netflix series.

A.D. Hemmings. August Dansworth. My heartbreak passed quickly, and I'm fine bingeing the series with everyone else. Who knows, I might even read *Blood Offspring* when it hits bookstores next summer. I'm curious about Inspector Hall's new widowed love interest.

I tuck Heathcliff in bed, leaving on only his night-light, which radiates the Bat signal onto the ceiling. Most nights he asks a hundred questions and gets up several times for water, but not tonight. Bonnie wore him out playing in the yard this afternoon. He's already falling asleep, talking sluggishly about a pill bug he and Bonnie found in my garden box. As his eyelids droop, I brush his blond bangs from his forehead. He looks like his father and grandfather in the dull light.

"I love you, Heathcliff."

As he drifts off, he rolls over in the bed, yawning widely. "I love you too. You're brave like Batman."

My heart full, I walk back downstairs, pausing in front of the fireplace mantel. The orchid Dad sent after Philip died still blooms. Framed photos line the rest of the shelf. Of course, there's a black-and-white picture of Philip and me cutting the cake at our wedding. There are photos of Philip, Heathcliff and me at the state fair, another of us dressed up as matching superheroes for Halloween. I'd been Poison Ivy in a silly and expensive wig. There's one of Heathcliff looking sulky and unhappy in a little seersucker suit at one of Mirabel's events. And now there's a framed photo of Heathcliff and a smiling Frank at a USC football game, both wearing team colors, garnet paint smeared on their cheeks.

I stare at the picture from Meg and Will's wedding. We're by one of the tiki torches, just before we slipped off for our walk by the river. Philip's kissing my cheek, looking like he's the luckiest guy in the world. I remember that moment, the feel of his chin stubble on my skin, how happy I was. Then the ache swells. I take a breath and return to the den.

After Patrick and Elaine leave, Henry and I sit on my front steps. The first episode of *Blood Oath* was about what we expected. Brad Pitt looked the part, ruggedly handsome as he drove back roads too fast in his sleek Bentley. But as Ms. Fernsby predicted, his Welsh accent stank. The chase scenes were fun and well edited, with Cardiff as a stunning coastal backdrop. But my thoughts kept drifting.

"Everything okay?" Henry asks.

"Yeah."

"You've just seemed a million miles away this evening."

My street is never as beautiful as it is at this time of year. Little bats flit around the streetlights; star jasmine spills thickly over front yard picket fences, swelling in these last breaths of summer.

"Some nights Philip just feels more in my thoughts than others."

Henry puts his hand on my knee.

"I know. Me too. Sometimes I just can't believe he's gone."

I put my hand over his. "I haven't told anyone this. But Philip and I talked once about how we would live if something happened to one of us."

"And how were you going to live?"

"With happiness and purpose," I say, before I kiss him.

After a few seconds, I pull away.

"What is it?" he asks.

"Let's take dancing lessons together. Soon."

He puts his palm gently on my cheek. "Anytime you want to, Lizzie."

Two Months Later

I WALK THROUGH THE NARROW, WINDOWLESS HALLS OF the administration building, and my brain hurts as I wonder why I would be called to Dean MacGregor's office the day before fall break. It seems far past the time when he would pressure me to retroactively pass Brad for the spring Jane Austen seminar. From what I've heard, Brad has other problems. According to Patrick, he's skipped at least a third of his poetry classes this semester; he streaked across the field at the last football game and was caught pouring soap into the campus fountain. Then there was a vaping incident in the campus bell tower.

I find Dean MacGregor sitting in his sprawling office, framed photographs of his wife, Annie, and Brad on his desk. He has lists of this academic year's dwindling donors in front of him as well as budgets for every academic department spread out on his desk. I see an X over *Gender Studies*, so I assume that department might be on the chopping block come spring.

"Hullo, Dr. Wells!" he exclaims cheerfully, hurriedly collecting the papers and sliding them into a binder. His iPhone lies face up on the desk, my Instagram account open to a photo of me sipping champagne with Bella Patel at a red-carpet event. Dean MacGregor blushes and quickly flips the phone over.

Maybe this is about me missing the last faculty meeting due to my televised interview with the cast on a morning news show in New York City.

"I just took a call from a prospective student wanting to come here to take your classes. You're quite a feather in our cap."

I smile, still confused. "So I suppose that means you're not firing me."

"Definitely not. But I am required to set up a meeting to respond to a formal complaint."

"I'm sorry?" Sure, I've slacked on some of my duties due to book and movie buzz, but I certainly haven't lost my shit in class (so far!) this year.

As if on cue, Bill Rhodes bursts into the office, glasses slipping down his nose, face red. He waves his phone like a gleaming trophy.

Smiling smugly, he sits in the chair next to me, just across from Dean MacGregor.

"As I said in my formal complaint, Dr. Wells has behaved *unbecomingly* during her leave and does not represent the values of Willoughby College. The evidence I hold here in my hand warrants her immediate dismissal."

"What the hell, Bill?" I say.

Then I see a paused video on his phone.

Oh.

Why didn't I think of that? Yes, of course I'll be fired. Although there's nothing specific in my contract, I'm pretty sure baring one's undies on a burlesque stage is not permissible as a Willoughby faculty member.

"Watch this! Just watch it!" Bill demands, thrusting the phone in Dean MacGregor's face.

Heat rushes to my face as I see myself dancing on grainy video in the flouncy costume. I'm belting out "Circus" and strutting about with the twirling ribbon. August lifts me into the air, and even now, I flush remembering the high of that moment, how I felt wonderful and confident and on top of the world.

"I really don't think we need to keep watching . . ." I mumble, not keen at all on Bill Rhodes and the dean seeing my silvery bra.

"We certainly do, Dr. Wells," Bill snaps.

"Bill . . ." Dean MacGregor warns. "I'm not watching any more of this . . ."

But Bill keeps the phone screen shoved in both our faces, and there it is—me ripping off the costume, baring myself to the crowd. Strangely, I'm not ashamed. I did it. It was liberating.

"Do you see? She's been playing the prim-and-proper grieving widow, dressing head to toe in black, but *this* is what she's been up to while she's been away!"

Dean MacGregor leans back in his chair and sighs loudly. "Come on, Bill, are you really one to cast the first stone? I had the xeroxed letter from 1987 in my mailbox detailing a fantasy between you and Dr. Caldwell involving togas and grapes."

"Ewww . . ." I mutter. "Also, where did you find that video?"

"What do you mean, where did I find the video? You're trying to divert from the fact that you were dancing about on a London stage in your *unmentionables*."

"It's a legitimate question," Dean MacGregor says, a twinkle in his eye. "How did you find the video—I can't imagine it would be on YouTube?"

"Fine, I stumbled upon it on a burlesque fetish site," Bill says, face as red as a beet. "It could happen to anyone."

There's two seconds of awkward silence before Dean MacGregor and I explode in laughter. I'm laughing so hard, a tear slides down my cheek. Never in a million years would I have expected a formal professional complaint to be made about me for burlesque dancing. And never in a trillion years would I expect to be having this conversation in my semi-reputable place of employment.

"Oh, *yes*, naturally. We all stumble on those sites, Bill," I say, wiping away the tear.

He stands, flustered, pointing his phone at the dean. "So you're not going to do your job and fire her on the spot?"

"Considering the notorious love letters between you and Dr. Caldwell, how about we call it a day?" Dean MacGregor says.

Bill Rhodes aims the phone at me now. "This isn't the end, Wells. You are not immune to termination or censure!"

After Bill Rhodes storms out, Dean MacGregor exhales loudly, a twinkle in his eye.

"Look, you're not fired. If anything, we need more faculty like you, Lizzie."

He gestures to the photo of his wife, Annie, hair windswept as she smiles widely from the seat in a pontoon fishing boat somewhere.

"Annie was just telling me the other day that we need to loosen up. She says we need to let our son fall on his feet for once. She said we need to stop putting off our trip to Greece, that we should fly there next summer and ride scooters along the shoreline."

This day continues to surprise me in so many good ways.

I smile as I get up to leave. "You should go and have a marvelous time."

From *Blood Offspring*:

Inspector Hall sighs as he watches Widow Warner walk out of his life, black skirt swinging, high heels clicking on the cobblestone sidewalk. If it were in him to love consistently, he would have loved her and only her.

Evening haze spreads over the bay. Cardiff is quiet on this warm September evening.

He wishes it could all be different.

He wishes *he* could be different.

But this is his destiny—always chasing a strangler, a sociopath, or, as is often the case, a woman. It's always the chase. He knows he was never meant for a quiet domestic life.

But bloody hell.

Penny was right. A woman would break him at some point. And the woman was Widow Warner.

Widow Warner is almost to the end of the street, and he fights the urge to go after her. She was the steeliest woman he'd ever met, with her dead husband's lock of hair tucked away in that little locket at the base of her lovely throat. He remembered kissing that throat in the pub booth as she helped him decipher the Uni Slasher's clues. What a woman! She'd helped him, and she made him feel more intelligent, stronger, and like he should at least try to be a good dad to the son Penny gave him.

He misses how she made him feel.

Once she rounds the corner, out of his sight—his *life*—for good, he sighs, and turns around to walk home.

From *The Catherine Saga*:

Finally, it happened. A century after Nelly's prediction, the Fae came for their due.

Cathy Earnshaw loved two men for decades. Linton had repented long ago of his arrogance, and Heathcliff's passion never waned. Between the three of them, they saved Great Britain over and over again from war and dark magic.

But then, one had to return to Penistone Crags. That was the price.

They'd fought endlessly over who would go. All were willing. But it was Heathcliff who gave himself, slipping away in the middle of the night to surrender, ensuring she and Linton could continue on together—*happily ever after*, as old tales promise.

Cathy often visits Penistone Crags at sunset, when wind and hazy light spill over the moors, the surrounding landscape shadowed. She takes her time along the rocky path, careful not to twist her ankle. Linton waits near the warm hearth at home, and she loves him dearly. She is happy. But her other soulmate stays here, eternally.

Cathy knows if her immortality comes to an end, neither heaven nor hell can keep her from this place. She's dreamed over and over again of dying and going to heaven with no peace. She feels only torment and loneliness there, and she weeps so loudly, the angels fling her right back here.

She reaches the face of Penistone Crags. But now the stone hole has closed. She can no longer reach the fairy bed, the tucked-away magical place she and Linton delighted in all those years ago. Now her Heathcliff is sealed within.

She sighs, pressing her cheek against the cold lichen-covered stone.

"*Heathcliff*," she whispers. And she knows he's just on the other side. The Fae thought they took him from her, but they didn't really. Their love was such that they were never really separate beings. Their hearts are still joined, and she knows he knows she's here.

"*Heathcliff*."

★ ★ ★ ★ ★

Acknowledgments

I am grateful to everyone who cheered me on as I wrote this book.

Thanks to Jessica Sinsheimer, who believed in this book from day one. You were incredible as I brought Lizzie to life. I'm grateful not only to you but to the entire Context Literary team who supported me and championed this book.

I'm so grateful for my fellow writers and early draft readers, Grace Worthington and Heather Hahn. Your insightful feedback helped give dimension to all my characters and believability to the plot. You advised me in the early drafts when it came to the delicate balance of portraying a grief journey with hope and joy and humor.

My lovely agency sister, Rowenna Miller, helped edit the burlesque-show fashions. Rowenna, you are the undeniable expert in all things vintage fashion. Thank you for checking on the accuracy of Lizzie's undergarments and costumes and for introducing me to the fascinating and essential busk.

ACKNOWLEDGMENTS

I don't think I would have had the courage to write this book without the wisdom of my priest and friend, Dorian Del Priore. You introduced me to the term *saudade*, and described it in a way that perfectly contextualized my feelings after losing Shawn. Thank you for letting Lizzie's priest, Chloe, quote brief lines from your definition of the word at Shawn's funeral.

I also want to thank the fantastic editor Sherri Puzey at *Zibby Mag* who published my essay, "How Victorian Rituals Helped Me Through Widowhood." Although *How to Grieve Like a Victorian* is a work of fiction, processing my own grief through the lens of rituals helped me with the brainstorming of this book. Additionally, I appreciate *Zibby Mag* giving me permission to retain rights to my work and include a few lines from the original essay in this book.

I want to acknowledge Lucasta Miller's *The Brontë Myth* for contributing to my understanding of the Brontë sisters.

I'd like to thank the entire Canary Street Press team. My editor, Cat Clyne, helped refine this book in so many wonderful ways. Taryn Ortolan's keen copyediting smoothed and polished the story. Yordanka Poleganova and Tara Scarcello designed a striking cover perfectly depicting Lizzie's strength.

Thank you to all my longtime friends and mentors who supported me during the writing of this book, specifically Nicole Fisk, Paula Feldman, and Dinah Johnson.

Thank you to my family; to my sister, Kristen, for reading early drafts; and to Henry, for providing plenty of coffee and dark chocolate as I wrote, revised, and revised again. Thank you to my daughter, Amelia, for journeying with me to Haworth so that I could see the paths Lizzie walked.

Finally, this book would not be possible without Shawn. We had a wonderful seventeen years together. I was so fortunate to be your wife, and I love you always.

Discussion Questions

1. In what ways is Lizzie torn as an academic and a creative writer? When do these two worlds merge and when do they conflict for her?

2. Why do you think Henry and Lizzie fall in love? Is it independent of their love for Philip, because of it, or both?

3. How might Henry and Lizzie be on separate journeys of self-discovery? In which ways are their journeys similar? In which ways are they different?

4. Henry experienced a different sort of loss than Lizzie. He was divorced as opposed to widowed. How do their different "losses" affect their journeys?

5. In what ways does Mirabel's desperate attempt to keep her secrets close to her chest intertwine with her grief?

6. How would you describe Mirabel's relationship with Philip?

7. How does Lizzie's relationships with the actors affect her during their journey? What role do they play in the book?

8. What role does creativity play in Lizzie's healing process?

9. Do you think any of Lizzie's academic friends evolve as a result of their interactions with her? Please explain.

10. Although Lizzie and Mirabel have very different parenting styles, are there any ways in which they might be similar?